Mending Fate

Elisabeth Waters

Marion Zimmer Bradley Literary Works Trust

MENDING FATE

by Elisabeth Waters

ISBN-13: 978-1-938185-43-4
ISBN-10: 1-938185-43-9

Trade Paperback Edition

August 9, 2016

A Publication of
The Marion Zimmer Bradley Literary Works Trust
PO Box 193473
San Francisco, CA 94119-3473
www.mzbworks.com

Mending
Fate

Also by Elisabeth Waters

Changing Fate

PROLOGUE

Zora was adding herbs to a mixture simmering over the fire in the stillroom when her cousins Kyril and Kassie appeared in the doorway. "Do you want to come flying with us?" Kassie asked. "Colin is coming too."

Do I want to change into an eagle and spend the rest of the day playing with the other shape-changers my age, or would I rather spend a beautiful summer afternoon as a human in a hot room mixing yet another batch of Marfa's potion? Silly question. I wish what I wanted was the deciding factor.

Kyril and Kassie were twins, and Zora, only two days younger, could have been their triplet. Colin was Kyril's foster brother and the fourth seventeen-year-old at Eagle's Rest. All of them were short, slender, and well-muscled—the result of using muscles most people didn't know they had. Kassie and Kyril had their parents' dark brown hair and brown eyes, while Zora was a blue-eyed blonde. Colin had grey eyes and light brown hair.

"I'd love to, Kassie, but I have to finish this potion for Marfa. She can't breathe without it."

"If that's what you're working on, I understand why you can't come with us. But I wish she weren't so sick. I like Marfa."

Thank you for not pointing out that she's dying. We all know it, but I don't like saying it aloud. "If you want my company, you could help with my work."

"If you need brute strength to stir something, I'd be happy to help you," Kyril said, "and so would Colin. But we all know Kassie is hopeless in a stillroom. It's a good thing *she* isn't going to be the next priestess of the Earth Mother." He ignored the face that Kassie made at him.

Zora felt an odd shiver pass through her. She forced herself to say lightly, "I don't think Kassie can tell one plant from another. If she ever changed into an herbivore, she'd probably poison herself."

"Probably," Kassie agreed. "That's the nice thing about being at the top of the food chain. If you're an eagle or a wolf, you can't go wrong with mice."

"Or rabbits," Kyril added. "Plants aren't food. Plants are what food eats."

"I dare you to say that to your mother," Zora teased. Zora's father Briam, who had died before she was old enough to remember him, had been twin to Kyril's mother Akila, who was the priestess of the Lady of Fire. Along with Marfa, priestess of the Earth Mother, she had taught Zora plant lore and how to make medicines in the stillroom. Zora's mother Druscilla had taught her a bit as well, but Druscilla was more interested in perfumes, lotions, and soaps.

Twins seemed to run in the family. Four of Lady Akila and Lord Ranulf's six children were twins. In addition to seventeen-year-old Kyril and Kassie, there were eight-year-old girls. The two non-twins fell between them. There was also Rias, Lord Ranulf's son by his first marriage, who was the priest of the Sky Father. His mother was dead, so he probably would have lived at Eagle's Rest with his father even if he hadn't been called by the Sky Father.

"Too busy to come practice with us, Zora?" Kyril asked.

"You mean come play with you, and I'm not one of the ones going out with the annual search," Zora pointed out. Again she felt that odd shiver run through her. "If my job is to be priestess of the Earth Mother, I don't need to be able to change shape easily and fly for hours on end. Marfa has been priestess since before our parents were born, and she isn't even a shape-changer."

"But it's fun!" Kyril protested.

"Yes, it's fun, and I wish I could go with you, but I have to finish this." Zora carefully stirred the mixture. It wouldn't do for it to stick to the bottom of the pot and burn. If that happened she would need to throw this out, scrub the pot clean, and make a new batch from scratch.

"Come on, Kyril," Kassie said. "Let her concentrate on her work. We'll see you later, Zora."

"Later," she agreed. *And thank you for getting him out of here before I ruin this.*

Zora continued to stir the mixture carefully, occasionally adding a bit more of one of the herbs or more water. Actually, it wasn't so bad working here. Yes, it was hot, but the task was soothing. And she was not alone; the Goddess was with her. Zora could not remember a time when the Goddess had not been there. Even if she didn't hear her voice, she always could feel her presence. She basked in the feeling of the Goddess's approval, not minding that it took her until almost time for the evening meal to finish her work.

The end of the evening meal was when Lord Ranulf made general announcements, things that usually involved most of the residents of the castle. Tonight he was announcing the students who would be going on the annual search, although he called it the annual supply trip. This trip was much more than a supply run, although many of the people on the estate believed that was all it was. These were the same people who thought Lord Ranulf had a zoo of tame animals. It kept them from attacking any wolf who walked through the castle gates as if it lived there. It also helped that the wolf was the animal on Lord Ranulf's banner; everyone knew not to try to harm one. Given the fact that a student caught outside with no clothing and not enough energy to make the flight up to the tower came home in wolf-shape, this was a good thing.

The annual trip to pick up supplies was also the expedition that looked for shape-changers who were in need of sanctuary and/or training. Some families—and some villages—didn't take it well when one of their children turned out to be a shape-changer. *Or at least that's what I hear,* Zora thought. *It's not as if I'm ever going to find out firsthand.*

The list of people going out this year included Kyril, Kassie, Colin, and just about everyone else close to Zora's age. *It's going to be awfully lonely around here until they get back.* And Zora knew some of them might not come back. Every year a few people chose to settle elsewhere. By the time Lord Ranulf allowed them to go on this trip, they were old enough to live on their own.

It must be exciting to go out and see the world beyond Eagle's Rest. I almost wish I could go with them. Almost, but not quite.

Perhaps the idea of the upcoming changes in my life is what caused those strange dreams, Zora thought as she woke the next morning. She lay in bed for several moments, trying to sort out what she remembered of them.

Do you truly wish to serve me? the Goddess had asked.

"You know I do. I've trained for it all my life!"

But is it what you truly wish for yourself? I will give you time—and space—to decide. I warn you: it will not be what you expect, and there will be danger to your lives and souls...

That was all Zora could remember, and she couldn't even begin to understand. She thought of the odd feelings she had been having lately when people said things she knew were true. Suddenly she wasn't so sure what was true and what wasn't. She couldn't even identify the shivery feelings she had now. Am I afraid?

CHAPTER ONE

Two weeks later Zora wished with all her heart that she were still mixing potions for Marfa. Now she stood in the chapel looking at the leaves carved into the top of the Earth Mother's section of the altar. Marfa had died two days ago, her funeral had been this morning, and Zora couldn't even remember what she had said during the burial when everyone shared memories of the deceased. All she could remember from the funeral was the feel of cold earth slipping through her fingers into the grave.

She felt like that earth now: cold and insubstantial. She'd been numb since Marfa's death, as she discovered that expecting someone to die soon and coping with the reality of it when they did were two very different things. She still couldn't believe that Marfa was gone. She kept thinking of things to ask or tell her, and she would start to turn toward Marfa's room before she remembered and stopped herself.

Now she was trying to prove that she was the Earth Mother's chosen priestess. She had spent the last several hours at the task. It was a simple test. All she had to do was press the proper two carvings on the top of the altar at the same time.

The altar was an octagon made of stone, standing as high as her waist. The north face of it showed the Earth Mother in human form at the center. She held a sheaf of grain, the fruits of the earth lay around her feet, and a tree stood behind her with its branches spreading out in all directions. The top of the altar held the few implements used in the daily ritual, and each section was carved with appropriate symbols. The Earth Mother's section was covered with dozens of leaves. All Zora knew was that when she pressed the correct pair of leaves, the library would open. She had asked her Aunt Akila, priestess of the Lady of Fire, for more details, but Akila had said only, "The Goddess will guide you."

Zora had been trained to be the next priestess, and everyone expected the Earth Mother to choose her—indeed, they had been expecting that for as long as Zora could remember. But something was wrong...

At first she had just pressed randomly at the leaves that spread out from the tree on the side of the Earth Mother's section across the top, at random, trusting that the Goddess would guide her hands. When that didn't work she methodically pressed every possible combination. That had failed as well, and now, feeling both frightened and desperate, she was wondering if there was a way to become a priestess without going through this particular test.

Akila became the priestess of the Lady of Fire when she was two years old. She can't have done this! The altar is waist-high on me—it would have been over her head. Even if she crawled across the top of the altar, and even if the flames were close enough together that she could press the right pair, she couldn't have gotten into the library without breaking her neck! So, either there's another way...

...or the Earth Mother doesn't want me.

The Goddess wasn't guiding Zora. She wasn't even speaking to her, and Zora was rapidly becoming panic-stricken. She tried to calm her breathing as she methodically pressed each possible pair of leaves. Nothing happened. She thought she heard the Goddess whisper *Not here*, but she couldn't be sure she was hearing anything over the pounding of blood in her ears.

Zora started shivering so hard she could no longer stand, and she sank down next to the altar, landing on the floor in a seated position with her back against the carving of the Earth Mother. Even the stone, which usually felt warm to her, was cold against her back.

I can't fail! This is the only way I can honor Marfa's memory: to use the skills she taught me; to take up the work she left. The daily ritual required all four of the priests—it was bad that there had been only three for the ritual last night, but Zora couldn't join them until the Goddess confirmed that she was a priestess. And now it looked as if she wasn't going to.

I want Marfa back. I can't bear never seeing her again, never hearing her voice, never being able to ask her about all the things she knew that I don't. I've lost part of myself—a large part of myself.

Zora was crying so hard that she didn't hear Kassie enter the temple. She wasn't aware of her cousin's presence until Kassie knelt in front of her, put a hand on her arm, and asked, "Zora, are you going to be all right?"

Thank you for not pretending I am now.

"In time, no doubt," Zora replied, "but apparently not soon." Then her brain woke up. *Kassie never comes into the temple!* "What are you doing here?" But Zora knew, even though it was hard to believe—and she certainly didn't *want* to believe it. "The Earth Mother has called you, hasn't she?"

Kassie shook her head. "I don't know. I had a feeling that I should come here, but it may just have been to help you."

"It's all right," Zora said, forcing her mouth to shape the words of the biggest lie she had ever told. She dragged herself to her feet, using the altar for support. "You *do* know how to tell if you've been called, don't you?"

"Not really," Kassie admitted. "I never paid all that much attention. I always thought you'd be the priestess and stay here, and I'd travel with my brother."

"We all thought that, but the Goddess appears to have different plans." Zora looked Kassie firmly in the eyes. "Do you intend to refuse if she has called you?"

"Why don't we find out first if she *has* called me?" Kassie seemed as stunned by the whole idea as Zora was—and almost as appalled.

"I'll wait outside and guard the door." *Dear Lady, this can't be happening.* "Press the leaves on the top of the altar. When you press the correct two at the same time, the entrance to the library will open. It doesn't work for me; I've tried every possible combination. If it doesn't work for you, I don't know *what* the Goddess wants."

"I guess we'll find out," Kassie said softly as Zora left the room.

Zora's legs still didn't want to hold her up, so she slid to a seated position on the floor in front of the door. She was nowhere near over the initial shock, but unfortunately her brain was starting to function again. *If I'm not the new priestess, what* am *I? Does the Goddess not want me at all?*

Kassie opened the door and nearly tripped over her. She held a scroll in her hand and looked at it as if it were the carved serpent from the side of the altar come to life.

"You got into the library."

Kassie bit her lip. "Zora, I'm so sorry. Believe me, I never wanted this. I never meant to take it from you."

"You didn't take it from me." Zora struggled to her feet. "The Goddess gave it to you."

"But I prayed." Kassie's voice was almost a whisper. "I didn't want to travel with Kyril and the rest, but I didn't dare tell him or Father that I'd rather stay here... I swear to you, Zora, I never thought *this* would happen!"

Neither did I, Zora thought. "I guess it's a case of 'be careful what you pray for.' Prayer really *is* answered, but frequently not in the way you expected."

Kassie looked down, seeming to find her own feet unusually fascinating.

"One word of advice," Zora added. "Don't *ever* tell my mother about your prayers. We both know that she wanted me to be the priestess so that I could never leave here."

Before Kassie could say anything, the other three priests arrived. "Zora, it's time for the evening ritual," Akila said. "Are you ready?"

"The Goddess has a surprise for us." Zora forced the words out through stiff lips. "You're going to have to teach the ritual to Kassie."

Somebody gasped. She didn't see who, and she didn't care.

She felt as though she had been punched in the stomach. There was no air. She couldn't breathe; she couldn't talk. She hurt more than she ever had before in her entire life. *How could the Goddess not want me? I spent my entire life training to be her priestess—and she chose* Kassie?

They were all staring—except Kassie, who was still looking at the floor. Akila opened her mouth, but Zora turned and fled up the stairs before she could say anything. She didn't want to talk to anyone about this, and—even if the Goddess had rejected her— she *could* manage that much. She was still a shape-changer, after all.

She didn't pause until she reached the top floor, and then she stopped only long enough to strip off her clothing before diving out the window. She was half tempted not to bother shape-changing, but self-preservation kicked in and forced the change to eagle-shape. *At least I remembered to take my clothes off. It would really be miserable to have to claw my way out of them before I hit the water.* She used her wings just enough to slow down so that she went *into* the water instead of going splat onto the surface. For a few seconds she was a very wet eagle, but then she quickly started the change to fish-shape.

Every adult shape-changer had taught that this was a *very* bad idea, but Zora didn't care. She had lost Marfa, the person she loved most in the world. *And now this. If the Goddess doesn't want me as a priestess after I spent my whole entire life learning how to be one, why should I stick around? If I spend the rest of my life as a fish... Well, there are worse fates—like being a miserable, unwanted human.* Zora shrank as small as possible and finished the change. There was a slight snap as the new shape set into place, and she could feel her body temperature dropping to match the water temperature as she sank deeper into the river and drifted downstream to the lake. But those were just physical sensations, and they passed quickly. Fish don't cry. Fish don't feel. Fish never suffer from being rejected. Since Zora didn't want to feel, she was content to be a fish. She didn't care how dangerous it was. She wasn't happy, but at least she wasn't *unhappy* anymore.

CHAPTER TWO

Giant claws grabbed Zora, dragged her out of the water, and dropped her on the shore. It was dark, and she couldn't breathe. She flopped around helplessly for what seemed like forever, until the giant eagle changed into a wolf, nosed at her, and flipped her over. As she landed on her other side, she found herself changing to wolf-shape. She scrambled weakly to her feet, and began the unpleasant process of coughing the water out of her burning lungs and replacing it with air. At least in wolf-shape her lungs were parallel to the ground, which made the process slightly easier than if she had been in human shape. When she could breathe air again, she flopped back down on the ground, gasping painfully for breath and unwilling to move. *Why did Uncle Ranulf bother to fish me out?* she wondered. *I'm no use to anyone now...*

Teeth grasped the loose skin at the back of her neck and dragged her back to her feet. The other wolf growled and nudged her—hard. She fell in beside him and walked—or, more accurately, staggered—back toward the castle. Her brain was still fuzzy from being a fish, but she still knew that she had better do what he wanted. Lord Ranulf was a very determined person. Sooner or later he would get his way, and it was easier on everyone if it was sooner.

He stayed at her side, making sure she didn't go anywhere but where he wanted her to go. Nobody paid attention as they crossed the courtyard. The fact that it was the middle of the night helped, but it wouldn't have been much different in the daytime. People who didn't know about Lord Ranulf's students believed he collected animals. He did, but not as many as most people thought.

Zora followed him to the suite of rooms he shared with her aunt. Akila was sitting in front of the fire, staring into the flames, when they came in. "Good. You found her." She rose, grabbed the scruff of Zora's neck, and dragged her into the dressing room. "I've got a nice bath waiting for you."

Zora changed slowly and painfully back to human form, and Akila helped her into the tub. When Zora gasped at the hot water and tried to get out, Akila frowned.

"That water is barely warm," she said. "What form were you in?"

"Fish."

Akila sighed. "Cold-blooded animals are *not* the best choice when you're upset. You *know* that."

Yes, of course Zora knew that, but she still didn't care. At least the physical pain was a distraction from a situation she still didn't want to think about.

"Tell me when the temperature gets tolerable," Akila added, "and I'll add more hot water. We need to thaw you out before you get sick."

Zora nodded. "It was such a shock," she said slowly. "First losing Marfa—" Tears filled her eyes and spilled down her cheeks. "I should have been able to cope. It's not as though we didn't know she was dying, but—"

Akila nodded, her face sober. "Even when death is expected, even when you don't want the person you love to suffer anymore, it still hurts to lose her."

"She spent my entire life teaching me to serve the Goddess." Zora gulped back the tears that threatened to choke her voice. "And the Goddess doesn't even want me! It's like she didn't care about Marfa, like she threw out over a decade of Marfa's work."

"Did she say she didn't want you?"

"She didn't say *anything*! She just chose Kassie. And I couldn't hear her voice—or even feel her presence in the temple, and I don't know why!"

"We often don't know why," Akila said. "That's why we have faith—for times when we don't know why. As for your training, nothing you learn is ever a waste of time. The strangest things, even things you think you will *never* need to know, can be your salvation."

Zora shook her head. It hurt. "I can't think of anything I've ever learned that's going to save me when my mother finds out about this. I'd be better off spending the rest of my life as a fish. I *really* don't want to tell my mother that the Goddess chose Kassie

17

instead of me. Mother may not care about the Goddess, but she *loves* the idea of my having to remain right here for the rest of my life."

Akila froze in place. "You have no idea, do you?"

"No idea of what?" Zora asked warily.

"No idea of how long you've been a fish."

Oh, no. Aloud she asked meekly, "How long?"

"Marfa's funeral was three days ago," Akila said. "Druscilla is frantic."

Zora groaned. "Of course she is. If I'd stayed a fish, at least I wouldn't have to listen to her. She's going to take this very, very badly, isn't she?"

"Yes," Akila admitted, adding more hot water to the tub, "your mother is upset."

When Zora was a baby, she and her parents had lived in a villa near the castle, but when she was about three years old there had been a big earthquake that had flattened the building. Her father had been killed, her mother's legs had been crushed so badly that she would never walk again, but Zora hadn't had so much as a scratch. That had convinced everyone she was specially favored by the Earth Mother.

Akila mourned the death of her twin brother, and she and Marfa did what they could to heal his widow. Lord Ranulf moved Zora to the nursery to join her cousins, and then supervised the demolition of what was left of the villa. Druscilla had lived in a suite in the castle ever since, while Zora grew up with Kyril and Kassie—and their siblings and Lord Ranulf's fosterlings. Ranulf taught all of them the fine points of shape-changing, and Marfa trained Zora to be a priestess.

Zora knew she was lucky to be with her cousins. Even years later, when her mother's health had improved as much as it was ever going to, she wasn't a cheerful person. Zora spent time with her, of course. Druscilla taught her to embroider, so they could do that together, but no matter how hard Zora tried—and she did try—she couldn't seem to make her mother happy. And nobody in the castle would deny that Druscilla had a tendency toward melodrama, and when she was really upset...

"Try not to worry," Akila said. "You don't have to face her alone. The rest of us will be here for you." She looked out the window into the darkness. "And you don't have to do it right now. It's the middle of the night, so dealing with your mother can wait until morning." Akila patted Zora consolingly on the shoulder and added still more hot water to the tub.

"Do you think— Do you think the Goddess has abandoned me forever?"

"No," Akila said firmly. "I am very sure the Goddess has not abandoned you."

I wish I had as much faith in that as you do...

When Zora considered the matter, she suddenly realized there was a reason she was lacking in faith. She had never developed a strong—or even a weak—faith because she had never needed it. *When you are constantly aware of the presence of the Goddess—and she talks to you—you have* knowledge, *so you don't* need *faith.* Obviously, however, her life thus far had not prepared her for her current situation. Zora had no idea what she was going to do now.

Zora looked at Lord Ranulf in horror. "What do you mean, 'grounded'?" It didn't sound good, and if it meant what she was afraid it did...

"I mean that you are going to spend the next three days in your mother's quarters, keeping her company."

"But why?" *I'd rather be a fish.*

He looked disgusted with her—and that had never happened before. Now that the Goddess didn't want her, everyone seemed to hate her. It was so unfair.

"I have spent the last three days searching the lake for you by day and listening to your mother have hysterics every time I came home without you. Do you realize," he added, "that if Colin hadn't seen you go into the river we would have had *no* idea where to look for you? Do you have any idea how close you came to becoming a fish permanently?"

"I'd rather be a fish than be shut up with my mother," Zora muttered resentfully.

"And you just missed a wonderful opportunity to keep your mouth shut," Lord Ranulf said calmly. "Nine days. Do you want to try for ninety?"

Zora shook her head and kept quiet. Obviously anything she said was only going to make things worse.

Lord Ranulf sighed. "It's not just punishment, Zora. You spent three days as a fish and completely lost track of time in the process. You need to stay in human shape for a while so that your body will remember that *this* is your true shape."

Nine days stuck in Druscilla's rooms might as well have been ninety—it certainly felt like it. Zora admitted to herself that if she couldn't walk, she didn't think she'd be cheerful either—even if her husband hadn't been killed in the same accident that crippled her. But it was really depressing to spend time in Druscilla's company, and Zora was already depressed by Marfa's death.

Now that she no longer had anything she needed to do, Zora slept until well after dawn. She dressed in whatever was laid out, which meant her mother's maids were choosing her clothing. She broke her fast with her mother, and then spent the morning working on the embroidery project Druscilla had given her.

Zora didn't share Druscilla's passion for embroidery, but it did have its uses. *If you leave your hair loose and bend your head over the work in your lap, nobody can see your face. You do have to keep your hands moving, but still, it gives you a sort of privacy, even in a crowded room.* Not that her mother's rooms were crowded, but because Druscilla couldn't walk unaided there were generally at least two servants with her.

After the midday meal, they usually continued the needlework, although sometimes Druscilla had Zora read to her. She liked poetry. Zora didn't care for it much, but it was something to do. It wasn't as if Zora had anything *else* to do. Her mother was the only one who wanted her for *anything.*

The Goddess rejected me, the priests are busy training Kassie, Lord Ranulf apparently isn't speaking to me, and all my friends seem to be following his example. I don't blame them—much. My reaction to Kassie's being chosen was childish, stupid, and dangerous. I know it, and I have no doubt that everyone else in the castle does too. Maybe I really deserve to spend the rest of my life doing embroidery and reading boring poetry. But why *did the Goddess reject me? What did I do wrong? It feels as though she doesn't care about me anymore, and I don't know what I did to deserve this! Lady,* please *tell me what I did to offend you, because I really don't know!*

Another frightening thing was that at the end of the nine days, when Zora was allowed to change shape and fly again, she couldn't do it, and she didn't know what the reason for that was either. She felt frantic—and even more useless. So she continued to sit with her mother and embroider, while her thoughts ran in unproductive circles in her head.

At least Druscilla didn't require her to talk. She just wanted Zora in the same room. This meant Zora could obsess over her problems without her mother's making a fuss about it. Druscilla hadn't even mentioned the fact that Zora wasn't changing. Of course, she had never wanted her daughter to be a shape-changer in the first place.

Another thing Druscilla didn't mention was that now that Zora was *not* the priestess of the Earth Mother there was nothing to stop her from leaving Eagle's Rest. *I think she hopes it won't occur to me if no one says anything about it. It did occur to me, but it isn't as if I have anyplace else to go. If the Goddess doesn't want me here, why would she want me somewhere else? Can't she at least talk to me? I'm going crazy here, and I've never been so miserable in my entire life. Lady, what did I do to deserve this?*

Zora had lost track of the days by the morning when Kassie came to her mother's rooms.

"Good morning, Aunt Druscilla," she said politely. "I apologize for disturbing you, but could I borrow Zora? I need help with a potion, and she's much better in the stillroom than I am."

As Druscilla inclined her head graciously in permission, Zora thought uncharitably that a squirrel was better in the stillroom than Kassie was. Still, she was happy enough to have an excuse to set her embroidery aside and follow Kassie from her mother's solar.

We'll go by my rooms first," Kassie said decisively. "I left the scroll there, and you need to change into something less—"

Zora looked down at her dress. She hadn't been paying attention to what she put on in the morning, so she couldn't tell what she was wearing *without* looking at it. Now that she had, however, she could see what Kassie meant. "Frilly?" she suggested.

"White," Kassie replied. "That dress won't take the amount of washing required to remove stillroom stains from it, and even the largest apron won't cover those sleeves."

"Not to mention the strong possibility of setting them on fire." Zora took another look at the dress. "Why am I wearing this?"

"I was wondering that myself. Is your mother picking out your clothes?"

Zora shrugged. "I just put on whatever's laid out in the morning. As long as I'm stuck with her, it doesn't really matter what I wear."

"Well, it's going to matter in the stillroom," Kassie pointed out as they entered her room. She rummaged in a clothing chest and pulled out a set of practice clothes: drab, loose pants with a drawstring waist, and a tunic of a similar color. Zora stripped off the dress she was wearing and tossed it on Kassie's bed as she reached for the pants.

"You've lost weight," Kassie remarked. "It didn't show under that dress, but you have."

Zora shrugged as she put on the pants and tunic. "What sort of potion do you need to make?"

"Not me. Us."

"Both of us?"

"That's what the Goddess said," Kassie replied. "It's the one from the scroll I found in the library. She said that *both* of us needed to be able to recognize it when we encounter it. Besides, potions are definitely something you do better than I do." She sighed. "I suppose I'll have to learn, won't I?"

"Herbs and other growing plants *are* generally considered to fall in the domain of the Earth Mother," Zora pointed out. "Don't worry, you'll pick it up. If I can do it, you can do it."

"Zora, there are a lot of things you can do that I can't."

"You'll learn," Zora said in her most consoling voice, "and if all else fails, you can always ask your mother—or even mine. Do you have the ingredients for the potion? I never did get a look at the scroll."

"I haven't looked at it either," Kassie admitted. "I've had other things on my mind."

The scroll for the potion was on Kassie's floor. Apparently she had dropped it there the night she was chosen and hadn't touched it since.

Maybe being chosen was as hard for her as not *being chosen was for me.*

They took the scroll down to the stillroom, where Zora quickly discovered that Kassie really *couldn't* tell one herb from another. Literally. *Maybe the Goddess wants me here to help teach Kassie. Somebody has to if she's going to be a good priestess. And even if I can't feel the presence of the Goddess, I'm still going to serve her to the best of my ability. I still feel— even after everything that's happened—that serving the Goddess is what I was born to do. But I'm so confused.*

Fortunately the jars in the stillroom were labeled, although seeing Marfa's handwriting on them made Zora feel like crying. Again. *I'm spending much too much time in tears these days.*

The bundles of dried plants hanging from the ceiling, however, were another matter, and failure to tell them apart could easily be fatal. Zora rummaged around in the back of the cupboards below the worktables until she found a set of labeled drawings Marfa had made for her when she was a child. She crawled backward out from under the table and lifted them up to Kassie. "Study these until you can recognize the plants without needing to look them up. You *really* need to learn this."

Kassie, miserable and overwhelmed, looked at the drawings and back at Zora.

"There's a trick I use when I'm making a potion," Zora added helpfully, "to make sure I don't forget anything or leave an item out. I take all the items on the list of ingredients and line them up in order on the worktable. Then, as soon as I add the proper amount of each ingredient I put that item away and pick up the next one. You don't want to finish a potion and discover you've left out a crucial ingredient." She unrolled the scroll, which Kassie had dropped on the worktable, and looked at the ingredients listed. "This is an odd list. It looks more like a soup than a potion. It uses beef broth as the base, adds finely ground walnuts, various herbs, and—" She stopped, staring at the scroll in disbelief.

"And what?" Kassie asked.

"A drop of blood from someone who hates you."

"What?"

"You heard me."

"Yes, but—is that a normal ingredient in a potion?"

Zora shook her head emphatically. "I've never seen one like this

23

before. And I don't know where we'd get it. I don't know of anyone who really hates us, do you?"

Kassie was silent, obviously trying to think of someone. "Does the person have to hate us forever," she asked, "or would being angry at us when we took his blood work?"

"The latter is probably the best we can do," Zora said, "given our lack of serious enemies here."

"Don't worry," Kassie said over her shoulder as she left the stillroom, "that's what brothers are for."

By the time she returned, dragging Kyril with her, Zora had assembled the rest of the ingredients and had the beef broth simmering.

"You want me to hate you?" Kyril was asking.

"Only temporarily," Kassie said brightly. "Oh, and we need your blood."

"Hating you is suddenly becoming easier," Kyril said. "How much blood?"

"Not enough to kill you," Kassie assured him. "Are we ready, Zora?"

"We're ready for you to start adding the ingredients," Zora replied. "I've got the base heated, and everything else is lined up right here."

"Can't you do it?" Kassie asked.

"Of course *I* can do it," Zora sighed. "The point of this is to teach *you* how to do it."

"Oh, very well." Kassie reluctantly stirred in each ingredient.

Zora confined herself to handing things to Kassie and putting them away afterward. *It would be so much easier to make this myself, but—just maybe—I won't be here doing it for her for the rest of our lives.*

"Last ingredient," Kassie said, straightening up and pushing her hair off her forehead with the back of her wrist. "Kyril, just think of everything either one of us has ever done that annoyed you."

"Well," Kyril began, "there was the time when—"

"Don't say anything aloud," Zora said quickly, "just think it. We still need to be on speaking terms when this is over."

Kyril glared at them for several minutes. "I think I hate you enough now."

Zora picked up a small knife, grabbed Kyril's left hand, and jabbed it into the side of his middle finger. Ignoring his sharp yelp, she held his hand over the pot and carefully squeezed two drops of his blood—*one for each of us*—into the potion and stirred them in. "All done. Thank you very much, Kyril. You can stop hating us now."

Kyril looked at Kassie. "You could have said you just needed a drop or two."

"Didn't I mention that?" Kassie said, the picture of sisterly mock innocence.

"No," Kyril said shortly. "But at least I get to watch you two drink the stuff." He grabbed a couple of clay cups from the shelf next to him, and ladled out two servings of the potion. "Here you go. Drink it while it's fresh."

"Do we have to?" Kassie asked.

"Yes," Zora said. "The scroll says that once the blood is added the potion has to be consumed immediately." She tossed the contents down her throat in one quick gulp, and Kassie reluctantly followed suit.

Then the potion took effect. Kassie sagged against the table, and Zora hit the floor like a puppet whose strings had been cut.

The next thing Zora knew she was upstairs in the solar, wrapped in blankets and in the lap of somebody sitting right next to the fire. She was still cold, so cold that she wasn't even shivering. Kyril was sitting next to Kassie, while Akila frowned over the scroll.

Zora heard someone say the word "antidote" and saw Akila shake her head. *I'm going to die. I'm going to die alone and cut off from the Goddess.* She wondered how long it would take, and if it was going to hurt anymore. She couldn't fight it, couldn't even reach out to the Goddess or pray for her mercy... Zora's eyes slid closed as her body went limp.

Someone was shaking her, and Akila was holding her face between her palms. "Listen to me, Zora," she said urgently. "You're going to be fine. This will wear off soon. Do you understand?"

Zora didn't really understand, but she nodded slightly and let her eyes close again. Somebody said something about "sleep it off." But as Zora slid gratefully into sleep, she wondered, *Why didn't this work on Kassie the same way it did on me? From what I saw, she barely felt it—she was sitting up while I was passing out.*

Zora came half awake at one point and heard voices near her.

"You were right." It was Kyril. "How did you know?"

The voice that answered was Colin's. "She hardly weighs anything, and I remember from my time in the kitchens the meals they prepare for Druscilla."

That was all Zora heard—or at least all she remembered.

CHAPTER THREE

When Zora woke again, she felt much better. She was lying on her side on the floor in the solar, next to the fire, propped up by Colin's hip at her back. She opened her eyes just a little bit, and saw Kyril sitting on the opposite side of the fireplace sharpening his dagger. He always sharpened the dagger when he was upset. Zora figured it was the male equivalent of embroidery—something to do with his hands.

She could hear the soothing, rhythmic stroke of the blade against the honing stone. She could also hear the fire, and the breeze that blew through the window, and she could see the motes of dust in the beam cast by the late-afternoon sun. She raised her eyes to look at the fire and realized that there was a face in the flames.

Not here, it said, and the face vanished. The voice, however continued. *You must choose freely.*

All right, maybe I'm not awake yet. There's no reason the Lady of Fire would be talking to me. But why does that phrase sound familiar?

"How are you feeling?" Colin's voice came from behind her.

"Well, I don't feel as if I'm dying anymore. For a while there, I thought I was." Zora shuddered. "It was pretty bad."

"It was strange," Kyril said. "When they left to do the evening ritual, they were still trying to figure out why it hit you so much worse than it did Kassie. I don't think it was the blood—I was much more annoyed with her than with you."

Zora thought about that, and she remembered how cut off from everything she had felt. "I think it was my training," she said thoughtfully, pushing herself slowly into a sitting position.

"What?" Kyril looked blank.

Colin put an arm around Zora's shoulders. It felt good, like an extra connection to the real world.

"Unlike Kassie, I've been training to serve the Goddess my

27

whole life. I'm used to hearing her when she speaks to me, and I've been able to feel her presence for as long as I can remember."

Kyril frowned. "Does the potion interfere with that?"

Zora nodded. "The potion severs the link instantly and completely." She could still remember vividly just how it felt. She wondered if she would ever be able to forget. "It was awful." *Even worse than the day the Earth Mother chose Kassie.* "I've never felt so alone in my entire life—and I never want to again." She leaned against Colin, grateful for the solid warmth of his body.

"So don't drink the potion again," Kyril said simply. "There's no reason you have to, is there?"

"I don't think so. I can't think of any reason why I'd need to use it again." Zora frowned, trying to remember exactly what Kassie had said about it. "I think the Goddess just wanted me to recognize it if I encountered it again."

"Would you?" Colin asked.

"Recognize it? Absolutely. First because the ingredients are not generally used in potions, and second because the last one—the blood—has to be added right before the potion is taken. If anyone drops fresh blood into a goblet in front of me, I'm *not* going to drink it."

"Good idea," Colin said grimly, "but I don't think it was your training, or at least not *just* your training. I think the fact that you're being starved has something to do with it too."

"What do you mean I'm being starved?" Zora asked in bewilderment. "I eat everything I'm served at meals, and I haven't been feeling hungry."

"You've been eating all your meals with your mother," Colin said.

Zora shrugged. "I *am* living with her at present. Am I supposed to be demanding special meals?"

"He may be right," Kyril said. "You haven't been out flying with the rest of us in weeks."

"I was grounded, remember?"

"That was over a month ago. You're not required to stay in your mother's rooms now. You're not forbidden to change shape, but you haven't done it, have you?"

Zora sighed. "I've been tired, all right? Kassie and I both have a lot to deal with."

"True," Colin said, "but have you been drinking that special tea Druscilla drinks?"

Zora's jaw dropped open and stayed that way until she remembered how unattractive she looked like that and hastily closed her mouth. *Mother's special tea. The first thing I learned how to make when I started working in the stillroom. The one I've made a batch of every month for more than ten years.*

"I am *such* an idiot. Yes, I've been drinking the same tea she drinks. I didn't notice because I never tasted it before, but I should have remembered how it smelled." The tea was designed to decrease Druscilla's appetite. Because she couldn't walk, it was important that she not eat too much. If she gained weight, it would make it difficult for her maids to help her move and to care for her.

Zora cast her mind over the ingredients of the tea. "Even you two wouldn't be hungry if you drank *that!*"

"And probably neither of us would notice anything was wrong until our wings got too weak to hold us up," Kyril said.

"The way you eat?" Zora scoffed. "Somebody would notice *long* before that happened."

"But you've been with your mother," Colin said grimly, "and nobody realized what was happening until I carried you up here and noticed how little you weigh."

"Actually, Kassie said something while I was changing clothes in her room this morning."

"About your being poisoned?" Colin asked skeptically.

"No, just that I'd lost weight. And the tea isn't a poison."

"If you die from drinking it," Kyril asked, "doesn't that make it a poison by definition?"

Actually, yes, it does. "Do you think Uncle Ranulf would let me go with you to look for new shape-changers, the way Kassie was supposed to?"

"Good idea," Kyril said. "Getting away from here would probably be good for your health. I'll ask him."

"And there are things I can do to help in the meantime," Colin said. "I still have friends in the kitchen."

Over the next several days, Zora realized they were right. Her mother had been starving her. She didn't know whether it was deliberate or not, but it really didn't matter. Whatever the cause, the results were the same—Zora was too weak to change shape—and definitely too weak to fly.

Colin had obviously talked to somebody in the kitchen. Zora's meals gradually got larger, although not so quickly that her mother would notice. And every night when she went to bed she found a basket of food—including the dried fruit and nut bars the shape-changers ate for extra energy—in her room.

Zora wondered what shape Colin was using to get them there unobserved. They didn't use giant eagle inside the castle walls because it would be too noticeable. Giant spider was a possibility if he waited until after dark—Zora smiled at the mental picture of a spider climbing up the castle wall to her window with a basket clutched at the end of one leg. There was an owl-shape that could be kept fairly small and still lift four times its own body weight. It also had feathers in varying shades of gray that made it invisible from twilight until daybreak, and it flew in silence. Unless it was literally right next to your head, you couldn't hear the movement of its wings. But Zora didn't care if Colin was using magic, she was just glad to get enough to eat. It was odd that she hadn't noticed she was starving until she actually started to get enough food.

Zora didn't have the strength for a complete shape-change yet, but she could change her eyes. She practiced cat vision at night, and eagle sight during the day, whenever she got a chance to stand at a window with her back to the room.

When Zora ate breakfast with her mother, she picked at her food, which seemed to please Druscilla, but only sipped the tea. Perhaps her mother wasn't deliberately trying to weaken her. Perhaps it was just that she didn't think about how being on her diet would affect a shape-changer. Druscilla had never been known for deep thought about the consequences of her actions. (Zora didn't know *exactly* what that meant, but she had heard Aunt Akila say it to Uncle Ranulf once when they didn't know she was within earshot.) Now her actions were limited and not likely to damage others. But, no matter how accidentally, Zora had been damaged. The only thing she could do was work to repair it.

She ate everything on her plate at the other meals, while being careful to avoid the tea. She also ate every bite that was smuggled into her room. She got out of bed after Druscilla and her maids had retired for the night and practiced changing shape. After a couple of weeks Zora had gone from being able to change her eyes or extend claws suitable for tree-climbing to being able to do the full change to wolf. Once she was secure with that, she changed to owl and practiced flapping her wings, very briefly.

Zora sat up in bed the next morning and suppressed a groan. Her back ached on both sides from her collarbones to her hips. *So much for thinking I'm not that badly out of shape.* She sat there for several long minutes, using her back muscles to move her currently non-existent wings until the worst of the soreness dissipated. *All right, I'm going to practice using my wings every night until this stops happening. Dear Goddess, if I tried to fly right now I'd probably plunge to my death.*

That night, mindful of the fact that a fall from the windowsill could kill her, Zora perched on the footboard of her bed and changed to owl-shape. The wings were doing better. The ability of her talons to grip the equivalent of a branch, however...

Zora wrapped her wings tightly around her and tucked her head as she fell. She hit the mattress and bounced. When she came to rest she realized there was no way she could move in owl-shape without her talons slashing the bedding. Disgusted with herself, she changed back to human shape and crawled under the covers.

The strange dreams Zora had before Marfa died resumed that night. The first one was vague: Zora seemed to be looking into a mirror and drinking something from a silver goblet while a dark shape hovered next to her. It was strange and slightly disturbing, but it wasn't exactly a nightmare, and it faded into the back of her mind soon after she woke up.

Zora ate breakfast with Druscilla, and then tried to leave her rooms. Admittedly the only time she had left them since Lord Ranulf grounded her was the day she and Kassie had made the potion, but she didn't think she was supposed to be a prisoner. Her mother thought otherwise. When Zora responded to her mother's demand to know where she was going by telling her that she wanted to see Aunt Akila, Druscilla informed her that Akila had better things to do now than indulge Zora's curiosity, especially now that she *wasn't* going to be a priestess. Zora fled back to her bedroom before Druscilla could see her tears. She didn't want to give her mother the satisfaction of knowing she had hurt her. Besides, it was true. Zora wasn't going to be a priestess, at least not here. *Not here.* She'd heard that before, but where?

After Zora was all cried out, she splashed cold water on her aching eyes and tried to think. What was it the Goddess wanted of her? She hoped the Goddess would give her further instructions.

Apparently the dreams were instructions, but they were so vague as to make oracles look specific. As they continued, night after night, Zora became aware that the dark shape was a woman, apparently about fifteen years older than she was. Then she started to hear a voice, but the only thing that was clear was her own face and her hands raising the goblet to her lips. She began to remember more of the dreams during the daytime, and she was pretty sure that she would know the goblet if she saw it in her waking life.

Someone, presumably Colin, continued to sneak food into her room each evening, and Zora ate everything he gave her in addition to what she ate with her mother. She practiced changing, and she flew out after dark to strengthen her wings. At least she was making progress as a shape-changer, if not as a priestess.

Then one night the voice of the dark woman in the dream went from an unintelligible mumble to something Zora could understand, and she woke up gasping in horror. *She called me Lina. That's not a reflection of me. That's another person who looks like me!*

Zora had no idea who her double was, but she felt compelled to find her. *I'll bet she is the reason the Goddess didn't want me—at least not here. Maybe she wants me to be with Lina, wherever that is. And, if Lina looks just like me, she is probably a shape-changer, too. It doesn't matter what my mother says about it, I need to take Kassie's place on this year's expedition. Lord Ranulf will probably agree. Kassie took my place, so it seems only fair that I take hers.*

Zora avoided dealing with her mother's unwillingness to let her leave her room by flying out her window and into the top floor of the old tower before anyone woke the next morning. There were always extra clothes there because the students used the rooms to change to and from eagle-shape. She dressed and went to the great hall in the main keep, where she could talk to Lord Ranulf when he came down for breakfast.

Lord Ranulf not only agreed with Zora, he went with her to talk to Druscilla and override her objections.

"She's too young," was Druscilla's first objection. "And it's much too dangerous. I'll never see her again if you make her leave!"

I'm as old as Kassie, and she *was going to go.*

"Zora is seventeen, which is definitely not too young. Several members of the group are younger than she is. And I don't believe she's going to get killed and you'll never see her again," he added. "If I thought it was that dangerous, would I have assigned both Kassie and Kyril to this year's journey?"

"But they were trained for it!" Druscilla wailed. "Zora has led a sheltered life. We never expected her to leave here—"

"And I expected Kassie to be able to go!" Lord Ranulf snapped back. "Zora has had the same training in shape-changing as all the rest of them, she's not going alone, and I need another girl to replace Kassie. Many of the shape-changer girls we find need another girl to relate to, not a pack of sixteen- to eighteen-year-old boys."

"You say *now* that you were going to send Kassie—"

"He announced it at the evening meal months ago, Mother— before Marfa died. He said it then, and everyone heard him, so you can't claim he didn't mean it or he's just saying it now. If the Goddess had chosen me instead of her, Kassie would be on the road this week."

"This week!" Druscilla shook her head violently. "No, you can't. You mustn't!"

"I can, I must, and I will," Zora said firmly. She turned to Lord Ranulf. "Uncle, may I move into the dormitory with the rest of the girls? It will help me prepare." *Not to mention allowing me to sleep in peace without having to listen to my mother wailing over my upcoming departure.*

"I think you had better," Lord Ranulf said as Druscilla succumbed to hysterics. "Call her maids to look after her, and come with me."

Zora was glad to obey him. *If I need anything from my room here, I'll climb the wall in the middle of the night to fetch it.*

Apparently Lord Ranulf really did need Kassie—or now Zora—because there was only one other girl in the entire group. Tekla was a few years older than the rest of them, and, thank the Lady, she had done the annual search twice before. One of the older boys had done it once, but the rest of them were making the journey for the first time. This meant a lot of lectures from Lord Ranulf about the surrounding territory—apparently he had traveled over or conquered a great deal of it in his younger years. Zora was learning all sorts of interesting new things these days. There were lessons on local customs, proper modes of dress, things you should say when meeting someone, things you should *never* say out loud to anyone, words that had different meanings depending on where you were...

It was a bewildering mixture of facts, and it was totally different from the sort of things Zora had been studying before. Fortunately Lord Ranulf put Tekla in charge of the entire search team, and he assigned the rest of them to sub-groups within the main group.

Zora was put in a sub-group with Kyril and Colin, who had the advantage of having lived in a city until he came here to study. Colin's job was to keep Kyril and Zora out of trouble, and they were sternly told to listen to him about anything to do with city life. Kyril muttered something under his breath at that order, but subsided when his father glared at him. "You don't know as much as you think you do, Kyril. Listen to Colin. If you think he's wrong and there's time and privacy to discuss the matter, you can. If it's an emergency, do as he says."

Zora made no protest. She didn't know anything about life outside Eagle's Rest, anyway.

A week later they all rode out the gates, past the lake, and onto the road that led south.

It was less than two days Zora discovered why Lord Ranulf thought it vital to have girls in the group.

They had just passed through a small village, which made Zora nervous because she found being stared at unsettling. Of course, this was the first time in her life that she had been a stranger to the people around her. She wondered if this was what Colin had felt like when he first came to Eagle's Rest.

The village—and its people—were out of sight behind them, and she was starting to relax when a young girl scrambled out of the woods beside the road, tripped, and fell almost under Zora's horse. The horse simply moved sideways to avoid trampling her. Lord Ranulf's horses were very well trained, not to mention being accustomed to much stranger things than this. It was much less happy about the man chasing after the girl with a whip, a dislike Zora heartily shared. She had never seen *anyone* go after a human with a whip. Whips were not used even on animals at Eagle's Rest, although the fact that there were people who whipped animals in the outside world *had* been part of the lessons.

Lord Ranulf said that people who needed a whip to make an animal obey them were not good owners, but that in most places their actions were legal. "You should, therefore, restrain your perfectly natural impulse to take the whip away from the human and use it on him. Use your brains first and your strength only if you must."

Kyril, who had been riding just behind Zora, tried to get his horse between her and the strangers. He managed to block the man temporarily, but the girl rolled under his horse and scrambled to her feet next to Zora. Her dress was torn and there were whip marks visible on her skin where the dress was about to fall off her. Part of her ribcage was visible, and not only could Zora see her ribs, she suspected she could have picked the child up by any one of them—assuming that it didn't snap in her grasp.

The man wasn't fool enough to use the whip on either Kyril or his horse, which was a good thing. The horse would have bitten him. Kyril might have too. By this time the rest of the group was surrounding Zora and Kyril as best they could on the narrow road. The man completely ignored Tekla and directed his attention to the oldest-looking boy. "Do you folks disagree with a father's right to discipline his child?"

"Depends on the discipline," the boy replied calmly. "What did she do?"

"She dabbles in witchcraft, and no daughter of mine does that!" He shoved in front of Kyril's horse and reached for the girl's arm.

For a moment Zora thought the girl was cowering on the ground, but then a kitten jumped out of the remains of the dress and landed on the front of her saddle. It overbalanced and fell into her lap, so she gripped it gently to keep it from falling off the horse.

The boy glanced from the rags in the road to the pile of fur shivering in Zora's lap. "Is that a cat?" he asked in a convincing display of surprise.

"Kitten," Zora said, thankful that the girl was young enough not to have turned into a cat. Cats went into heat all too often, and always at the most inconvenient time.

"My young friend appears to be attached to the animal, wherever it came from, and clearly it cannot be your daughter. Your daughter would be human." He paused, and then continued as if the idea had just occurred to him. "Would you sell the kitten to us? I expect the girls can train it to be a decent pet."

"Pet!" the man protested. "I'll have you know that's a valuable, hardworking—"

"Oh, is she a good mouser?" Zora muttered.

"Quiet!" Colin hissed.

Colin never talked to her like that, so Zora figured he knew something she didn't. She shut her mouth and lowered her head to look down at the kitten in her lap, gently stroking it while keeping watch on the father through her eyelashes. One of the many benefits of being a shape-changer was having long eyelashes at will.

She sat quietly holding the kitten while the "men" concluded the deal, and the girl's father went back into the woods, probably happier with the coin than he'd ever been with his daughter.

"All right, people," Tekla commanded as soon as he was gone, "we're going to ride as fast as we can and get well clear of this area before he comes back with his friends."

"A man like that has friends?" Zora was astonished, and it showed clearly in her voice.

Tekla sighed. "I keep forgetting what a sheltered life you've lived. Yes, he'll have friends—or at least drinking companions who will take his side in a quarrel, especially a quarrel with outsiders. I want to put as much distance as possible between him and us before we camp tonight. Pass the kitten to one of the boys; you're not an experienced rider."

Zora noticed that both Kyril and Colin winced. "I may not be the best rider, Tekla, but I'm probably the one most willing to have a nervous animal with sharp claws in my lap."

Tekla looked at the boys and laughed. "I suspect you're right. Tell us if you have trouble keeping up, and I'll take her."

Colin bent to scoop up the remains of the dress and tossed it to Zora. "Wrap her in this. She's shivering."

Zora suspected that was due to nerves more than cold but thought it better not to leave the dress in the road, where it would be evidence to support the man's story. The rest of the group apparently felt the same, because the boys rode in such a way as to obliterate any clear tracks where they had stopped and to muddle the trail as the group moved out after Tekla.

They continued down the road until the light failed. By then the kitten had fallen asleep, so Zora stayed in the saddle while everyone else dismounted and led the horses even farther away from possible pursuit. The horses couldn't see in the dark, of course, but the rest of the group didn't have that problem. They finally ended up going single-file along a very narrow path that ended in a clearing in the woods.

Tekla had obviously been there before. She issued a series of instructions about watering the horses, pitching tents, and unpacking cold food. "It's too late to hunt tonight—or at least it's too late to cook what wolves can bring back. Zora, you stay on your horse until our tent is pitched. We can deal with our newest student while the boys handle the camp routine."

When Zora finally dismounted, still carrying the kitten, Kyril was nearly carrying her. To say that she had stiffened up during all the hours in the saddle was an understatement. She was very thankful to be in a dimly-lit tent with Tekla, the kitten, their supper, and a jar of liniment for her sore muscles. She collapsed onto one of the bedrolls Tekla had laid out (she had added a third one tonight), and stretched out her legs, alternating the stretching with applications of the liniment.

While Zora was trying to get her body back into working condition, Tekla split the food into three portions and tried to convince the kitten that it was safe to turn back into a girl. Zora watched with interest. This was the first time she had been around a new student—assuming that the child wanted to be a student. Maybe she didn't. It wasn't as if anyone had asked her what she wanted. She had made no effort to move out of Zora's lap once she landed there, but that only meant she felt safer there than with her father, and anything with a desire to survive would feel that way.

Tekla lifted her and placed her gently on the third bedroll. "Look," she pointed out, "we have clean clothes for you, just like the ones we wear. We have plenty of food, and we can easily get more when we need it. You don't have to do anything you don't want to. If you don't want to come study with us, we'll make other arrangements. But would you please turn back into a human?" The kitten seemed to pull herself into an even smaller ball, and Tekla frowned. "I think she may still be in shock." She poked her head out of the tent. "I need a couple of volunteers to fly back to where we found her, see what her home was like and whether there are any *other* children we need to get out of there. Whoever goes needs to be back here ready to ride by morning. News of whether anyone is coming after us would be appreciated as well. Who's fastest, quietest, and best able to ride half-asleep the next day?"

Zora heard a few chuckles and some low-voiced discussion, but she didn't know who they decided to send. She didn't hear flapping wings either, so she presumed that whoever left had used owl-shape.

Tekla turned back and tied the tent flap closed. "It's too bad there's no way to get a cat to change back to human."

Zora laughed. "You haven't heard the stories of my early childhood. My mother mastered that trick before I could walk. Not that I remember it, but I've heard the story."

Tekla looked hopeful. "You can get her to change back?"

"It can be done," Zora said, "but I'm not prepared to apply my mother's methods to anyone who's already traumatized. Let me try something else first." She lay flat on her stomach and looked the kitten in the eyes. "I won't force you to change, but here's what happens if you don't. First, you'll probably be called 'Kitten' for the rest of your life. Second, as long as you're in cat-shape, you can't eat a lot of the food we do. It's not that there's anything *wrong* with raw meat, but it's a limited diet. Third, if you stay in cat-shape too long, you'll forget how to turn back into a human, or into anything else." *Fourth, you'll eventually get stuck as an adult cat, but I'm not getting into the disadvantages of* that *now.* Then Zora realized something. Tekla had told the child that they came from a school for shape-changers, but...

Zora peeled off her shirt and changed shape to a cat similar in size and coloring to the one in front of her. Another benefit of shape-changing kicked in: she could stretch much more effectively as a cat, and changing shape also healed simple injuries. She stretched for several minutes, and then changed back, put her sleeping tunic on, and reached for a dried fruit bar.

"Well, that fixed my sore muscles, but now I'm hungry. Good thing I can eat dried fruit." She bit off several bites and shoved them into her cheeks in the way that had gotten her the nickname "chipmunk" as a child. It did, however, let her eat and talk—more or less at the same time. "If you turn human now, the damage from today's beating should heal, and you can have these." She held out a fruit bar.

The kitten sniffed at it and turned away in favor of a strip of dried beef. She dragged the meat to the foot of Zora's bedroll, turned around several times to make herself a comfortable place to curl up, and started chewing.

Zora shrugged. "All right, Kitten it is. You can sleep with me tonight, and we'll see how you feel in the morning." *And how I feel. By morning I may be willing to use my mother's solution: dip cat in water until it changes back.* She ate the rest of her food, giving Kitten a generous share of the dried beef, and crawled into the bedroll, being careful not to kick her.

Tekla got into her own bedroll, and blew out the candle.

Zora must have slept soundly indeed; when she woke in the morning Kitten had moved inside the bedroll and was curled up against Zora's side. She woke up the instant Zora stirred and watched her carefully. Avoiding any sudden movements, Zora got dressed and took her "pet" outside, where the kitten promptly scrambled up Zora's body as a pair of wolves trotted into the clearing, carrying dead rabbits in their jaws.

"Are we allowed to cook breakfast?" Zora asked.

"That's an excellent question," Tekla said, following her out of the tent. "What's the report?"

"It's your decision," Kyril said, taking the rabbits away from the wolves, who disappeared to change to human shape and get dressed. "The scouts you sent out last night say that she's an only child, and her father spent enough of the money in the local tavern to ensure that he and his friends won't be up before noon, much less coming after us."

"Very well," Tekla said. "Build a fire, skin and cook the rabbits. We'll continue on after we eat."

"How long is she going to stay a cat?" Kyril asked.

Zora shrugged. "Until she feels safe being a human, I guess. In the meantime, I'm calling her Kitten. By the way, are we likely to be buying more people?"

Tekla winced. "Actually, we do have a budget for it. There are a lot of places where it's legal to sell children, and people are most willing to do it at this time of year, when the crops are all in and they're thinking of children less as workers and more as extra mouths to feed all winter. That's why we make this trip in the autumn."

"They're not considered precious members of the family?" Zora asked in astonishment.

"Not once the family gets too big," Tekla said gently. "When a family has a large enough number of children, the parents start forgetting which one is which—and that's the *best* case."

It was another three days before Kitten changed back to human shape, and even then, she refused to answer to any other name. Tekla took it in stride, telling Zora privately that in cases like this, a new shape-changer often wanted a complete break with her old life. Well, Kitten was certainly getting that. The life they led on the road couldn't have been anything like her previous existence. It wasn't even much like Zora's.

They spent several more weeks travelling and collected eight more shape-changers. Two of them were girls and only slightly older than Kitten, and she started to spend time with them instead of following Zora's every step.

At the halfway point between the Winter Solstice and the Spring Equinox, Tekla decided they were ready to head back to Eagle's Rest, getting all the supplies they had ostensibly been sent to fetch on the way. That was when Zora discovered that she, Kyril, and Colin had been assigned an extra errand.

"Father wants me to deliver a letter to his niece Catriona," Kyril explained, "so we'll be going farther south, along the river road."

They packed enough provisions so they wouldn't have to stop and hunt for food—the rest of the group would have plenty of time to do that on the way home, and it would be training for the new ones. Then they mounted three of the horses and headed along the road that ran next to the river.

"Where does Catriona live?" Zora asked, wondering how far they were going and what their destination would be like.

"A place called Diadem," Kyril said. "It's a city-state, with the city at the point where the river becomes navigable down to the ocean. It's a matriarchy, and apparently it's also where your mother grew up."

Zora thought that sounded interesting. She had no idea what an understatement "interesting" was going to be.

CHAPTER FOUR

A week later they were approaching the northern border of Diadem, and Zora discovered there was one more thing Lord Ranulf had not warned her about. She, Kyril, and Colin were sitting around a small fire after having cooked their dinner over it. They were well off the road and out of sight, because apparently this was going to be their last chance for any real privacy for a while. Kyril had said that his father had a house in Diadem where they would be staying. It came with a housekeeper who didn't know they were shape-changers, and they all wanted to keep it that way.

"Father had more instructions for us," Kyril said. "He gave me letters for each of us, to be opened right before we arrived in Diadem." He pulled three sealed packets out of his saddlebag, distributed them, and opened his own. Colin followed suit.

Zora looked at her name, written in Lord Ranulf's bold hand, with foreboding. Somehow she knew that if she opened that letter, her life would never be the same again. *And why would you want it to be?* her inner voice asked.

Dear Zora, the letter began, unexceptionally enough, *I am sending the three of you to Diadem for a variety of reasons. Some of them have to do with a trading partnership I have with the city—the boys will handle that end. But some have to do with you personally.*

I hope you know that I love you as if you were my own daughter and that Eagle's Rest will always be your home. But something is not in balance, and I believe you have an important part to play in what is to happen. Go to Diadem, look around, and keep an open mind. I cannot tell you my suspicions, and they may be unfounded, but...

I have one initial instruction for you, and it is VERY important. Do not enter Diadem in your true shape, and do not change back to it until you understand why this matters. I would suggest that you take dog-shape— something reasonably non-threatening (yes, there actually are people who are afraid of dogs). Colin will pretend to be your owner, as he has lived in a city before and understands how people regard "pets." Kyril, having lived all his life at Eagle's Rest, would forget to maintain the pretense. City people may talk to their dogs, but they don't expect them to understand much, and they certainly don't expect them to answer questions!

Go with the Goddess, my beloved daughter. I am sure that she will be with you, especially in Diadem.

"Has he gone crazy?" Colin looked up from his letter. "Why would he want you to be a dog?" He frowned. "And I don't really want to own you. I mean, that's like slavery."

"It would actually *be* slavery," Kyril pointed out, "except that you don't own her. You're only supposed to *pretend* you do. Why is that, anyway?"

"Dogs have owners—that would be a human who is responsible for the dog and its behavior. A dog running around loose in a city is likely to be impounded."

"Impounded?" Zora had never heard the word before.

"It's like jail, only worse. If the owner doesn't show up to claim the dog, it can be put to death."

Zora gulped. "It's a good thing it's hard to imprison a shape-changer."

"Unfortunately," Colin added, "city-folk tend to regard many animals as vermin. Mice, rats, bugs of any sort—anything small enough to stomp on often does get stomped. Cats are iffy. Some people like them and some people hate them, and there's no legal penalty for killing one—unless it has an owner who objects, which generally happens *after* the fact. You are safest as a dog, and hunting dogs are valuable, but you need to stay with one or both of us. If you do get separated from us, do *not* bite anyone—vicious dogs are put to death no matter what the owner does. If they impound you, stay calm, and act like a well-trained and valuable animal. If you go missing, Kyril and I will ask the Guards if they have you. Remember that, Kyril."

Kyril nodded, looking shaken. "Are they really that barbaric?"

Colin sighed. "Try to remember that most of the world regards people who let their animals run around loose as barbaric—after all, they're not used to animals with human intelligence. Remember Lord Ranulf's lectures on the importance of conforming to local customs. Just stay with me, Zora," he continued, "and for the love of the Lady don't bite anyone. Try to refrain from growling or appearing unfriendly. People tend to react badly when they are frightened or nervous." He reached out and patted her knee. "It will be all right. I'll take good care of you."

The rest of the conversation was devoted to what dog-shape would be least frightening to strangers while still maintaining Zora's general size and weight.

"It won't work to turn you into the sort of little bundle of fluff that ladies keep for lap dogs," Colin remarked, "because anyone trying to lift you into their lap would notice that you're much too heavy." They finally settled on a type of hunting dog with short curly fur in a rather pretty shade of apricot. "...and that sort of fur doesn't shed," Colin finished.

"Now that's a real advantage," Kyril remarked. "Most of our dog-shapes shed enough fur each week to make a new dog. Certainly our wolf-shapes do."

Zora went into her tent and stripped off her clothing. *It's much simpler to undress before changing shape, rather than changing first and having to find a way to get the clothes off. It's also not as hard on one's wardrobe.* She packed her things neatly away, and then changed to dog-shape. When she came out, the boys were still discussing how to handle a dog in the city.

"We had better agree on some basic commands and hand signals before we go into town," Colin said to Zora. "Somebody is bound to want me to demonstrate that you're under control."

Unfortunately a dog's face was not capable of conveying just how Zora felt about this statement. Fortunately, however, nobody else was around now to see her non-verbal reaction to it.

Colin patted his chest, just over his breastbone. "This means 'come here,'" he started to say.

Zora launched herself at him, hit him with her front paws on his shoulders, and knocked him flat on his back.

"Zora!" Colin protested. "Get off me! 'Come here' means stand or sit in front of me, not 'jump up and knock me flat.'"

I know what 'come here' means, silly. You appear to have forgotten that I was the one who helped you train Lord Ranulf's dogs. I also remember sit, stay, lie down, and heel.

"Shouldn't we have some other name for her?" Kyril asked,

grinning at the sight of Colin pinned to the ground by the harmless-looking dog. "If we call the dog Zora, how do we explain why we're calling the human the same thing?"

"We'll think of something else to call her before we get there," Colin said impatiently. "In the meantime, Zora, let's go over the rest of the commands—starting with *get off me!*"

Laughing inside, Zora scrambled nimbly off Colin and moved a few yards away so that he would have room to get up—and to brush the dirt off his clothing without getting it into her fur. Most of the dirt, of course, was on Colin's back, so Kyril had to help him. Colin, trying to retrieve his dignity, ignored Kyril's snickering.

Going through the remaining commands took all of five minutes, and it took that long only because Colin went into considerable unnecessary detail as to exactly where Zora was supposed to be in relation to his left leg for heel.

And I already know to sit when he stops walking. He doesn't need to tell me that.

The boys loaded her baggage and the tents onto the now-extra horse.

"Before we get to Diadem," Kyril said, "I need to tell you what Father told me about their religion. It's a bit odd by our standards. They choose a Year-King in the late spring and sacrifice him at the end of summer. Father was one—that's when he was married to Rias's mother. He said it was a very strange experience, because there's some sort of magic that makes the Year-King fall completely in love with the Queen." He grinned suddenly. "Mother calls it 'Year-King idiocy.'"

Colin frowned. "How do they choose?"

"There's some sort of ritual," Kyril replied. "Father couldn't remember the details, but he said if it happens to either of us, we don't need to worry. They may not even be doing it yet, because the Queen he married died about sixteen years ago, and they don't do it while the Queen is a child."

"Why not?" Colin asked.

"The Queen has to be old enough to marry. That's the whole point—the Year-King marries the Queen."

They continued on toward the northern boundary of Diadem. "It's the one closest to the city," Kyril remarked, "so we don't have far to travel. But, Zora, if you have trouble keeping up, let us know."

If I have trouble keeping up, you'll know because I'll be back somewhere behind you.

Zora was glad they didn't have too far to go. She wasn't used to moving at a horse's speed. *Talk about an unfair advantage—they have legs at least three times as long as mine.*

The boys figured this out pretty quickly and slowed the horses. Even at a walk, however, the milestones seemed unnaturally close together. Just as they passed one of them, Zora suddenly felt dizzy, her paws tangled, and she tripped, landing rather hard on one side. She thought she heard a woman's voice say *here*, but she was much too confused to be certain. As she lay there, wondering what had just happened, she felt a familiar but completely unexpected sensation: the snap of a shape-change finishing and settling into the new form. *But I changed shape* miles *ago!*

Kyril reined in his horse and looked back at her as she lay in a puzzled and awkward sprawl across the road. "What happened?"

"Zora!" Colin was off his horse and kneeling beside her. "What happened? Are you hurt?"

Given the fact that Zora was a dog at the moment, that wasn't a question she could answer in any detail. Being a shape-changer did have a few disadvantages. She had definitely just felt the sensation of a change finishing and locking into place. But there was no reason she should have felt like that—and certainly no way she could explain it to the boys.

Colin ran his hands gently down her legs and along her ribs to check for broken bones. When he finally said, sounding worried and a bit doubtful, "I don't *feel* anything wrong," Zora rolled and got to her feet.

She gathered what was left of her dignity, glad to find that her legs worked properly now and she didn't have to think about them or suddenly re-learn how to walk. She butted her head against Colin's leg in what she hoped he would interpret as reassurance. He scratched her behind the ears. Colin was definitely her favorite human.

That was odd, she thought, *and it happened when I passed that milestone. I wonder if there's something special about it.* She walked back to the stone, followed by a puzzled Colin. Kyril stayed back to make certain the horses hadn't been spooked by whatever it was that had just happened.

When she examined the stone, Zora discovered that this was not just a milestone. It was also a boundary marker. *Whatever that was, it happened when I crossed the border into Diadem. I wonder what would happen if I crossed out and then in again.* She stepped forward, and jumped back, startled and with a sore nose. It felt as though she had walked—nose-first, of course—into a wall. Apparently a wall made of solid air. She slowly slid a front paw out ahead of her. The air still felt like a wall, but at least she hadn't hit it hard this time.

By now Colin had noticed the problem. "Can we not cross the boundary?" he asked anxiously. Zora managed a sort of shrug and pushed him forward. He walked across the boundary and back as if there were nothing there. "Try it again," he said, frowning thoughtfully.

Zora did, but the results were the same.

"All right, you can't cross on your own. What happens if someone carries you?" He lifted Zora, slung her across his shoulders, and headed slowly toward the boundary. He got his front foot planted on the other side with no problem, but when Zora's body hit the wall, they were stopped in their tracks. Zora had prudently tucked her nose and most of her head into his armpit, so at least she wasn't hurt this time. "Kyril," Colin called, "come here and bring a horse with you."

When Kyril did they ascertained that he could cross the boundary, both on foot and mounted. But when Colin tried to pass Zora up to lie across the saddle, Kyril balked.

"It didn't work when you carried her," he pointed out. "I'm willing to try the same experiment, but *not* with one of my father's horses. If it gets stuck halfway, it's likely to panic."

"You're right," Colin agreed. "It is a very odd feeling, and I knew what I was doing. It appears there's some force that doesn't care about us, but doesn't want Zora to leave Diadem."

Zora tried to remember exactly what it was that Lord Ranulf had said in the letter. "...something not in balance..." *Well, there's certainly something odd happening here.*

The boys argued for a few moments, but there was really

nothing they could do but continue on to the city. They decided to leave Zora in Kyril's lap so they could make better time.

The sun was quite low in the sky when they reached the city's north gate. The walls, Zora noticed as they approached, were made of gray stone, and the crenellations gave the appearance of a giant crown. Kyril handed a letter to the guardswomen on duty. Zora noticed as it passed by her nose that it carried a scent other than Lord Ranulf's.

"Lady Sigrun gives you and your party permission to use her house?" the guard asked. "What is her relationship with you?"

"She is my aunt, my father's sister."

The guard looked at Kyril's face for a moment. "I see," she said, stepping aside to allow them to pass through the gate. "Be welcome in Diadem."

"Thank you," Kyril replied as they passed.

Colin nodded a silent greeting, while Zora wondered what was happening. She was very thankful she didn't feel any new sensations as she went through the city walls, but it looked to her as if the guardswoman had recognized Kyril. Granted, he looked a lot like his father, but one trading partnership was unlikely to have made Lord Ranulf so well known that the city guards would recognize his son. *At least I hope it wouldn't. What kind of deal was that, anyway? And why is the house Sigrun's and not Ranulf's? Do men need female sponsorship to enter the city?* Zora knew that Diadem was a matriarchy, but she had no idea what that meant in terms of daily life.

They found the house without difficulty—apparently Kyril had been here with his father at least once before, and the housekeeper knew him. He introduced Colin to her, but didn't say anything about Zora. *Of course, at this size it's hard not to notice me. On the other hand, we should have come up with a name for me while I could still talk— Lady only knows what Kyril will make up on his own.*

Unfortunately, the housekeeper insisted that the dog stay in the kitchen, much to Zora's annoyance. But she was tired, and so were the boys, and at least the housekeeper fed them well.

Colin at least thought to put out food and water dishes and made up a bed of old blankets by the kitchen fire. *Definitely my favorite human.*

Zora was actually quite comfortable—if a bit lonely after everyone else had gone off to bed.

Zora woke up at sunrise, as she had done for most of her life. She was suddenly feeling better than she had since Marfa died, almost overflowing with a restless energy that would not let her sleep or even lie around. When the housekeeper came into the kitchen to build up the fire, she let the supposed dog out into the garden without comment.

The earth should have been cold under Zora's paws, because the sun hadn't reached it yet, but there was a warm patch—no, a warm path—that led across the garden. She followed it, jumping the waist-high gate between garden and alley, and continued to follow it along the cobblestone streets of the city. It was pulling her somewhere—somewhere important.

She ended up in a plaza in front of what she somehow knew was the palace, even though she had never seen it before. She wondered if this odd sudden knowledge was a way for the Goddess to speak to her when she was stuck in animal form and couldn't hear her words the way she could when she was human. Zora had barely heard the Goddess or felt her presence since the day Kassie was chosen, but now she had *something*—not the usual strong sense that the Goddess was with her, but just a faint impression that told her she was where the Goddess wanted her to be. Zora felt now that at least she knew *where* she belonged, although she still had no idea as to *why*.

The palace was the largest building she had ever seen; it was at least twice the size of the entire keep at Eagle's Rest. It was built of large pale stone blocks, with wide, low stairs leading up from the plaza to the main doors. The windows on the ground floor were a normal size, but when Zora tilted her head back she saw that the ones on the upper floor were enormous, even larger than the main doors. It appeared that the upper floor was twice the height of the lower one. The arched windows above the doors opened onto a large balcony that ran the width of the building.

Zora had never seen anything like it, but something inside her said "home." This was even stranger than when she had crossed the boundary into Diadem. She felt changed, as if some permanent alteration had been made inside her. She didn't understand it at all. She was nervous, but fortunately dogs didn't get the human "butterflies in the stomach" feeling. Her fur seemed to be trying to stand on end, but it was early enough that there were still plenty of shadows, and Zora was careful to stay in them. She wanted— needed—to see, but she didn't want to be seen. Belatedly, she remembered Colin's warning about going out alone. She carefully avoided the townspeople who stood in the square in front of the palace balcony, obviously waiting for something.

The something was apparently an announcement.

"Harken to our Queen, Chosen Daughter of the Goddess," a voice called from the upper windows.

Zora looked up just in time to see the Queen come out onto the balcony. It was Lina.

If Zora had been in human form, she would have gasped aloud. At least everyone in the plaza bowed when the Queen appeared, so nobody was paying any attention to Zora. But the Queen and Zora really *were* identical—or would be once Zora was in her true form again. *At least now I know who Lina is and where to find her. But maybe I should stay a dog. I'm not certain that changing back to human is such a good idea after all. Now I understand why Lord Ranulf told me not to show myself here in human form!*

Lina was leading a morning ritual, and it seemed familiar, even though it was not one of the ones Zora had learned at home. She could even hear the words in her head just before Lina sang them, both the Queen's part and the people's responses. When the ritual ended and the Queen went back into the palace, Zora turned to go home to Kyril and Colin, with her mind full of questions—and possibly a few answers.

It might feel right and natural to be in Diadem, but now Zora *really* wondered just why the Goddess wanted her here.

Unfortunately, Zora didn't make it back home before the boys woke. Apparently Lady Sigrun's house didn't have the same pull on her that the palace had, and she got turned around. She wandered for what felt like hours, getting more tired and lost, until she found herself back in the plaza in front of the palace. By now it was midmorning, and she wasn't hidden in a crowd anymore. If she hadn't believed what Colin said about cities and animals before— and she'd had some doubts—it was certainly clear to her that he'd been correct when the guardswomen started chasing her.

If she hadn't been in the plaza she wouldn't have had a prayer of eluding them, but somehow being there gave her just a bit more energy—and the large front doors to the palace were open.

Following her instincts, Zora ran between the guards, through the doors, and up a very shallow staircase to the second floor. The double doors at the top of the stairs were open as well, so she kept going into a large, high-ceilinged room. The light from the enormous windows at the far end of the room was in her eyes, but people were moving out of her way—or maybe they were moving out of the way of the guards chasing her. She tried to stop before she hit the wall, but the floor was marble and very slippery. She skidded and then slid until she crashed into someone's knees.

Zora and the woman she hit went down together in a tangle, but the woman rolled smoothly over to pin Zora on her back with her ribs trapped between the woman's knees. From what Zora could see of her clothing, she was a guard—so why was she staring at Zora as if she had seen a ghost? Zora was pretty sure she was an ordinary-looking dog—the boys would have said something otherwise—unless something had changed in the last few minutes.

Behind her the pursuing guards came to a stop more efficiently than Zora had done, and one of them said something about a stray dog, interspersed with an apology for interrupting the court.

"Are you certain she's a stray?" the woman kneeling over her asked, looking up at them.

"Wasn't on a leash, Sword-Bearer, and we didn't see a collar."

Zora closed her eyes and desperately pulled whatever energy she could find, praying to make one minor change. When the woman's fingertips ran through the fur at her neck, there was a collar. Zora really hoped the woman would be too busy looking at what it said to notice that it was a part of Zora's body.

"'Colin of Eagle's Rest,'" Sword-Bearer read. "Sound familiar to anyone?"

"Isn't he your cousin?" one of the guards blurted out. "He said he was."

"What? When was this?"

"He came through the north gate yesterday, with another boy and a dog that looked like this one. Genia and I were on duty."

"They did arrive yesterday," Genia confirmed—she had been one of the guards chasing Zora. "But it's the other boy, Kyril, who is your cousin. He had a letter from your mother giving them permission to stay in her house."

"It probably is my cousin," Sword-Bearer said reassuringly. "I do have a cousin by that name, and I don't expect that a couple of strange boys would know enough about my mother for the letter to be false. Adyta, go to the house on Poplar Street and see if he's there. If he is, please ask him and his friend to come and collect their pet." She moved to sit beside Zora, keeping a hand on her neck, but no longer forcing her to lie on her back. Zora flopped onto her side with a sigh of relief.

"But Sword-Bearer," a semi-familiar voice protested, "*should* she be returned to them?" The Queen knelt in a froth of skirts and her blonde hair fell forward as she bent over Zora. "Look at her! She's obviously not being fed enough, and"—Zora cringed as the girl reached for the fake collar—"this collar is so tight it's a wonder she can breathe! What kind of a brute treats a helpless animal this way?"

Zora caught a repressed choking sound from Sword-Bearer. *She's Lord Ranulf's niece, all right. Probably doesn't think I'm a real dog. And she'd be right.*

The Sword-Bearer tried to stop the Queen from touching Zora's "collar"—but this resulted in their fingers tangling into Zora's fur, putting all three of them in contact with each other. Although she knew she was lying perfectly still on the floor, Zora's brain and body were convinced that the room was whirling around them. She felt so awful that for a moment she was afraid she was going to pass out. Lina swayed against them, and Zora opened her eyes long enough to see that the girl was pale and had her own eyes squeezed tightly shut. *This can't be good. What in Earth is happening to us?*

"I would suggest this matter wait until the young man is present to defend himself," an older woman said, bending down to lift the

Queen to her feet and steer her back to her seat. "In the meantime, perhaps the animal could be removed so that court can continue."

"Of course, Shield-Bearer." The Sword-Bearer—Zora now realized that these were titles rather than names—rose to her feet, pulling the dog up by the scruff of the neck.

While Zora was grateful for the support, the Queen, of course, didn't understand. Apparently she didn't know much about dogs. "Don't hurt her!" she protested. "And get that horrible collar off her!"

"Yes, Lady." The Sword-Bearer bowed and quickly removed both herself and Zora to a small side office, closing the door behind her.

Zora flopped to the floor again as soon as she was released. *Suddenly I have about as much mobility as a puddle of water*, she thought anxiously. *What in Earth is* wrong *with me?*

The Sword-Bearer knelt beside Zora, looking anxious. "I'm Catriona, and you're Zora, right?"

Yes, she knows I'm not a dog—but how does she know who I am? I could just as well be Colin or Kyril, or any of Lord Ranulf's students.

"The Queen is right about one thing; you do look horrible. Can you get rid of that collar? It's got to disappear before anyone else notices that it's actually part of your neck."

Zora tried to undo the change she had made, with absolutely no success. She sighed and shook her head very slightly.

"There's no help for it then," Catriona said grimly. "Hold still and try not to make any noise. This may hurt."

It did hurt. Zora had no clue what Catriona was doing, but it felt like fire wrapped around her neck. She did manage to keep the noise to a very soft whimper, and eventually the pain subsided. She was dimly aware of Catriona gently stroking her ribs and murmuring "Good girl" as everything went black.

When Zora came to again, she was wrapped in a cloak and lying on a cot at the back of the room. She was alone in the office, but apparently the sound of footsteps just outside the door was what had wakened her. The door opened to admit Catriona, who was carrying some sort of shallow bucket with a lid on it. She set it on the hearth, unwrapped Zora and set her down next to it, and then removed the lid. "It's beef stew," she said. "Eat as much as you can, but please don't eat so quickly that you'll get sick."

As far as Zora was concerned at the minute, that meant 'chew once before swallowing.' The stew smelled delicious and tasted even better. *Why am I suddenly so hungry? I thought I'd gained back most of the weight I lost...*

"All right," Catriona said, regarding the empty container. "If that stays down, you can have another helping in an hour. Fortunately nobody has found Kyril yet, so we may have a bit more time—"

Given that he wasn't even awake when I left this morning, we may have quite a bit of time...

"—or not," she finished as Kyril's protesting voice sounded from the main room. "Can you stand?"

Zora struggled to her feet and slowly followed Catriona back into the main room. It was amazing how incredibly tired getting lost and wandering around the city had made her. *I think I felt better right after I changed back from being a fish for three days.*

The crowd that had been there earlier had dispersed, leaving only a handful of people. Kyril was escorted by two guards, neither of whom looked happy with him. The feeling was clearly mutual. The Queen was flanked by the Shield-Bearer, a veiled women in green, and a bitter-looking lady-in-waiting at least a decade older than the Queen. The lady-in-waiting was dressed in mourning, complete with black veils, although the face veil was thrown back at the moment. *She seems familiar, but there's no way I could possibly have seen any of them before today.*

The Queen glared at Kyril. Kyril stared dumbstruck at the Queen for a moment before recovering enough to remember to bow. "Lady," he said, almost reverently.

Colin had accompanied them, but he was letting Kyril be the visible one while he slipped quietly along the side of the room. He joined Zora and gave her an anxious look. Zora tried to look reassuring, which was rather difficult in dog-shape. Feeling scared herself didn't help either. Catriona did much better; she smiled at him and nodded before turning her attention to the group surrounding the throne.

"Good morning, Kyril," she said, and he turned to see her and then Zora.

"Oh, thank the Lady, you found her," he said, crossing to stroke Zora anxiously. "Is she all right?"

"All right?" the Queen asked incredulously. "She looks half-starved, and she's been running around the city with nobody to look after her! Is this how you take care of a helpless animal?"

Kyril was momentarily struck dumb by the injustice of this. "We've been taking good care of her," he protested.

"You haven't done a very good job," the Queen said. "I'll bet *I* could take better care of her than you do!"

"I don't think so," Kyril snapped. Whatever his initial impression of Lina had been, Zora thought, he obviously didn't like being criticized by her. "I don't think you'd know the first thing about taking care of her!"

"What is her name?"

"What?" Kyril sounded stupid, which was only slightly unfair. He and Colin couldn't very well use Zora's real name. Catriona might not be the only one to recognize it.

The Queen sighed in exasperation. "Does she even *have* a name, or do you just call her 'dog'?"

"Look," Kyril said, obviously trying to be reasonable. "I wasn't the person who half-starved her, and if you think she looks bad now, you should have seen her before. We've been taking very good care of her."

"Until this morning, apparently," the Shield-Bearer put in. "How did she get away from you?"

Colin shook his head. "The housekeeper let her out into the garden before we woke up, and when we went to look for her, she wasn't there. I have no idea how she got out—the garden is fenced—and we've been looking for her all morning."

"Apparently she doesn't want to stay with you," the Queen said smugly.

It was unfortunate that Kyril's response to this was to clench the hand holding Zora's fur into a fist so tight that he pulled her fur and she let out a yip of protest.

"See what I mean?" the Queen said triumphantly.

If they were cats, the fur would be flying by now. Please, Goddess, do something!

"How about a compromise?" Catriona said. "Leave her with me, I'll look after her, and all of you," she looked at the Queen, Kyril, and Colin in turn, "can check on her every day to make sure she's being treated well."

"All right," Kyril said. "As long as I can visit every day, I'll agree to leave her in your care."

Thank you so much for giving up without even a token protest, Kyril. Unless your father told you to do that, I'm seriously annoyed with you.

Colin looked less happy with that solution, but he had also looked much less impressed by the Queen's beauty. Zora wasn't impressed by her beauty at all. The Queen looked just like her. She got the impression that Kyril was happy to have an excuse to see more of Lina, but Zora couldn't begin to imagine why. *Love at first sight?*

"She still needs a proper name," the Queen said. "We'll call her Princess—it will give her something to grow into."

The lady in black muttered something that sounded to Zora like "A bitch would be a suitable Heiress for you." If anyone else in the room heard her, they ignored it, and the lack of reaction left Zora wondering what it was she had heard. It *couldn't* have been what it sounded like.

Lina might be young and maybe even a bit scatterbrained, but she *was* the Queen. Even if nobody respected her as a person, they should respect the title and what it represented. Judging from the morning ritual, the Queen wasn't just the temporal ruler, she was the high priestess as well. Was she also considered an avatar, the physical presence of the Goddess in this realm?

"The dog stays here, then," the Shield-Bearer said. "Now that that's settled, Lady, you had better get some luncheon unless you want to do your afternoon meditation fasting."

The Queen nodded. "Take good care of Princess, Sword-Bearer. I'll check on her after meditation."

As she left the room, trailed by her entourage, Catriona took a grip on Kyril's arm. "I'd like a few words with you two before you leave." She dismissed the guards with thanks for having found Kyril. Then she took both boys and the dog back to her office and closed the door.

CHAPTER FIVE

"All right, Kyril, what is going on here?" Catriona demanded. "I gather that this is Druscilla's daughter Zora."

"Yes," Kyril said, "but how in Earth can you tell?"

"Mixed blood," Catriona explained. "My mother's a changer, but my father is a mage. I don't have much magic, but I do have a bit. I can see a changer's true shape if I touch her, and I can do a force-change if I absolutely have to."

"What's a force-change?" Zora was glad that Colin asked because she couldn't in her present form, and she felt too tired to change back to human just then. She also had no particular desire to be naked in front of two boys her own age—even if she did regard Kyril as a brother, or perhaps especially because she regarded Kyril as a brother.

"Changing someone else's shape," Catriona explained. "It only works on a changer, and the person doing the force-change has to be a changer *and* have magical abilities."

"That would explain why Lord Ranulf didn't teach us that," Colin said. He doesn't have magic, does he?"

"No, and neither does my mother. But when the guards chased Zora in here and said she was a stray because she didn't have a leash or collar, she somehow managed to produce a collar while everyone was looking at the guards. I'm fairly sure I'm the only one who noticed that it was actually part of her neck, but the Queen touched it and thinks it was brutally tight. And then Zora didn't have the strength to get rid of it, so I had to do it for her, after which she passed out for nearly an hour. So," she glared at the boys, "if you've been taking proper care of her, why is she so weak that she can't do a simple change? And just how long has she been a dog?"

"She's only been a dog for the last a couple of days," Kyril tried to explain. "Father said that she must not enter Diadem in human shape. He wouldn't say why, but now that we've seen the Queen, we can guess. He knew they looked alike, didn't he?"

Catriona nodded. "So why is she having trouble changing?"

"Trouble changing?" Kyril asked. "I don't know. She could change yesterday."

"She seemed to be recovering while we were travelling," Colin said, "but before that, her mother was starving her. We don't know if it was on purpose or not."

"I've met her mother," Catriona sighed, "and you're right. It could be either."

"Maybe the fish had something to do with it," Kyril added.

"Fish?" Catriona asked incredulously.

"She spent three days as a fish—but that was months ago. As far as I know she was human from then until we left on the annual shape-changer hunt." Kyril frowned. "There *was* that strange potion that she and Kassie made. It made her really sick and she slept for most of a day before it wore off. And that was when Colin realized that her mother was starving her, so he started sneaking more food to her after that."

"Where does Kassie fit into all this?"

"My sister Kassie is the new priestess of the Earth Mother, which was really a surprise because everyone expected it to be Zora."

Catriona stroked Zora's head. "So you're saying that in a period of a few months, Zora has had her life turned upside down, spent much too long as a fish, been poisoned while in human form, and become so weakened that she is having trouble changing shape until she recovers from near starvation."

"She *was* doing much better until we got here." Kyril clearly did not want to sound neglectful. "Maybe it's something about being in Diadem."

"She did trip over her own feet when we passed the boundary stone," Colin added.

Catriona's eyes widened. "Did she now? That's interesting."

"What does it mean?" Colin asked anxiously. "She couldn't cross back over the boundary either, even when I was carrying her."

Catriona shrugged. "Perhaps nothing. It's too soon to tell. But I think having her spend time with the Queen will be good for both of them. I'll take care of Zora. You two go home and get some rest yourself. And when you come back here, remember that you are coming to court and dress accordingly. The clothes you wear to search the city for your lost dog are not appropriate for court."

Kyril nodded. "Mother did pack proper clothes for me, but when I woke up this morning and found Zora missing I was so worried..."

"Remember that the dog's name is Princess," Catriona warned him. "If you start calling her Zora, we'll have a problem when she turns human."

"And the Queen would probably get mad at me again." Kyril sighed. "Do you think she'll get over being angry? I mean, you can explain to her that I wasn't mistreating 'Princess'—I want her to like me, and this was a lousy beginning." He sighed again. "She so beautiful."

Catriona looked questioningly at him. "Doesn't Zora look just like her?"

"There's a resemblance, I guess," Kyril admitted, "but Zora is like a sister to me."

"I supposed she would be." Catriona smiled wryly. "We'll see you later. Tomorrow will be soon enough."

Colin knelt and hugged Zora, very gently. "Take care, and for the Lady's sake, eat!"

After they left, Zora followed Catriona down the broad staircase, around to the left side of the building to the kitchens, where she ate another bowl of stew. When she finished that, Catriona took her outside to a large enclosed garden between the wings of the palace. Near the back of garden was a pool with a benches beside it and bushes that provided shade for the benches.

Catriona flopped down on a bench and sprawled on her back. "I would suggest a nap."

That sounded good, and Zora curled up on the ground near the bench. It was very peaceful there; nobody else was at this end of the garden. Beyond the bushes was a wall, and the river was obviously on the other side of the wall, although it sounded as if it were lower down rather than right next to them. The sound of running water was there, but it was muted and came from below.

Even in the shade the ground still felt warm to Zora. Now that she thought about it, the ground in Diadem seemed to be unusually warm...and comfortable...

When Zora woke, Catriona took her back to the kitchen and fed her again. Zora was still eating when the Queen came looking for her.

"She's still too thin," the Queen said, "but at least you got rid of that awful collar. Should I have a new one made for her? I could get several, so she'd have one to match each of my gowns."

Zora gave a soft growl of protest. *I might be a dog, but I'm not a fashion accessory.*

Catriona said quickly, "I wouldn't advise putting a collar on her before we know what size she's going to be. I don't think she really needs one, anyway. She seems well-trained and intelligent. I've been telling her what I want her to do and she's been doing it, so I think she probably understands quite a bit of what we say to her."

Not to mention everything you say to each other.

"Well if she'll follow me without a collar and leash, I won't put them on her now," the Queen said. "Come on, Princess, it's time to go to bed."

Zora followed the Queen, who had apparently ordered a bed set up for 'Princess' in a corner of her own bedroom. It was a nice, thick cushion covered with soft blankets. Zora curled up on it and fell asleep almost immediately.

When Zora woke up the next morning, she was alone in the Queen's bedroom. She was feeling better than she had the night before, but then, she had felt pretty good yesterday morning before things went wrong. She thought she had been afraid that day in the temple at Eagle's Rest when she couldn't open the library, but she was even more frightened now. *I'm in a strange city, where I don't know the people or the customs, something here is sapping my energy and making me sick*—her stomach was one big knot, and she tried to force herself to breathe slowly and evenly so her throat muscles wouldn't go into spasm—*the Goddess wants me to stay here, which means I may keep getting sick for the rest of my life, and on top of everything else, I'm stuck as a dog!* She didn't want to even try to imagine what the people around her would say if she changed back to human. *And if I'm accompanying the*

Queen everywhere, I'm not going to have much privacy.

As if summoned by her thoughts, the Queen returned to the bedroom, followed by a veiled priestess dressed in green. Zora couldn't tell if it was the same one as yesterday or another woman; the loose robe and the veils would do a good job of hiding anyone's identity.

"Good morning, Princess," the Queen said. Her voice was cheerful, but Zora thought the cheer seemed forced. "You were sleeping so soundly when it was time to do the morning ritual that I left you here to sleep, but now that you're awake we can have breakfast together!"

Why is this girl so desperate for someone to talk to that she doesn't even care if they're human? Granted, I haven't seen any of the priestesses talk yet, and that woman dressed all in black—the one who called me a bitch yesterday—doesn't seem like cheerful company, but Catriona's nice, and the Shield-Bearer seemed decent enough...

Zora followed the Queen to a small parlor next to Catriona's office. A servant put a tray of food in front of her and another bowl of meat in front of Zora and left the room. Catriona, hearing Lina's voice, came in to check on Zora/Princess.

"You're eating here instead of the hall?" she asked the Queen. She didn't wait for an answer before turning her attention to Zora. "Still, the dog is looking better this morning. I think the fresh air yesterday helped. There's no court this morning, so you can take her out in the garden after breakfast."

"All right," the Queen agreed. "But what if that boy comes back?"

"*Lord Kyril* will undoubtedly be back today. That was the agreement, that both of you could make certain Princess was being well cared for. Be thankful I persuaded him not to come back last night."

The Queen scowled. "He really doesn't deserve to have her."

"If the two of you are going to squabble over her as if you were toddlers, I'll find someplace else for her to live."

"You wouldn't do that..." The Queen didn't sound very sure.

"I'd do it in a heartbeat," Catriona said promptly, "and the Shield-Bearer would support me."

"Just because my mother died and made her my Regent," the

Queen sighed. "I'll bet my *mother* would have supported me in this."

"I wouldn't bet on that." Catriona looked the Queen straight in the eye. "What did I just say the young man's name was?"

"Who cares?"

"You do, if you want to share custody of Princess."

"Kyril, wasn't it?" The Queen scowled. "Considering the fact that any man unfortunate enough to be involved with me has the lifespan of a crop of wheat, it's much easier if I *don't* try to remember their names."

"*Lord* Kyril." Catriona paused. "Like *Lady* Esme."

"But Esme got her title because her father was the Year-King!"

Her father was a Year-King?

"So did Kyril. His father was married to your mother."

"When? Kyril looks about my age!"

"He is."

"But he can't be!"

"Lina," Catriona said gently. "Not *all* Year-Kings die. Occasionally one of them does survive the Sacrifice. Kyril is the son of Lord Ranulf, Beloved of the Goddess."

Sacrifice? "Beloved of the Goddess"? What exactly is a Year-King? Could this be any more confusing? I wish Kyril had told us more before we got here.

"How nice that *he* got to grow up with a father," the Queen said bitterly.

Catriona sighed. "Just eat your breakfast." She looked down at the full bowl still in front of Zora. "You, too."

Lina and Zora finished their respective meals in near silence, broken only by an occasional sniffle from Lina.

The idea of a Year-King certainly seems to upset her. A lot. I really need to find out about this—too bad I can't just ask the Goddess. At the moment I can't even ask Kyril how much more his father told him than he told us before we got here. Knowing Lord Ranulf, I bet he told Kyril quite a bit that he hasn't shared with Colin and me.

"Come." Lina shoved her plate away and made a hasty retreat from the room. Zora scrambled to keep up as they made their way to the far end of the garden.

Lina sat on a bench near the pool with her back to the sun—and the palace—while Zora sprawled on the ground, basking in the warmth. Lina sat quietly, her eyes fixed unseeingly on the bushes in front of her.

She still doesn't look happy, but at least she no longer looks totally miserable. And she's one of those lucky girls who can cry without getting red-rimmed eyes. I think I could learn to hate her if I didn't feel so sorry for her. She's even more trapped here than I am.

Kyril and Colin arrived at midmorning, and Catriona escorted them back to join Lina and Zora. Catriona sat on the bench next to Lina, while Kyril perched carefully on the rim of the pool and Colin, heedless of his—or possibly Kyril's—good clothes, sat on the ground next to Zora and scratched behind her ears. She resisted the impulse to climb into his lap. That particular impulse was not a good sign. *I've stayed too long in this shape if I'm starting to feel its instincts.*

Kyril was explaining to the Queen that Colin was his foster brother and was very fond of animals. Catriona was presumably mentally translating that into "one of Lord Ranulf's shape-changer fosterlings" as she reported that Princess's condition seemed to be improving.

"She slept with me last night," the Queen said smugly.

Kyril almost succeeded in biting back a grin. "Lucky dog."

Was that a straight line he just couldn't resist, or is he really interested in her? There were more boys than girls at Eagle's Rest, and Kyril had never seemed interested in any of the girls there. Then again, Lord Ranulf's normal training sessions didn't leave any of his students with a lot of extra energy. Maybe that was deliberate. Zora didn't know what Lord Ranulf told the boys, but Lady Akila's lectures to the girls on shape-changer pregnancy did *not* encourage experimentation—especially in the girls old enough to remember the birth of Lady Akila's youngest children. Carrying a shape-changer child was difficult for the mother, and the risk of death was much higher than it was for the mother of a human child.

Colin kept a hand on Zora's head, which was still resting on his knee, but Kyril seemed more interested in talking to the Queen than fussing over "his" dog. He told her stories of his travels with his father, who seemed to have taken him to every estate he owned. "...but I like Diadem. It's a beautiful city."

While they made conversation, Colin bent his head over Zora's and spoke very softly. "I'm glad that you're doing better. Just remember that if you don't change back soon you'll risk getting stuck. So eat and rest as much as you can, all right?"

Zora nodded very slightly, and he whispered "Good" as he returned to scratching behind her ears. She leaned against him and, at least for the time being, was content.

Kyril and Colin stayed to eat with the Queen. Apparently she didn't have a choice as to where she ate lunch; the meal was served in the great hall. It was near the kitchens, so at least the food was still hot when the servants put it in front of them. Lina and the boys sat at a table on a dais at one end of the room, flanked by the Shield-Bearer and the Sword-Bearer. Everyone else sat at two tables that ran the length of the hall. Lady Esme sat at the near end of one of them, and the ubiquitous green-robed woman sat opposite her at the other table. Zora quickly discovered that under the high table was the best place to stay out of the way. Lina was a bit quiet at first, but Kyril told jokes that had her giggling through the rest of the meal.

As soon as the meal ended, however, Catriona sent the boys home, explaining that it was time for the Queen to meditate in her private chapel. She did not, however, object when Lina insisted that Princess accompany her. She didn't even wince when Lina started talking about matching hair ribbons.

Zora did wince. *Where is she planning to tie hair ribbons on me? My ears?* She accompanied Lina and Catriona through a confusing series of hallways and passages. *It is much too easy to get lost here.* Of course, before Zora came to Diadem she had lived in the same place her entire life, so learning her way around new buildings hadn't been a skill she had any reason to cultivate. *I'm still realizing how much my life changed when the Goddess chose Kassie.*

Finally they came to a small chamber—or maybe a cave. Zora had the distinct feeling that this was original and the rest of the palace had been built around it later. Much later. There was a plain wooden bench at one side, a tunnel leading away on the other, and a thick wooden door in front of them. Catriona opened the door and lit a torch set in a bracket beside the door with a flint from her belt pouch, and then took a seat on the bench with the air of one prepared to spend a long time there.

Lina took the torch and entered the chamber. Zora followed her, and Catriona closed the door behind them.

This room was unmistakably a cave, although someone had leveled the floor and polished a section of it. Lina headed straight across it toward the far end of the cavern, but Zora stopped at the edge of the polished area, feeling a sudden surge of warmth. *This feels like the ground in the garden, but much stronger—and there's no sun here.* She looked down and saw that there was a pattern set into the floor, made up of darker and lighter stones. The pattern was vaguely tree-shaped, but somehow the path wound along all of the branches, ending at the top of the tree, where it fed into a half-circle that enclosed what appeared to be a round boulder that had been cut in half and a wooden bench along the back wall. Lina was already sitting on the bench, looking bored.

Zora found herself following the path, unable to step off it, until it ended at the boulder. For some reason the path seemed familiar—yet another familiar thing that she had certainly never seen before. *Either there is something very strange going on here, or I am losing my mind.* She wasn't sure which alternative disturbed her more.

The top of the boulder had been polished to form a smooth, dark mirror-like surface and appeared to be a very shallow, almost flat, bowl covered with water. There was a deeper indentation cut into the center with a handful of smooth small stones in it. Wondering how the water had stayed so clear in a place where most of the floor had a layer of dust, Zora examined the rough sides of the rock. They were wet over every bit of the surface, and she realized that this was not a sculpture. It was a fountain.

She touched her nose to the water flowing across the top of the rock, and then—

There was a flash of bright green light and a burst of the strongest energy Zora had ever encountered. Then she was lying flat on her back on the rock floor, naked. Her back hurt—all along the length of her spine—and Lina was screaming. Even though Zora was now a human instead of a dog, her ears hurt. The screams were excruciating.

Zora tried to lift her head, but her neck muscles refused to work. After a few days of her using the muscles at the *back* of her neck to lift her head, she found the muscles at the front weren't quite up to the task. There was a sharp pain in her breastbone when she tried to sit up, but she finally managed to prop herself up on her elbows. She could turn her head, but moving it hurt her neck. She looked anxiously toward the door. It was thick, but Lina's screaming was pretty loud.

Sure enough, the door opened a crack and Catriona's head appeared. Lina, mercifully, fell silent when she saw her.

"I heard a scream— Oh." She looked from Zora to Lina and back. "You two can work this out between yourselves." Her head disappeared and the door closed again.

"I can't believe she just left like that—she's supposed to be my bodyguard!" Lina stared at the door in disbelief.

At least she's not still screaming. "I guess she doesn't think your body is in any danger from me."

Lina studied Zora from head to toe. "You obviously don't need *my* body," she said slowly. "You've got one that looks just like it. How old are you, anyway?"

"Seventeen," Zora replied. "How old are you?"

"I turned eighteen three days ago."

Zora did a quick calculation. "That makes you four months older than I am."

"I guess we're not twins, then," Lina said wistfully. "Too bad. I'd like to have a sister."

Zora nodded. It hurt. She pushed herself painfully into a seated position, and touched a cautious fingertip to the top of the rock. This time there were no strange lights, and the energy was gentle and cool. It flowed through her body, chasing the pain away. "What is this?"

"What?" Lina stared at her blankly.

"This." Zora traced her finger through the water across the smooth surface of the stone.

"It's a rock. With water."

Isn't she supposed to be some sort of priestess? "Why is it here? What does it do?"

Lina shrugged. "I don't know."

And it doesn't sound as though you care either. This might be a problem. I wonder if it's why I'm here. Given that I'm suddenly human again, maybe it is.

"So," Lina asked, "should I worry about your taking my clothes?"

I'm getting the impression she's really not a deep thinker. Also, I'm really glad that the floor in here is warm. "No." Zora shook her head, thankful that it didn't hurt anymore. "I expect to be a dog again by the time we leave this room, so I won't need to borrow your clothes."

"What in Earth are you?"

"I'm a shape-changer."

"So you can choose to be a dog, or to be me..."

"Not exactly. I didn't intend to turn human just then. I think the Goddess did that."

"Why would she turn you into me?"

"She didn't. This is what I really look like—at least as far as I can tell." Zora rolled to her knees and twisted to look at her reflection in the water. "Yes, that's my face." Lina bent to look over her shoulder, and both faces were clearly visible in the smooth sheet of water on top of the polished black rock.

"We have the same face," Lina said flatly. "And I'll bet you *could* wear my clothes."

"Probably, though they might be a bit loose at the moment."

"Are you calling me *fat?*" Lina asked indignantly.

"No, of course not. The trouble with changing shape is that it requires a *lot* of energy," Zora explained. "I was sick a while ago, and just when I was starting to get better... Can you see all my ribs again?"

Lina leaned back against the wall behind the bench. "Yes. You looked better as a dog!"

Zora sighed. "Well, I did have fur. That helps some—at least it hides the protruding ribs."

"Not enough. Is that why you were a dog?"

"No. I think I was a dog because I look so much like you."

"That doesn't make sense," Lina complained.

"You're the Queen," Zora pointed out. "How would people here react to the arrival of a foreigner who looks just like you, but doesn't know anything about life here? Lord Ranulf gave strict orders that I was not to enter Diadem in human shape or to change back to human until I understood why it mattered what I looked like."

"But why a dog?"

"At home I'd be a wolf—actually I was a wolf the night before we arrived here because I was hunting."

"Hunting what?" Lena sounded nervous.

"Rabbits." Zora laughed. "It's fairly easy to hunt in wolf-shape, and the person who hunts doesn't have to cook or clean up afterward. So once I brought the rabbits back, the boys did all the rest of the work, while I lazed around next to the fire."

"If you had come to the city as a wolf," Lina said, "I think most people would have been terrified of you."

"That's what Colin said. He's the one who lived in a city before. Kyril and I grew up at Eagle's Rest. It's probably not *the* end of the world, but I think it's *an* end of the world." Zora laughed. "Colin told Kyril that his problem was that he looked at a wolf and expected it to be a member of his family, and Kyril said that at home it usually was."

"Is Kyril your boyfriend?"

Zora shook her head, smiling at the idea. "No. He's my cousin, but we were raised more like brother and sister. He worries about me because if anything happened to me while I was in his care my mother would kill him—well, not literally. His father would stop her, but my mother can throw tantrums like you wouldn't believe."

"Is that why you ran away? Don't you realize how lucky you are to even *have* a mother?"

"You haven't met my mother. Besides, the Goddess wanted me to leave home, and my mother was being totally unreasonable about it. She wouldn't even let me out of her rooms, and she was the one who was starving me."

"But why would the Goddess want you to leave home?" Lena asked, obviously confused.

Zora shared her confusion. "I don't know," she admitted. "All I know is that she seems to want me to be here."

"Why?"

Zora shrugged. "I guess we'll find out in the Goddess's own good time."

"What makes you think she wants you here, anyway?" Lina asked.

"Doesn't she talk to you?" Zora asked in surprise. "Your

position is much more important than mine, so I'd expect her to."

"What do you mean by *talk*?"

"I hear her, like a voice in my head."

"Actual words?" Lina sounded skeptical.

"Yes, usually. Sometimes I can't hear her—being an animal keeps a changer from being able to hear the Goddess—but normally, I hear what she says to me."

"If she's so willing to talk to you," Lina said bitterly, "ask her why she wants me to be a murderess!"

"What are you talking about?"

"Every spring I have to marry some man, and then at the end of the summer he gets sacrificed!"

Married? She's only my age! When Kyril told Colin and me about the Year-King, he didn't say that the Queen had to marry him so young! It also didn't sound like anything that involved death when he described it, and he said that Lord Ranulf was one. Zora tried to come up with some sort of coherent reply, but what came out was "Sacrificed how?"

"Pushed off the terrace into the river at the waterfall."

Zora couldn't help it; she started laughing hysterically.

Lina glared at her and then slapped her across the face.

"I'm sorry," Zora gasped. "I know it's not at all funny, but now I know what Catriona meant about Uncle Ranulf."

"What does your uncle have to do with this?" Lina was still annoyed.

"She said he was a Year-King, and she must have been right." Zora drew in a deep breath and bit the inside of her cheek to keep from going into another fit of giggles. "He trains shape-changers, and one of his tests—well, somebody drugs your wine at dinner, and then you get dragged out of bed in the middle of the night and tossed off a cliff with a river way down below it. You have to be able to turn into a bird on the way down and then into a fish when you go into the water. Then you have to swim downstream to the lake, make your way to the shore, get out of the water, and change to something that breathes air. Until you can do that, you don't pass the test."

Lina stared at her in horrified fascination. "How many students die in that test?"

"None," Zora assured her. "If you're too drugged to make the change in the air, a couple of the stronger changers will catch you, and if you don't change into a fish—or if you forget to change *out* of a fish—somebody will drag you out of the water. It would be easy without the drug. Being drugged means that you have to be good enough to change automatically, without thinking about it."

"The king is drugged," Lina said softly. "I'm not sure if it's so he won't suffer much or so he won't struggle and upset the ritual."

"Maybe a bit of both, but I'll bet that's why Lord Ranulf drugs the students for that test. Any student of his—" Zora froze suddenly, realizing what she was saying. "Any of Lord Ranulf's students should be able to survive the Sacrifice. The waterfall would make it harder, and there are probably rocks at the base of it, but even so..."

"Too bad the Year-Kings aren't his students," Lina said bitterly. "As it is now, being Queen is a curse."

There was a sharp rap on the door, and Catriona poked her head in. "It's time to go back upstairs," she said. "Zora, do you need help changing back?"

Zora still remembered vividly the pain of the force-change to get rid of the collar. She rolled to her hands and knees and touched her lips to the water flowing across the top of the rock. *Please, Lady,* she thought as she visualized the dog-shape.

The change came so quickly she was scarcely aware of it before she was in dog-shape again.

"I wish I could do that," Lina sighed.

I wish I had more control over it, Zora thought anxiously. *What can I do stuck in this shape?*

CHAPTER SIX

Apparently what Zora could do as a dog was follow Lina everywhere she went. *I could even say that I'm dogging her heels.* It was very informative. Zora had thought at first that Lina was a spoiled brat, and there were still times when she reminded her of Druscilla, but Zora slowly began to realize that Lina had almost no privacy. The only places she was left alone were the Queen's chapel and in her bedroom at night. Even then a priestess, one of the veiled women in green, slept in the antechamber between the bedroom and the hall. Lina also had no control over her own life beyond choosing which item on her plate to eat first at meals and deciding what to embroider in her "free" time, when she sat with at least one priestess, Lady Esme, and usually a guardswoman in attendance—and this was in the walled garden of her own palace! *It's as if they're afraid she'll run away if they take their eyes off her. Come to think of it, she's so unhappy that she might actually try it. I think I might be tempted in her place, not so much because of her duties, but because of the obvious lack of trust from everyone around her.*

Kyril showed up every day, ostensibly to check on the dog, and spent his time flirting with the Queen. Colin, who always accompanied him, was the one who actually *was* checking on the dog.

"Lady," Colin said to Lina, after nearly a week had passed, "would you allow us to take Princess home with us—at least for tonight?"

"Why?" Lina asked, looking wide-eyed and innocent.

"Uh...because we miss her," Colin stammered. Zora was glad that dogs couldn't burst out laughing uncontrollably.

"You see her every day," Lina pointed out. She was the very picture of reason, but Zora's ears, well attuned to Lina's voice by now, caught a very faint quaver.

She's having trouble keeping a straight face. I wonder how much longer she can keep this up.

Lina didn't try very hard. "She does make a beautiful dog, doesn't she?"

Colin tensed, and Kyril frankly gaped. "Don't you mean *is* a beautiful dog?" Kyril asked.

Lina started laughing. "If you two could see your faces!"

"What makes you think she's not a dog?" Colin asked cautiously.

"She turns human in the chapel."

Colin exhaled sharply and shivered as the tension left his body.

"Why were you so worried that I'd find out— Oh!" Lina realized what the problem was. "You were afraid she was going to get stuck in that shape."

"Yes," Colin said, "but if she's spending a couple of hours a day as a human, she should be all right."

"If she needs more time," Lina said practically, "I can always lock my door at night so she can sleep in human shape."

"You'll tell her if you need to do that, right?" Colin said firmly to Zora.

Zora nodded. It was nice to have someone who cared about her here. She wondered if anyone worried about whether Lina, not just the Queen, was well and happy.

"Do you like Kyril?" Zora asked Lina as they sat in the chapel the next afternoon.

Lina blushed and looked down at her hands. "Yes," she admitted. "But it doesn't matter if I like anyone or not. I'll have to marry again in a few months, and the Goddess will choose the man. If I'm lucky, he'll be really old and somebody I've never met before."

"Why would you want an elderly husband?" Zora asked. "It sounds dull."

"If I don't care about him, it hurts less when he dies," Lina said crossly. "The last thing I want is a husband I actually *like*."

Zora had actually forgotten about the Sacrifice. "Sorry. I see what you mean."

"The other one, Kyril's friend—what's his name?"

"You mean Colin?"

Yes. How did you meet him?

"He's one of Lord Ranulf's students. We've known each other for years."

"So it isn't really *animals* he likes," Lina said archly. "He likes *you.*"

"I *think* he might like me. But he does like animals. All of us do. You can't change into the shape of something you don't like—not easily, at least. Besides, anyone who lived at Eagle's Rest and didn't like animals would be miserable."

That gave Lina something to discuss with Kyril the next day. She asked him about the animals who lived around Eagle's Rest, and then gazed raptly at him for the next three hours while he talked.

Zora lay in her usual place—with her head in Colin's lap—and worried. *What if Kyril is chosen to be the Year-King? He'd probably be fine, but I'm afraid Lina would take it badly. Very badly.*

Zora's life was falling into a routine—or perhaps a rut. By the end of the second week she had memorized the pattern of the labyrinth set into the chapel floor. She always walked along its path—she felt compelled to—while Lina just walked straight across it as if it weren't there. Zora could tell the fountain was important, too— aside from enabling her to change shape, which she still could not do outside the chapel. Lina ignored both the fountain and the labyrinth, as if neither had anything to do with her.

"Living water," Zora remarked one afternoon, as she ran a fingertip across the top of the surface, briefly making a trail in the water. She did that a lot; she found it soothing. Lina never touched it. *I wonder why.*

"What?" Lina may not have been interested in the chapel or whatever meditation she was supposed to be doing, but she did seem to like having a girl her own age to talk to. Zora didn't blame her. Everyone else around was old enough to be her mother. *That might be why she's so friendly to Kyril, too, although she pretty much ignores Colin. Of course, he pretty much ignores her too.*

"The water is the blood of the land," Zora murmured, mostly to herself, because this wasn't the sort of thing that interested Lina. "It wells up in the center of the rock, which comes from the earth, and then it spreads out and runs down along the sides." She put her face practically on the floor to look more carefully at the base of the rock, which would have been easier if she'd been a dog at the moment. "And then the water returns to the earth." She sat back on her heels and stretched. "I wonder if this is what the Queen is supposed to contemplate."

Both of you should be contemplating it, the voice of the Goddess said in her head.

Zora jumped. It was the first time the Goddess had spoken to her since she arrived in Diadem.

"What is it?" Lina asked.

"Didn't you hear her?"

"Hear who?"

"The Goddess. She said that both of us are supposed to be contemplating the water and the earth."

"Are you sure it's not just your imagination?"

"Positive."

"But that's stupid. It's just a rock!" Lina said in frustration. "You sound like the First Priestess. She's always trying to tell me that stupid things like that are important."

Your lives and your souls depend on your understanding...

Zora closed her eyes for a moment, thankful beyond words that the Goddess was talking to her again. She decided, however, that she wasn't going to share that last remark with Lina—at least not now. Lina was already a nervous wreck. Truthfully, Zora was frightened as well. She had a strong feeling that something was very wrong at court, but she hadn't yet been able to figure out what it was. Maybe this was something that could help.

"What did the First Priestess say about it?" Zora asked.

"I don't remember," Lina said crossly. "If you could stay human long enough, you could ask her yourself, if you care all that much." She slumped back against the wall, crossed her arms across her breasts, and glared at the water.

"Or you could ask her while I'm with you," Zora said, trying to cajole Lina into a better mood. "I can hear and understand just fine when I'm a dog."

Lina looked curious. "Can you read? When you're a dog, I mean."

"Not really. Large, simple signs, yes. Scrolls, books, or anything like that...unfortunately not." Zora looked at her hands. "Paws are no good for writing or turning pages. 'Speaking' is limited to 'one bark for yes, two barks for no' answers to questions, and that's only when people aren't around to notice that the 'dog' is acting odd. When you're a dog you get pretty good at listening. It's what you do best." *Is that* why I'm a dog? *Is the Goddess trying to get me to listen? If so, to what?*

"It must be frustrating," Lina remarked.

"Very."

"I don't think I'd like it. It would be nice to turn into a bird and fly away from here, but I guess I'm glad I'm not a shape-changer."

Zora opened her mouth and then quickly shut it. *You look* like a *shape-changer. You have the same body type that I do, that all of my cousins so—even Catriona has it. Under all the clothing you wear it doesn't show, but even though you look slender, you have muscles instead of fat—and you don't do the kind of exercise that we do to get them. I wonder...*

What she said was, "Could you ask the First Priestess? About the rock and the water?"

Lina sighed. "All right, if you really want me to. I have a lesson tomorrow, anyway."

Zora was prevented from asking what sort of lesson by Catriona's calling Lina. As she walked in dog-shape back through the labyrinth she thought, *Whether the Goddess intends to teach me to listen or not, I'm certainly being forced to learn patience. I just wish it was easier. But then I guess it wouldn't be patience.* She grinned to herself, thinking what a prayer for it would sound like. *Lady, grant me patience—right now!*

To Zora's surprise, Lina actually did remember her question. After breakfast the next morning they went down to the chapel's antechamber—but instead of going into the chapel, they went down the tunnel that stretched off to the side. Catriona waited on the bench in the antechamber behind them. *Presumably wherever we're going is safe enough that Lina doesn't need a bodyguard.*

They came out of the corridor into a largish room, rather like an underground version of a solar. There was a rectangular table with six chairs around it, a couple of padded couches along the walls, a sideboard and several tall cabinets, and a lot of curtained doorways. Five of them were on one wall, and their curtains were drawn back, displaying small rooms with simple furnishings. Each one held a bed, neatly made and covered with a wool blanket, a clothing chest, and a washstand. Light came in through some sort of translucent crystal high on the wall of each room, providing illumination in the main room as well.

A woman, presumably the First Priestess, stood at the table waiting for Lina. She wore the green robe and veil that all the priestesses wore, but the veil was thrown back so that her face was visible. She had the look of someone resigned to the duty of teaching but with no great hopes for her student.

"First Priestess," Lina said politely, taking a seat at the table. The woman sat opposite her.

"Is there anything particular that you would like to discuss today, Lady?" The priestess clearly expected either a 'no' or perhaps no reply at all.

"Yes," Lina said.

Zora was lying on the floor beside Lina's chair, so she saw the priestess's muscles twitch under her long tunic as if the woman was startled—as if the furniture suddenly spoke. *She doesn't seem to expect much of Lina. I think she'd be less startled if I had asked the question.*

"I was wondering about the rock in the chapel. The one with the water. What does it do?"

"It's an anchor point, Lady," the priestess replied, suddenly sounding much more interested in the lesson.

I bet she was getting even more bored and frustrated than Lina was.

The priestess continued, "It's a place where two elements— earth and water, in this case—mix smoothly together. Earth and Water are female elements—"

That would be a surprise to Galin—and the Lord of Water, Zora thought, remembering the temple at home.

"—while Air and Fire are male elements."

—and to Akila and the Lady of Fire.

"The rock in the chapel represents the body of the Goddess, while the water represents her blood. When they are mixed in such a fashion, they are a source of power, as well as a reminder that the Queen's body serves the same function during major rituals."

Rituals, plural? How many are there?

"The reason that you spend time next to them each day is so that your body will have the strength and knowledge it needs for these rituals. Does that help with your question?"

"Yes." Lina's voice was oddly subdued. "Thank you."

She sounds as if something is troubling her. Zora was surprised to find that she was feeling protective toward Lina. She had started out thinking Lina was a useless idiot, but spending all that time with her—and having her be the only person Zora could talk to—was creating a bond between them. *She might be an idiot, but she's* my *idiot.*

"First Priestess?" Lina asked tentatively. "Is it *really* necessary to have the Sacrifice? Does the Goddess need it?"

"I don't know whether the Goddess does—perhaps not, given that the occasional king does survive. The people, however, definitely do."

"The people?" Lina sounded incredulous.

Why would the people need the Sacrifice if the Goddess doesn't?

"Why do you do the morning and evening rituals on the balcony in front of the palace each day?"

"Uh...because you told me to?"

Dear Lady, it's like listening to Kassie! Why does the Goddess choose the ignorant? Did all the studying I did disqualify me?

The priestess sighed audibly. "Well, at least you do them. No, Lina, the reason you do them is so the people know and are reminded each day that the Queen is their intermediary, that she stands between them and the Goddess. As for the Sacrifice, there have been attempts to end it, but they have not gone well."

"What happened?" Lina asked curiously. Zora was wondering that too.

"A couple of generations ago one of the Queens decreed that the Year-King not be sacrificed. We have no idea why—perhaps she fell in love with him. On the proper day the people dragged them to the terrace and pushed *both* of them into the waterfall. And the harvest was particularly good that year, so the next Queen didn't try to argue about it."

"They killed a *Queen?*"

"Need I remind you that the Queen *cannot* simply decree anything she wants? The Queen reigns at the will of the Goddess, but also at the will of the people."

"That doesn't make sense."

"Does it make any more sense if I say that the Queen serves both the Goddess and the people?"

That makes sense to me. I wonder if that's true at Eagle's Rest—it always seemed to me that the gods cared much more about the rituals than the people did. I think a lot of the people just take the gods for granted and think that dealing with them is the job of the priests and priestesses.

"I guess it makes more sense that way." After a moment of silence Lina added, "Do you think it would have made a difference if the Queen had tried to end the Sacrifice *before* the Choosing?"

That's a really good question.

The First Priestess gasped. "Don't even think of that!"

"Why not? I can see that once a Year-King had been Chosen—"

"Did you know that you were born in a famine year?"

What does that have to do with anything?

"What? Did my mother do something wrong?"

"No, your mother was an excellent Queen. The problem was her Heiress, who apparently felt as you do. She tried to stop the Choosing."

"Is that possible?" Lina asked, with a faint note of hope in her voice.

"No, it is *not*," the priestess replied firmly. "Druscilla, unfortunately, seems to have paid even less attention to her lessons than you sometimes do."

The Heiress was named Druscilla? Like my mother? *She can't mean my mother—it must just be someone with the same name. I've never heard of anyone else named that, but that doesn't prove anything.*

"What did she do?"

The priestess's voice was clipped and disapproving. "She made a scene during the ceremony itself."

Actually, that does *sound like my mother. And I do look a lot like Lina, which would make sense if we're relatives. But...*

"The Shield-Bearer had to knock her out and remove her from the plaza," the priestess continued. "She was packed off to her country estate the next day, but apparently it wasn't enough. Even though the Sacrifice was performed, there was unseasonal rain. Part of the harvest couldn't be gathered, and the weather was so wet that much of what had been gathered rotted in the barns. We had to import food to get us through the winter, and we were lucky we were able to do that."

"Do you think the Goddess will ever end the Sacrifice?"

"I don't know, Lina. Ask her."

To Lina's ill-concealed dismay, Kyril was not at the palace when she went up to the main floor after her lesson. Apparently there were no petitions to be heard that morning, so there was no court, and Lina had nothing better to do than her needlework. So she and Zora ended up in the courtyard between the wings of the castle, sitting with one of the silent green-robed priestesses—Lina always had one as a shadow whenever she was not in either her private rooms or the underground temple complex—and Lady Esme.

Zora didn't like Lady Esme. She reminded Zora of the dark shadow from her dreams at Eagle's Rest, and she smelled of bitter burnt herbs, as if she spent her spare time brewing something nasty in a stillroom. She never seemed to miss an opportunity to "accidently" kick Zora, and she wore hard shoes, rather than the soft slippers that most of the women at Court wore. The Guards wore boots, of course, but they paid attention to where they were putting their feet and made sure to avoid things like Zora's tail. By now, of course, it was difficult for anyone to step on Zora's tail because she had learned to keep it pulled in next to her body. But there was no way for her to protect her ribs from Lady Esme's swinging feet.

Kyril turned up in time for the midday meal, but Colin wasn't with him. Zora was very glad when it was time to go back to the chapel for the afternoon meditation.

"Zora," Lina said when they were alone in the chapel and Zora was in human shape again. "Can you change on your own, without the—whatever the First Priestess called it? Kyril seems to think you should be able to."

"She called it an anchor point, Lina. I don't know if I can change anywhere else; I haven't tried to change unless I'm in here and touching the water." Zora considered the matter. "I think the Goddess wants me to stay a dog in order to learn something."

"Like what?"

Zora shrugged. "Patience? How to listen?"

"Speaking of listening, did you hear what Kyril said about the famine?"

"No. When was he talking about that?"

"At lunchtime. I guess you were busy concentrating on wolfing down your food." Lina grinned. "Pun intended."

Zora chuckled. "Are we being a bad influence on you?"

"It's nice to have someone my own age to talk to," Lina said. "Anyway, he said that his father sent grain here from his estates so people didn't starve. Apparently that's why his aunt has a house here—she was the one handling the details."

"It's certainly convenient for Kyril—it gives him a place to stay, at least."

"As well as a place where he can change shape if he needs to," Lina remarked. "You said that you could turn into a wolf—what do you look like that way? You can change in here. Can you show me?"

"I don't know if it will work, but I'll try it." Zora rolled to hands and knees and then touched her lips to the water while concentrating on wolf- rather than dog-shape.

The change was easy and smooth, but Lina gasped as she finished. Zora looked up to see Lina staring at her, the fingers of her left hand pressing against her open mouth. A quick glance at the water, now still again, reflected the wolf.

"Z-Zora?" Lina sounded a bit afraid.

Which is silly, because she asked me to do this. And once again, I can't talk, so I can't use words to reassure her. Zora paced around the stone until she was directly in front of Lina. With the wall behind her, she had no place to go, but she looked as if she would back into the wall if she could. Zora pushed her head under Lina's right hand and butted up against it in the unspoken "Pet me, human" command. Lina automatically began stroking the wolf's head and laughed shakily.

I wonder if I can— Zora visualized the change from wolf to dog. To her surprise—and Lina's—it worked. *Now let's see if I can make it back to human.* She managed, but this time it took real effort. Zora sagged against the bench next to Lina's legs and tried to catch her breath.

"You did it without touching the water," Lina said, obviously impressed.

"True, but it used to be much easier than this." Zora stopped talking and concentrated on breathing. *Lady, why did you do this to me? What do you want me to learn?*

Humility.

Oh. As in, helpless and having to wait for the people around me to take care of me, and unable to talk so that I have to learn how to listen?

That's a fair description.

Do you think I've learned enough so that I can be allowed to change normally again? I agree that Princess is a good shape for following Lina around, but perhaps there are some things I should be learning in Diadem as a human.

Are you asking me to allow you to change as you could before you came here?

Please, Lady. I'm getting very tired of being a bitch.

Lina jerked suddenly. "Did you hear that? It sounded like someone laughing."

"Oh, yes," Zora said. "I heard her. The Goddess has an unusual sense of humor."

"Does that mean that she's done keeping you a dog?"

"Yes, I'm pretty sure that it does. And if she's letting me change to human again, that means there's something she wants me to do in that shape."

Lina frowned. "But how do we explain having *two* of me?"

"We don't." The Goddess didn't have to tell Zora this. "The fact that we look alike is something we need to keep secret. I have a feeling we're going to need to use that, which we can't do if people know there are two of us."

"So what do we do?"

"First, you give Kyril his dog back." Lina opened her mouth to protest, so Zora added quickly, "He can still bring me to visit you, but the palace has too many people—and too little privacy—for me to be changing back and forth outside this chapel."

"I guess you're right," Lina said reluctantly. "I'll let Kyril take you home with him tomorrow—but you had better visit me!"

"I will. I promise."

Kyril looked bewildered at Lina's sudden willingness to send Zora home with him. Colin was quicker on the uptake. "Thank you very much, Lady," he said fervently. "I appreciate your confidence, and I'll take very good care of her. I've missed her."

Lina stared into Colin's face for so long that Kyril looked annoyed. Apparently whatever she saw satisfied her, for she said, "I'm sure you will."

"I'll bring her to visit you," Kyril said. "If you permit, I'll continue to visit you myself, even if I can't bring her with me."

Lina smiled faintly. "I'd like that."

"I'll take the dog home now," Colin volunteered. "You can stay here with the Queen until they make you leave."

"Fine," Kyril said absently, his eyes still on Lina.

Colin and Zora left them together.

When they got home, Colin took Zora up to his room, gave her a pair of his pants and a tunic, and went into the hall while she changed.

"I'm sorry," he apologized when she let him back in. "All of your clothes are still packed."

"That's actually a good thing." Zora had been planning her sudden appearance as a human as they walked home. "Send the housekeeper out on an errand. While she's gone, I'll dig out traveling clothes, rub some dust on them, and put them on. By the time she gets back, I'll be sitting with you in the parlor, having just arrived, complete with my baggage—you do have that stored somewhere, right? We'll stick to the truth. I'm Kyril's cousin and I've come to live here. By the time she's arranged for the bath I am going to demand, made up a room for me, and redone the menus to feed three of us instead of just you two, she'll have forgotten any questions she might have had."

"Including why a woman is traveling alone?"

"This is Diadem, Colin. It's a matriarchy, haven't you noticed? She won't expect me to have a chaperone."

"And the dog?"

"Warn Kyril to keep his mouth shut, and she'll think the dog is still at the palace. As long as he keeps visiting the Queen, who's going to notice? Everyone will think Princess is someplace else.

Also, now that I can change back and forth, I can go out in the garden in dog-shape first thing in the morning, and then change back to human for the rest of the day." Zora twisted a strand of hair in front of her face and regarded it thoughtfully. "The only major problem is my resemblance to the Queen." She changed her hair from blonde to dark brown and made it about six inches longer. "Does this change my appearance enough, do you think?"

Colin looked startled. "Well, it doesn't look like you, that's certain."

Zora shrugged. "Then it doesn't look like her. I guess it will do."

The plan worked as Zora had predicted. She spent the afternoon soaking in a warm bath, washing her hair for the first time in weeks, and using pumice on her hands and feet. *Not bathing didn't bother me when I was a dog most of the time, but as soon as I start to think of myself as a full-time human, my grooming standards change.* She unpacked the saddlebags she had put her belongings in before they entered Diadem, arranging her clothing and making a pile to be washed. That night she slept in a bed that was not at floor level. It felt a bit strange after weeks of blankets and cushions on the floor, but she told herself to enjoy it. The Goddess only knew how long this phase of her life would last.

Princess accompanied Kyril to court a few mornings while his cousin Zora was ostensibly sleeping late, and the Queen looked both relieved and delighted to see her.

There was only one thing Zora had failed to take into account, and that wasn't her fault. She hadn't known anything about it until the guard showed up at their house.

CHAPTER SEVEN

It was midmorning, and Kyril had gone to court, as usual. Colin was out on some errand or other, and Zora was in the front parlor reading one of the books from the house's well-stocked library. She heard a knock at the front door, and then the housekeeper escorted a guardswoman into the parlor. She was short, with a wiry build and cropped dark hair just starting to go gray. Zora didn't recognize her, either from court or from the handful of guards she had seen in the city.

"I understand that it is your intent to make Diadem your permanent home," the guard said. "Is that correct?"

Well, it certainly seems to be the Goddess's intent. "Yes."

"The laws of Diadem require that all women between the ages of twelve and fifty spend a month each spring at arms training, so that they may serve in the Guard and defend the city at need," the guard went on. "Was that explained to you?"

"No." Zora looked at her in surprise. "I've only recently arrived in Diadem. And I'm afraid I've never had arms training." *I doubt that turning into something with claws and teeth whenever I feel threatened counts.* "What I am supposed to do?"

"We're doing preliminary orientation today for women who are in their first year."

I guess that means me and a bunch of twelve-year-olds. Why didn't Lina— or Catriona—mention this to me?

The guard eyed the dress Zora was wearing. "I would suggest that you change into pants you can move in easily. I need you to accompany me to the training grounds."

"Of course." Zora marked her place in the book and set it aside. "I'll be with you shortly."

She dressed in a pair of drawstring pants and an old shirt, thankful that Akila had packed some of the student practice clothing. Leaving a message for the boys with the housekeeper,

Zora followed the guardswoman down the street toward the part of town where the Guard barracks and training grounds were located.

The guard, whose name turned out to be Ciara, was friendly and—when Zora expressed her concern that she wouldn't be able to keep up with the twelve-year-olds—reassuring. "There's a certain amount of general training," she said, "but nobody expects you to be expert at everything. Also, you may have more useful skills than you realize. For example, can you swim?"

"Like a fish." *Literally.*

"So that's one thing you won't need to be taught. And we can always use a good swimmer. We get girls who are afraid to put their faces in the water—in fact, we get girls who are afraid to put their *toes* in the water."

Zora laughed at that, beginning to feel that she could cope with training. Then they walked through the gate into the compound. Ciara dropped back slightly as they entered, so she was behind Zora when the attack happened. A woman charged straight at them with a raised sword in one hand and a dagger in the other.

Zora clawed her way up the wall of the nearest building— fortunately there was enough space between the stones for her fingers, so actual claws weren't required—and was on the balcony before the woman reached Ciara. She stopped, and both of them looked up at Zora.

"Well, that certainly demonstrates your basic reaction to danger," Ciara called up. She turned to the swordswoman, laughing. "I haven't seen anything like that since the day Catriona first came here!"

"I think this one is even faster," the swordswoman said with a chuckle. She looked up at Zora. "Can you get down on your own, or do you need help?

"I can get down." *I think.* Zora reversed her path down the wall, moving more slowly and carefully now that she was not in a panic.

"You're Zora, right?" the woman asked once she had reached the ground. "You're a good climber. Do you do a lot of it?"

"A fair amount," Zora admitted, not mentioning that she was usually something with claws when she did. "At home I used to climb trees, and the wall here has enough space between the stones for my fingertips."

"But not for your toes when you're wearing shoes," Ciara remarked. "You must have very strong arms and shoulders to be able to make that climb with only your hands."

"Being scared helped," Zora said ruefully. *So does being able to fly—apparently I haven't lost all my muscle tone.*

"So were you simply trying to escape," Ciara asked, "or to find a good vantage point?"

Zora frowned, considering both the question and her actions. "I think it might have been a bit of both. If it had been pure escape, I'd have kept going up and then across the roof, not stopped to look down and see what was happening."

"You didn't feel any urge to stand and fight?" the swordswoman asked.

"I'm small, I'm not trained to fight, and I'm not armed, so no."

The swordswoman looked appraisingly at Zora. "You've had no training at all, not even for self-defense?"

Zora shook her head.

"Well, at least you won't have anything you'll need to un-learn." She turned to Ciara. "Start her in the beginning classes—tumbling, basic hand-to-hand, knife work, sword fighting, archery, and running."

"She says she can swim," Ciara reported.

"Excellent. Test her for that, too. She's all yours until she's advanced enough for me to work with."

Zora suppressed a sigh of relief. She had a feeling that even the beginning classes were going to be a challenge. "Why tumbling classes?" Of all the things on the list, that seemed strangest.

"It's important to learn to fall without hurting yourself, and being able to roll away in any direction is useful as well." Ciara smiled. "I think you might be good at tumbling, so we'll start there. Come with me."

The rest of the morning was spent working at basic tumbling—Zora wasn't too bad at it, but she knew she was going to have bruises the next day. She also ached in muscles that she hadn't known she had—and she hadn't thought there *were* any muscles that Lord Ranulf's training had missed.

She was thankful to follow Ciara into the dining hall attached to the barracks, where they each grabbed a tray of food (Zora just copied what Ciara chose) and joined a group of women seated at one of the long tables that ran the length of the room. Zora collapsed onto the bench next to Ciara, thankful for the opportunity to sit down, if only for a little while.

"This is Zora," Ciara said to the group. "Today is her first day, but she says she can swim."

Six pairs of eyes regarded Zora with interest, appraising her body.

"She's small, but she looks strong enough," somebody muttered.

"Zora," Ciara said, "this is our swim team. They are our best swimmers, so they handle most of the jobs that require that ability."

"And we can certainly use more swimmers," one of the women said. "Are you bringing her with us this afternoon, Ciara?"

"That's the plan," Ciara said cheerfully. "We'll go down to King's Cove, and she can join our practice session."

King's Cove was near the south end of the lower city, outside the walls and downriver from the waterfall. The river carved an arc out of its left bank, and there was a small, sandy beach.

The women had walked down from the barracks at a reasonably slow pace—"To give our food a chance to settle," one of them explained—and they began by doing stretches to loosen up their muscles for swimming.

In Zora's case that also helped to loosen the muscles that had gone tight in the wake of the morning's activity. Then everyone removed at least one layer of clothing, leaving the women in pants that were a shorter version of Zora's, and breast bands. She followed their example, glad that she had put on a breast band when she dressed to accompany Ciara. Zora didn't have much in the way of breasts, so frequently she didn't bother with a breast band, but it would have been embarrassing to have been naked from the waist up when nobody else was. She followed the other women into the water until it was up to their hips and her waist.

"We're doing strength practice today," Ciara said. "As soon as you get out of this cove you'll be in the main current. Swim upriver as far as you can, and then return to the cove. Just follow the other women, and don't worry—I'll stay with you in case you have any trouble. Remember, coming back downstream is the easy part, but you don't want to miss the cove. If you catch the current just right, it will practically drop you on the beach here. Otherwise you'll have to swim in. Any questions?"

Zora suspected that "Why is this called King's Cove?" wasn't the kind of question Ciara had in mind, so she shook her head and followed the rest of the group into deeper water.

The current wasn't too strong at first, but as they got closer to the waterfall, the water ran faster and got rougher. Habits Zora had developed from years of competing with the other shape-changers kicked in, and she pushed herself harder, using the arm muscles developed from years of flying and running on all fours. Gradually, she pulled ahead of everyone else. It wasn't until she hit really rough water that she realized she was almost under the waterfall, and then she barely had time to gulp a lungful of air just before the turbulence pulled her under and banged her hip into a rock.

Ouch! I'm lucky that wasn't my head, and I'd better get out of here before it is. Zora pulled into a tight little ball, and then used her legs to push off the rock. She dove as deep as she could in search of calmer water, keeping her eyes open to look for obstacles. It was hard to see much through the turbulence, but it looked as though someone had planted a garden of standing stones underwater. She used the current to navigate through them as best she could and worked her way downstream, bouncing off quite a few rocks in the process. *I am going to have so many bruises tomorrow...*

When her lungs started to burn, she pulled her way up to the surface. *Changing into a fish now would be a* really *bad idea. If I ever have time, I think I'll try to come up with a shape that can breathe underwater and still look human—maybe add gills just below my ribcage...*

Zora came up in mid-river, gasping for air, and discovered that her hair had come out of its braid while she was underwater and was now plastered across her face. She hung upright in the water, kicking just enough to stay afloat while she took deep breaths and worked on getting her hair out of her face. She had just managed to get the whole mass of it to run back from her hairline and down her neck and back when Ciara grabbed her arm.

"Are you all right?" she asked anxiously.

"Yes, I'm fine." Zora said. "I should have tied my hair tighter, that's all." She was certainly in no danger of drowning.

Ciara jerked her head in a 'follow me' gesture and angled downstream toward the cove. Zora trailed after her, scarcely needing to move to stay on course.

Everyone else was already on land, doing arm and leg stretches. "Be sure to stretch out your arms very thoroughly," Ciara told me. "I'm amazed you got as far as you did without having them cramp up on you."

"Where did she get to?" one of the others asked.

"Farther than I can go," Ciara said grimly. "Next time, Zora, do *not* outpace your partner."

"I apologize," Zora said hastily. The last thing she needed was to have the people she was training with angry with her. "I was concentrating on swimming, and then I got pulled into—is that a rock garden below the waterfall?"

"You got into the rocks?" Ciara asked in horror. "You should never go that close to the waterfall. It's *much* too dangerous!"

It certainly is, and you didn't answer my question. This probably isn't a good time to keep asking. I'll find out another way. Somehow. Aloud, Zora simply said, "I'll remember that."

The next few weeks were some of the happiest in Zora's life. The training was challenging—and she had never realized how much she could do while still remaining in human shape. She started spending more and more time training with the guards. It wasn't that she was naturally good at anything other than swimming—not at first. The most difficult part at the beginning was remembering to do everything in human shape. Zora had never realized before just how much she and her friends relied on shape-changing abilities at home. She had never had to stand her ground and defend herself using nothing but human shape. *But if a normal human can learn to do this*, she thought grimly, *I can learn it too.* It was hard work, and she had bruises on top of her bruises, but each day she got a little bit better. And that encouraged her, so she worked even harder and made even more progress.

She was telling Colin about it one night at the supper table, which was the only time she saw the boys now. Colin was interested; Kyril wasn't. He was practically sulking because he couldn't spend much time with the Queen. Apparently she was required to train this month as well, which made sense to Zora. If all the women were required to train, certainly the Queen should be setting an example. *I wonder if arms training is more to her taste than her other duties. I'll have to ask her when I see her next.*

"I haven't seen her," Zora remarked, "but I suppose she's in the advanced classes."

"No," Kyril said. "All they let her do is archery, so that's the only class she's in. She was complaining about it the other day—she says it's boring. But at least she doesn't have to hold court and hear petitions. All the women who would be bringing them are in training all day."

"I certainly am," Zora said, "and I'm going to bed as soon as I finish eating. I didn't think there was anything more exhausting than shape-changing, but this comes *very* close to it."

Kyril shrugged. "Father wasn't training us for war."

"That's the disadvantage of a matriarchy," Colin remarked. "You may not need a chaperone, but you can't count on the men to defend the city."

"But it's their home too," Zora said. "Why wouldn't they be willing to defend it?"

"It's not really theirs," Kyril said. "Men generally don't even own property here. It's not illegal for them to, but it's not customary. We may call this Father's house, but it actually belongs to Catriona's mother." He lowered his voice. "We can't even trust the servants."

"Sure we can," Colin said with a grin. "We can trust them to tell Catriona everything that goes on here." He added softly, "Everything they know about, anyway."

It seemed to Zora that there would be disadvantages to those restrictions, but she fell asleep while she was thinking about it. And in the morning it was back to the training yard as soon as the ritual in the plaza was over. Zora was doing well with tumbling, and she was also taking basic hand-to-hand combat and beginning knife fighting. The swimming sessions after lunch were almost a break for her, since they used skills she already had.

She was learning the fighting skills, and her teachers seemed happy with her progress. She was already valued for her swimming ability, but she was starting to be appreciated for other skills as well, and she realized that it was the first time she had really felt useful since Kassie's Choosing. Zora hadn't realized at the time how much of the pain she had felt had come from feeling useless and unimportant.

After swim practice Zora used the Guard bathhouse with the other swimmers, which gave her an excellent opportunity to observe the guards who worked in the city and to pick up news and gossip. She learned the names and faces of the guards—as well as the fact that the Shield-Bearer, in addition to being the Queen's Regent, was the head of the Guard and the Queen's official bodyguard. Catriona, the Sword-Bearer, was second in command, and her official duty was to guard the Queen's Heiress, as the Shield-Bearer guarded the Queen. In the absence of an Heiress and with the Shield-Bearer busy with her duties as Regent and counselor to the Queen, Catriona ran the Guard, but Zora was so junior that she never encountered either of them, and she suspected neither of them would notice her if they did happen to see her.

After Zora was finished at the compound, she went back to the plaza in front of the palace for the evening ritual, and then went home, ate whatever the housekeeper put in front of her, and collapsed into bed.

So when the end of training was announced for everyone but the swimmers, who had a holiday before their summer training, Zora didn't question her good fortune. She planned to spend at least two days catching up on her rest. After that, she would see what was going on in Diadem outside the Guard compound.

Zora managed to stay in bed until midday the next day, but Kyril was still home when she got up.

"I thought you were at court," she said, surprised to find both him and Colin in the dining room.

Kyril shook his head. "The Queen was busy with something this morning, and she told me she wouldn't be able to see me until after her daily meditation. So I'm going to see her this afternoon instead.

Will you come with me, Zora? Please? I think something is bothering her, but she won't talk to me about it. Maybe you can find out what it is."

So Zora changed to dog-shape and accompanied Kyril when he went to visit the Queen. Lady Esme was with her, doing needlework. She wasn't very good at it and kept pricking her fingers, which made Zora wonder why she didn't find something else to do. In addition, one of the green-robed veiled priestesses sat next to the Queen, and members of the Queen's guard walked through the courtyard at irregular intervals. Kyril and the Queen had discovered a mutual passion for a board game he had given her. Apparently they had been playing it every afternoon for the last month from the time the Queen finished her meditation until she had to prepare for the evening ritual.

The thing that told Zora what was worrying the Queen, however, wasn't at the palace. It was in the streets. Every house, garden, and street in the city was cleaned, and flowers surrounded windows and doors. *One of the Great Rituals must be nearly upon us.* Nobody mentioned any ritual in front of Kyril, of course—Zora had noticed during her time as the Queen's dog that there were no priests in Diadem, only priestesses—but flowers didn't last long once they were cut and made into decorations. As long as Zora was a dog, she couldn't say anything, but she made mental notes of what to tell Kyril when they got home.

As the Queen and Kyril were finishing their game, the Queen asked Kyril if he would do a favor for her.

"Of course," Kyril said promptly. "Anything. What would you like?"

"It's silly," the Queen said, "but nobody has had time to go hunting lately, and I have a sudden craving for venison. You said you can hunt, and I wondered if you would be willing to go out tomorrow and bring back a deer. There should be some in the woods to the east."

"It would be my pleasure," Kyril assured her, kissing her hand as he rose to take his leave. "You shall have venison for supper tomorrow."

"The day after tomorrow will be soon enough," the Queen said earnestly. "After all, it will need to be cooked."

Zora started laughing as soon as they got home and she changed back to human. "I'm glad you didn't tell her how much better venison tastes when it's raw and fresh."

"That's only if you're a wolf," Kyril pointed out.

"So? Are you planning to hunt for deer as a human? You'd be out all day—" Zora stopped, hearing what she was saying. "She's trying to get you out of the city for the day. The festival all the houses are decorated for—it's tomorrow. Whatever it is, it's tomorrow, and she wants you out of the way."

"The Choosing?" Kyril said in surprise. "It can't be time for that already..." His voice trailed off.

"Didn't you see all the flowers around the windows and doors of every house we passed? Flowers don't last long once they're picked. What exactly is the Choosing?"

Kyril grimaced. "The Choosing is the ritual by which the Goddess, through the Queen, chooses the Year-King."

"That would explain why the Queen is trying to make sure you are far away. The last Year-King died, and she's still upset about that."

Kyril frowned in thought. "So you think she's trying to get me out of the way so I won't be Chosen?"

Zora remembered the way Lina had talked about murder in the chapel. "Absolutely."

"Does she think I'll spend the summer watching her with another man?" Kyril asked, suddenly furious.

"If the Goddess wills it," Zora said firmly, "you had better."

"We're all going hunting at dawn, then," Kyril said grimly. "I'll be back for the ritual, and we'll just see what the Goddess wills."

True to his word, he dragged Colin and Zora out of bed an hour before dawn. "Eagle to spot the deer," he said, "wolves for the kill. I'll bring clothing, so I can change to human without having to come home first. Colin, you can change to a horse, can't you? We can deliver the venison to the palace kitchens, then we all meet back here and clean up for the ritual."

"Use claws for the kill—or a knife if you can," Colin said. "A deer with its throat torn out by a wolf would be hard to explain to the kitchen staff."

"All right, I'll get a knife," Kyril said. "Just hurry up!"

Colin and Zora went upstairs, climbed out of their respective windows onto the roof, and changed to eagle-shape. A few minutes later, Kyril came out of the house, carrying his dagger in a leather sheath, and went into the stables. A minute after that a wolf carrying a sack in its mouth came out of the stables, looked up at the eagles, and set out quickly through the dark streets. Colin and Zora dove off the rooftop, struggled to gain altitude, and then flew above Kyril to watch for anyone who might see or try to stop him. Fortunately the three of them appeared to be the only people out that early.

The sun had barely cleared the horizon when Zora spotted a group of deer drinking from a stream. Colin doubled back to lead Kyril to the spot, while she climbed above the deer and dropped to strike a nice fat buck, hitting it at an angle that knocked it over and broke its neck. *Sometimes weighing much more than a natural eagle has advantages.*

Kyril arrived as Zora picked herself up. Since she doubted she was going to be able to get back into the sky from the ground, she changed to Princess, while Kyril changed to human, dressed in a tunic from his sack, and dealt with the buck. Colin landed and changed to a horse, and Kyril slung the deer over the horse's back.

They returned to Diadem without incident and dropped the deer off at the palace kitchen. Fortunately the servants were too distracted to see that the horse had no bridle or reins, and the three of them hurried home before anyone noticed anything odd about them.

While the boys bathed and dressed in their best clothes, Zora considered what shape she should take for the ritual. She knew she needed to be there—even if it wasn't required for the entire population of the city, Zora felt sure that the Goddess wanted her there. She didn't think going as a dog at Kyril's heels—especially if he was likely to be chosen—was a good idea, but she wasn't sure that attending in human form was any better. At the daily rituals it had been becoming harder each day to make sure that the Queen's part, the one Zora was *not* supposed to be singing, remained inaudible to everyone around her, and she didn't know how a Great Ritual would affect her. *But I have already changed shape three times in one day. I'll go as a human—and trust in the Goddess.*

Zora dressed in her good clothes—after all, this was a festival— and followed Kyril and Colin to a plaza in the middle of town where the ritual was being held. *Even if we had just arrived in town, we could have found the right place merely by following the people.* Everyone in the city seemed to be crowded into the plaza; the only empty space was on top of a wooden platform where the Queen stood. Kyril, who was standing next to Zora, stared at the Queen and apparently forgot to breathe.

She really is beautiful. Suddenly she doesn't look like me at all. Lina's hair was loose and falling around her shoulders, and she was dressed in a simply cut but richly embroidered gown of deep purple fabric. It was sleeveless, with a V-shaped neckline cut down to her breasts, and it was held together with a golden cord tied just under her bust. She looked remote—as if she was listening to something other than the hymn the people were chanting—and so calm that Zora wondered briefly if she had been drugged. *Surely not. She needs to be able to hear the voice of the Goddess.* Then the people fell silent, and the Queen began to sing, and only the song existed.

It was like nothing Zora had ever heard before, and it was beautiful beyond belief. It seemed as though all of creation was singing, and the music filled her body and soul. She had become hollow, providing a space for the music to echo back and forth in. The words were in a language she didn't understand, but still she found her lips starting to shape them. Fortunately, before she actually uttered them, power swept through her in one great overwhelming wave, and she lost consciousness.

CHAPTER EIGHT

Zora woke up alone in the dark. She was lying on flat stone, and there was some sort of linen fabric draped over her. Her first terrified thought was that she had been entombed alive. She had no idea where she was or how much time had passed. She tried to open her eyes, and she discovered that they were already open. Changing them to cat-shape was no help. *Cats can't really see in the dark—that's just superstition. They have to have* some *light, even if it's not as much as a human needs, to see. And why am I worrying about the structure of a cat's eyes when I'm...* The feeling of panic reclaimed her.

Zora had never felt like this before; her body felt as if a fire had burned *inside* it and now all that remained was empty space waiting to be filled—but by what? She tried to force herself to be calm. *Start with the basics: breathe in, breathe out; breathe in, breathe out...*

I should have stayed a dog.

Something—the taste of the air, perhaps, along with a sense of the amount of space around her—made her suspect that she was in a cave, but it didn't feel like the chapel. It really *did* feel like a tomb. She was lying flat on her back on a smooth stone surface, and her arms were at her sides, held down by a linen sheet that came up to her chin. She was pretty sure she was naked, but presumably she could wrap the sheet around herself when she got up, so it could have been worse. And she could feel movement in the air, so even if she *was* in a tomb, she hadn't been sealed into it.

That realization helped her calm down a little bit, and Zora was thinking about getting up and exploring her surroundings when she noticed she was starting to be able to see. Some source of light was heading her way. Zora decided the best thing to do was to pretend to be asleep for the time being—at least unless somebody *did* try to entomb her. The fact that the only sound she could hear was a girl sobbing hysterically made her very uneasy. She struggled to remember what had happened to her.

The last thing I remember was the beginning of the Choosing. Did I do something wrong and disrupt the ritual? Am I being punished for something?

Zora closed her eyes to shield them from the light and concentrated on using her ears, trying to pick up anything other than crying. But all she could hear was the still-hysterical sobbing. It not only drowned out all other sounds, it made her head hurt.

She tried to get her hands free so she could put them over her ears, but the linen was either wrapped or weighted. She could probably fight her way free, given time, but she wasn't sure that was the best move at the moment.

The sobs were interspersed with the word "no" repeated over and over, and Zora finally recognized the voice. It was the Queen's—it just sounded younger than usual. *What in Earth is going on?*

"I don't know why the Goddess chose her," an older woman's voice finally carried over the sobs, "but there is no doubt that she did." She paused, took a deep breath, and continued. "Now will you please say the Calling so that all of us can get out of here. We have a lot to do today."

"I can't," the Queen sobbed. "I can't bear this! It's all just too much! Why didn't he go hunting for venison when I asked him to? He would have been safe then!"

I guess Kyril won't have to watch her with another man all summer. Why don't I remember his being chosen? What is my *part in all of this? Whatever it is, I don't think I can do it stuck here, so...*

"Lina," Zora said firmly, loudly enough to be heard over the sobbing. Everyone in the room gasped. *Either I wasn't supposed to speak, or I wasn't supposed to know the Queen's name. If anyone asks, I'll tell them the Goddess told me.* "Lina, I'm here to help you, but I can't do anything as long as we're stuck here. Please say whatever it is you're supposed to say."

Lina's sobs muted to sniffles. "All right," she said, coming forward to stand at the foot of whatever Zora was lying on. Two women carrying candles flanked the doorway, while two others moved forward to stand at Zora's shoulders. There was enough light now for her to see that she actually *was* lying on a stone bier— or an altar—in a small crypt. *At least I'm the only body in it, and it appears they are preparing to let me out. But to do what?*

"Chosen of the Goddess," Lina began, in a thin, uncertain voice. "Dead to the world, arise to new life."

The women at Zora's shoulders pulled the linen down her body. They wore the green gowns of the priestesses who attended the Queen, but they were unveiled.

"Arise," the Queen said. "Be reborn in the service of the Goddess." Her voice was distinctly lacking in enthusiasm, but apparently the words were correct.

When the linen was completely clear of Zora's body, the priestesses helped her to sit up and then stand. She was a bit dizzy, but they seemed to expect that, and they supported her as the Queen led them out of the crypt and up a passage carved out of rock, heading toward daylight. The two priestesses with the candles followed them. As the dizziness passed, Zora noticed that the stone under her bare feet was not cold, but warm, and that power seemed to well up from the floor. She felt better and stronger with each step she took. *Given the energy coming up from the floor, we must be somewhere near the chapel, but I haven't been in here before.*

They came to a small chamber with an underground stream running through it, and the priestesses who were guiding her indicated that Zora was to step into it. It came up to her knees, and it was *freezing*. Gently, but firmly, they pushed her down to her knees and then forward. She didn't think they were going to drown her, but she strongly suspected that she wasn't getting out until her entire body had been completely submerged. *Of course! It's a rebirth ritual—and the sooner I'm completely immersed, the sooner I can get out of here.* While they didn't use anything like this at home, she could guess at the principles. She couldn't get into the temple library there herself, but Marfa had given Zora many books to read over the years.

So now Zora filled her lungs with air and allowed her body to slip under the surface. After several long seconds—she guessed they were making sure all of her hair was underwater—they pulled her up. Zora gasped from the cold—and the pain of being submerged in such cold water—but didn't say anything. She suspected she really wasn't supposed to be talking yet.

The priestesses lifted her out of the stream—Zora could hardly move by herself—and then took towels and vigorously rubbed her body dry. When one of them started toweling her hair, she panicked again for a moment, wondering what color it was. Had she reverted to her true shape while she was unconscious? *But if I had, surely someone would have commented on my resemblance to Lina.*

When she was dry, they dressed her in a green gown like the ones they were wearing. Lina was wearing one as well, and Zora hoped it was just for this ritual. If she and Lina had to spend a lot of time together while dressed identically, just having different hair colors and lengths might not be enough.

When Zora was dressed, the priestesses with the candles led the procession further down the hallway until they finally reached someplace she recognized: the room where Lina had come for her lessons. The candles were extinguished and put away, Lina collapsed onto one of the couches, crying as if she would never stop, and everyone else sat down at the table. One of the women, the one Zora remembered from Lina's lessons, indicated the chair at the foot of the table. Zora sat there, hoping that somebody was about to explain what was going on.

The Shield-Bearer came in just then. Not counting Zora and Lina, there were now five women in the room, looking at the Queen with attitudes ranging from dismay to disgust.

"Do you want venison, Lady?" one of the priestesses asked. She sounded as if she were trying to placate a fractious toddler.

"I don't *care* about the venison!" the Queen screamed. "I just wanted him to be out of the way!"

"Are you talking about Kyril?" Zora asked.

Lina looked up at her. "Who are you, and what do you know about the king?"

Surely Lina knows who I am. Granted, she hasn't seen me before with dark hair instead of blonde, but does she really not recognize me? Lina had not stopped sobbing since Zora first heard her, and now she was becoming totally hysterical again. Zora was starting to appreciate why the priestesses wore veils in public, especially given the way they were looking at the Queen. Their expressions would definitely not inspire public confidence in the monarchy—or the priesthood.

One of the priestess said quickly, "I'll get a healer," and ran from the room.

"I wouldn't tell him you don't want the venison after he went to the trouble of getting it for you," Zora said. "He dropped it off at the kitchen this morning...it *was* this morning, wasn't it?"

"No. The Choosing was yesterday." The Shield-Bearer looked suspiciously at Zora. "What do you remember?"

The only time the Shield-Bearer had seen her, Zora had been a dog, so she probably didn't have much to worry about from her. "I remember going to the plaza. It was crowded, and the Queen stood there and started singing..." She closed her eyes and concentrated, but nothing more came to her, just faint memories of singing and rising power and a feeling... There wasn't anything more. Zora shook her head. "That's all I remember. What happened? Did I faint?"

"Something like that." It was the eldest priestess who answered. "It seems the Goddess has called you to her service. It's a great honor—it's been twenty years since she last called a new priestess." She looked sternly at Zora, apparently not wanting to have *two* girls in hysterics. "What is your name?"

"Zora."

Lina lifted her head and stared in astonishment. Tears still ran down her face, but now her main emotion appeared to be bewilderment.

"So, Zora, are you willing to serve the Goddess?"

Zora opened her mouth to say "Of course I am!" It was, after all, what she had been trained to do from infancy. But she remembered that this was not Eagle's Rest, where she knew exactly what was expected of her.

Maybe I should ask a few questions before I make any vows.

Zora looked down at the gown she was wearing and up at the priestesses. She had never seen them without veils, nor had she ever heard any of them utter a single syllable outside of this... "Where are we? Is this some kind of temple?"

"After a fashion," the eldest priestess said. "We're in a complex of caves and tunnels under the palace. The Goddess is the Earth, and she is usually worshipped outdoors. Properly speaking, this is not a temple, but it's easier to call it one. There is a meditation chapel for the Queen, the chamber where you woke up, a library, and living quarters for those of us who attend the Queen."

"So if I say yes, am I stuck down here for the rest of my life?"

Zora thought of the friends she had started to make during guard training, of the swimming that would continue through the summer, and of Kyril and Colin. "And if I say no, can I go home?"

The priestess sighed. "If you say no, we won't force you to stay here. But if the Goddess really wants you here... As for being 'stuck down here' for life, this isn't a life sentence. We are here to support the Queen while she is young and growing into her role. Once she has learned and embraced her role, we are allowed to retire and return to life outside if we wish."

It's a life sentence. The girl she had spent so many afternoons in the chapel with wasn't going to "embrace her role" in any future Zora could foresee. But somehow Zora knew this was where the Goddess wanted her—*and maybe I can get time off for swimming practice with the team.*

"Yes." Zora's voice wasn't quite as steady as she could have wished, but it was audible. "I will serve the Goddess."

Lina switched to anger faster than Zora could blink. "You don't know what she's going to make you do!"

"I trust her." *I believe that she has a plan for me and this is part of it.* "Don't you?"

"No, I don't!" Lina snarled. "It was bad enough last year when I had to marry an old man and then watch him die, but this year—" She went back to sobbing hysterically. Again.

"This year you have a Year-King your own age. Is that the problem?"

The Shield-Bearer looked at Zora in horror. "Do you know Lord Kyril?"

"Yes." Zora couldn't lie about that; Kyril would give her away the minute he saw her—assuming he recognized her. With her luck, he would.

The Shield-Bearer's eyes narrowed. "Don't tell me he's your brother," she said grimly.

"He's not," Zora assured her. "We just grew up on the same estate."

"What about your family?"

"My father is dead, and my mother promised me to the Goddess before I was born. I was raised to serve her."

"I hope it works better with you than it did with *her*." The

Shield-Bearer looked at Lina and sighed.

Zora contemplated the Queen, who was once again sobbing into the side of the couch. It was odd to see Lina enacting the exact same sort of scene that Zora's mother did when she got upset. "I hope so, too," she said soberly.

The missing priestess returned with a healer. The healer carried a vial of pink liquid, which she poured unceremoniously down the Queen's throat. After a few minutes Lina stopped crying, but her eyes were still red and swollen.

"Put a veil on her," the eldest priestess ordered, "and take her back to her rooms. We don't want anyone to see her looking like this."

"Why don't we just keep her here?" one of the other priestesses asked, and then looked at Zora. "Oh, that's right. We don't have a spare cell anymore."

"Until one of us dies," another priestess muttered nervously, watching as two of the priestesses pulled Lina to her feet, put a veil over her head, and escorted her out of the room.

"Why should one of you die?" Zora asked, now completely bewildered.

"There are usually four priestess, plus the Queen, who is the High Priestess," the one who had suggested keeping Lina there explained. "So there are five cells." She gestured to five curtained doorways along one side of the room. "In the past a new priestess has been chosen when one of us has died, but I've never heard of one being chosen *before* one of us died."

"Maybe the Goddess wants me for something else, then." Zora hoped she sounded calmer than she felt. *Yes, I wanted to serve the Goddess, but this isn't at all what I expected.*

"Then why are you here?" the nervous one asked.

"To learn?" It was all Zora could come up with at the moment.

"That makes sense," the eldest priestess said. "We'll train you as we would any new priestess, and in time we will know what the Goddess wants."

"Have her attend the Queen as soon as possible," the Shield-Bearer said. "Having someone closer to her own age may help—there isn't one of us not old enough to be her mother—and Zora can also serve as an example of wholehearted obedience to the will of the Goddess."

"As opposed to token obedience with whining, sulking, moping, and the occasional fit of hysterics to liven things up," the Eldest sighed. "I haven't seen behavior like that since the year her father was chosen."

"Don't remind me," the Shield-Bearer groaned. "I had to choke Druscilla unconscious to keep her from disrupting the ritual."

"She would never have done as Queen," one of the priestesses sighed.

Do they mean my mother Druscilla? I can't imagine her as Queen here; she'd be worse than Lina.

"But is what we have any better?" another asked.

"Presumably this is the will of the Goddess," the Eldest said. "We must have faith."

"It's not as if we have anything *else*," someone muttered.

"In a way it is a shame about Lord Kyril," the Eldest remarked. "She was actually behaving better when she had him for company."

"But she'll still have him for company, won't she?" Zora said. "The king has his Companions to spend time with, and the Queen doesn't actually *have* to see much of him if she doesn't want to."

"I guess that would help if it was somebody she hated. But she already knows and likes him, so there's no point in avoiding him now, is there?"

"Unless she thinks avoiding him now will make his death easier to bear," the eldest priestess said.

I'm not supposed to know about this, so I had better pretend I don't. "His death?"

"The king is sacrificed at the end of the summer."

"Sacrificed as in *killed?* I thought it was symbolic—after all, his father was a Year-King, wasn't he?" *I'm supposed to know that, I think. This is getting confusing.*

"The Sacrifice is not an empty ritual," the priestess said sternly. "The king is given to the river, to mingle his blood with that of the Goddess."

"What does that mean, exactly?"

It was the Shield-Bearer who answered. "There's a terrace next to the river, just above the waterfall. The king steps off that and is swept over the waterfall."

"Right into the rocks below, probably." Zora remembered them vividly from her first day of training. "And the water is very rough there. So the king would have to be a really good swimmer..." She was reminded of Lord Ranulf's advanced swimming lessons. "Kyril *should* be able to do it."

"Just because his father could doesn't mean he can."

"True. But if he doesn't, his father is going to be seriously annoyed with him."

"He told him how he survived," the Shield-Bearer said.

"His parents knew that he was coming here, so I'd guess his father told him everything he thought he might need to know. Besides, Lord Ranulf teaches every child on his estate to swim. Even I can do it."

The Shield-Bearer sighed and shook her head. "He would." She frowned at Zora. "You must remember, Zora, that this subject is taboo here. It is a sacred mystery, and it is not to be spoken of outside the temple. Whatever you know, or think you know, or guess, do *not* speak of it!"

"When she leaves these rooms," the eldest priestess pointed out, "she'll be veiled."

The Shield-Bearer nodded, looking relieved, and the priestess turned to Zora. "We don't speak when we're veiled. We attend the Queen, but we don't take an active part in public life."

"What do the priestesses do?" *What have I agreed to?*

The eldest priestess actually smiled. "That's what you're here to learn."

"If I might make a suggestion," the Shield-Bearer said, "teach her everything that the Queen is supposed to know. If we are incredibly lucky, perhaps she can pass on what she learns to the Queen."

"It's worth a try," the priestess agreed. "Goddess knows the wretched girl refuses to learn what she needs to know from any of us."

CHAPTER NINE

Zora's lessons started the next morning, and nothing at Eagle's Rest had even begun to prepare her for them. She woke at dawn in what was now her room. The light came from a short, wide window placed high in the stone wall above the bed. The ceiling overhead was made of wooden planks supported by thick crossbeams, but the rest of the room appeared to be cut out of rock. It was small, little wider than the bed was long. At the foot of the bed was a plain wooden chest used to hold clothing, and the only clothing in it was a spare set of green robes. *I wonder what happened to the clothing I wore to the Choosing. I hope that I'll get it back at some point; it's my best outfit.* There was no other furniture in the room, unless one counted the dark curtain which served as a door.

Being trained by the priestesses in Diadem was different from anything she had previously experienced. At home, even though the priests and priestesses had been teaching her to be a priestess, it was—well, not as formal. Zora had lived with her family, or stayed in the girls' dormitory with Lord Ranulf's other students, and lessons had been part of her normal, if occasionally chaotic, life.

Here, however... *All the Goddesses are one Goddess.* Zora had been told that before, both by her human teachers and by the voice of the Goddess. *That may be so, Lady, but I think you left a few details out. Why am I here again? Not just in Diadem, but why am I in this place?*

The Goddess didn't answer. Zora wished she would, because there was a lot of silence in the temple complex, and it was driving her crazy.

It wasn't that anyone was unkind to her, but...there were a lot of little things for her to learn in addition to what the priestesses thought she was supposed to be learning. Silent meals, for example. Zora had never been at any meal that was eaten in silence—back at Eagle's Rest most meals were noisy, with everyone talking at once. But the priestesses here valued silence. They said it made them more receptive to the voice of the Goddess.

Zora asked during one of her lessons if they heard actual words and was startled to be told that they didn't.

"Very few people actually hear the Goddess talk to them," the First Priestess had explained. "Some of the Queens do—though I'm fairly sure Lina isn't one of them, at least not yet. The rest of us keep silence so that if the Goddess does choose to speak to us, we can hear her. If we don't hear actual words or see visions, we contemplate what we know of the Goddess, what she has taught us in the past through the Queens, and we consider whether our actions will be pleasing to her."

I'm not certain that the way you've been treating Lina would please the Goddess, Zora thought. *I believe we are supposed to be supporting the Queen, not making her miserable. To be fair, however, there is a lot more making Lina miserable than the way the priestesses act. They may not help much, but they aren't the main cause of her misery.*

Silence started with evening prayers and didn't end until after breakfast the next day. All meals were eaten in silence—except when Zora knocked her spoon against the side of her bowl, or set down a cup so hard that everyone heard the clunk it made as it hit the table. No student of Lord Ranulf's actually *was* clumsy, but trying to keep silence while surrounded by women who had probably been doing so for longer than she had been alive certainly made Zora feel horribly clumsy, noisy, and self-conscious. An additional challenge was trying to eat at the same rate as everyone else; the other priestesses had a rhythm that eluded her. Zora wondered despairingly how many years it took to finish eating at the same time as everyone else—the four priestesses seemed to finish together effortlessly, and then they waited for Zora to finish. *Nothing in* that *to make a person feel awkward...*

The priestesses were kind enough, but it was only too obvious that they hadn't expected her and were at a loss as to where to put her. The room Zora slept in—they called it a cell, and she certainly didn't disagree—was the one used by the Queen, although nobody had explained why the Queen had a room down here when she had a perfectly good bedchamber upstairs. The large table in the common room where they ate had a chair at the head, which was the Queen's, two chairs on each side for the four priestesses, and a chair at the foot of the table that had been brought in from someplace else (it didn't match the ones that were there already). The really annoying thing was that when Zora sat in it, her feet didn't quite touch the floor.

At the end of the night silence, after breakfast, the priestesses met together in the common room to discuss the day's schedule and divide up the tasks to be done. Having Zora to train was apparently a substantial addition to their work, but she had to struggle not to laugh when she overheard one of them mutter "At least she can read."

"These are the proper forms of address," said the First Priestess. "The Queen is addressed as *Lady* if you are talking to her and referred to as *the Queen* when you are talking about her. Her personal name is *not* used outside the temple. The Year-King is called *Lord Kyril*, and if he has siblings or children here in Diadem, they are called *Lord* or *Lady*."

"So Esme wasn't *Lady Esme* until her father was Chosen, right?" Zora asked. "And if a Year-King survives, does he keep the title, like Lord Ranulf?"

"Yes, those are both valid examples. The priestesses," she continued, "are more complex than usual right now. Normally there are four of us, and we are referred to as First Priestess, Second Priestess, Third Priestess, and Fourth Priestess. I am also called *Eldest*, and the Fourth Priestess is called *Youngest*. But you would technically be the Youngest, and you would be the Fifth Priestess if there were such a title." She paused and shook her head. "For the time being we will not use the title *Youngest*, and we will simply call you *Sister*, as we wait for the Goddess to clarify what role she has chosen you for."

At least the Goddess has finally chosen me for something, *whatever it is.* Even though Zora felt awkward and uncertain in the temple, she was relieved by that. *It's better than being a dog—at least I hope so.*

"Follow me," the Eldest commanded, rising and leading Zora down an underground hallway to a small room that apparently served as the temple's library. It had shelves along the back and right walls, and a long desk was attached to the left wall. "Since you can read, we'll let you learn as much as you can that way." She pulled several volumes from the shelves and placed them on the end of the desk farthest from the door. "Start with these, and ask me later if there's anything in them you don't understand. We will be questioning you on the contents to be certain that you remember and understand them."

She left, and Zora happily immersed herself in the books. These were "everything you wanted to know while you were a dog and couldn't ask about it." The subjects included the history of Diadem, the lineage of the Queens (apparently after they were dead, using their names was allowed, or maybe these books just never left the temple), and several centuries worth of harvest records with notes about the corresponding Year-Kings. Zora found the last particularly fascinating.

In addition to the crops, weather conditions, and harvest yields, the scroll gave the name of each Year-King, his age, whether he was from Diadem or elsewhere (if he wasn't from Diadem, the scroll simply said "foreign"—apparently they didn't care where he came from), along with any special comments about the Choosing and Sacrifice rituals. Zora started with the previous year ("Pelar, age 50, Diadem, widower, survived by daughter Esme, age 31, all taxes forgiven for her lifetime"), and worked her way backward through years marked "interregnum" and the last Sacrifice of the previous Queen's reign. Then she came to the Sacrifice that took place ten months before her birth.

The entry started innocuously enough: "Briam, age 18, foreign," but the notes were a real shock. They included "survived by sister Akila," and they described the Choosing in detail. Zora had been wondering on and off if the Druscilla they talked about was her mother and had begun to suspect that it was, but she could never have imagined the rest. *How could Father have been a Year-King? And how did Mother end up married to him, especially if she's the Heiress? And he wasn't a shape-changer, so how did he survive the Sacrifice?*

Reading the account of the Choosing ritual, she wasn't surprised that they'd sent Druscilla away—the surprise was that they hadn't strangled her permanently on the spot. *No wonder everyone agreed that Druscilla would be hopeless as Queen. They probably wouldn't want her back even if they knew she was still alive. But Lina is a lot like her.* Then Zora realized something that should have been immediately obvious. *We have the same father. That makes us half-sisters. And if my mother is the*

Heiress... She turned back to the book about the Queens. *The last Queen and my mother's mother were sisters. I guess that explains why Lina and I look so much alike. It's not some sort of divine action. It's simple inheritance.*

But how did Father survive the Sacrifice? And if he was supposed to die then, is that why he died in an earthquake a few years later? Somebody had said something... *Now, if I could just remember what... It was something about a famine the year the Queen was born. Is this why Mother promised me to the Goddess—to try to make up for whatever it was she did? But what in Earth did she do?*

Zora was thankful that lunch was eaten in silence, because she was afraid to open her mouth. *My father was supposed to have died before I was even conceived, and judging by the records, everyone here thinks he did. Put that together with what the Eldest told Lina about the people needing the Sacrifice...*

Zora resolved not to mention her parents. To anyone. She wished fervently that she were still back at Eagle's Rest having lessons with Marfa. Marfa—and the rest of the priests—had expected to her study hard and learn, but life there hadn't been as...well, treacherous. Doing the wrong thing there would get you corrected, or possibly scolded, but being grounded after the fish incident was the only time Zora had been punished. Here, if she said the wrong thing to the wrong person, she didn't know what would happen, but she was horribly afraid that somebody could die.

Zora realized the room had become totally silent and looked up from her plate. To her embarrassment she discovered that everyone else had finished eating and they were waiting for her, so all of them could leave the table. Again. Lowering her head so she didn't have to look at them, she ate as quickly and quietly as she could. As soon as she had finished, they all stood, and the Eldest said the post-meal blessing. Zora stumbled over the responses. *I can't do anything right today!* She did manage to copy the way the others stacked their dishes together so she didn't drop anything as she followed them down a short hall to a small anteroom where they left their dishes on a tray on a wooden shelf next to a closed wooden door. *Somebody else must bring our food and take our dishes,* she thought. *Is there a hall to the main kitchen on the other side of that door?*

As they returned to the common room, the Third Priestess fell back to walk next to Zora, who, as the Youngest, was at the end of the line. "Don't worry, child. It takes a while to learn the rhythm of life here, and nobody expects you to be perfect at the beginning. I had a horrible time getting used to the silence when I first came here. You'll do fine." She gave Zora a consoling pat on the arm, and Zora blinked back tears.

"Thank you, Elder Sister," she whispered. "It does all feel a bit strange right now."

They joined the First and Second Priestesses in the common room. Before anyone could ask Zora about her morning's reading, the Fourth Priestess stalked into the room from the other side, from the tunnel that led to the Queen's chapel, if Zora was remembering the layout of the rooms correctly.

"We had no idea how lucky we were with Queen Zoradah," she snarled, "and I would believe that wretched girl is not her daughter if there hadn't been so many witnesses to the birth."

For one horrible moment, Zora thought that the priestess had said "Queen Zora," but then she remembered that she had seen the name of Lina's mother in the Book of Queens. She just hadn't realized that it was pronounced so much like her own.

"May I assume, since you are here, that the Queen is meditating in her chapel?" the Eldest said sternly.

"She's in her chapel," the Fourth snapped, "but if she's not crying her stupid little head off, it will be the first time she's stopped since the Choosing."

I wonder how Kyril is taking that. He's bound to be upset.

"What of the king?" the Second asked. "Is he any help?"

The Fourth collapsed on the couch. "He tries, but she's still blaming him for not staying out all day hunting so he wouldn't be Chosen. It was a ghastly morning." She leaned back and closed her eyes. "I'm getting too old for this."

"Headache?" the Third asked sympathetically.

"I wish it would just finish splitting my head open and let me die."

The Second was already moving to a cupboard against the wall. She opened it and pulled out a small bottle. "Here," she said, "drink this."

The Fourth poured it straight down her throat—*as if she's trying to avoid tasting it, which would make sense because it's probably distilled willow bark and very bitter.*

"Just lie there and keep your eyes closed," the Second continued. "We'll let you know when you need to get up again."

The Fourth thanked her in a faint voice and then went limp. Zora looked at her in alarm, but the Third said softly, "She has put herself into a trance, that's all. It's a useful trick for dealing with pain. We'll have to teach it to you."

"It sounds as though I may need it," Zora replied, keeping her voice low. "Should I go back to my reading now?"

"Yes, do that. I'll call you for supper."

"Sister? Am I allowed to attend the evening ritual?" Zora wanted to see for herself how Lina was doing.

"Not just yet, I'm afraid. Probably in a few weeks, but you'll have to be veiled."

Zora retreated to the library to see if she could find anything on the training of a priestess or the rules they lived by. Her search came up empty, so she took a history of Diadem and started in on that. *I need to learn more about how things work around here, and I need to learn it fast.*

It was the middle of the night, and Zora couldn't get to sleep. She was worried about so many things she couldn't even sort them out, resulting in an overwhelming feeling of panic. *And I'm shut away from anyone who could give me answers. I wish I could go home and talk to Aunt Akila, or Uncle Ranulf, or even my mother—although she'd probably just have hysterics and refuse to tell me anything.* But that reminded her that there was a place in Diadem she had been calling home. *As long as I'm back before anyone misses me...*

She changed shape into an owl, counting on the shape's silent flight and the fact that most people didn't look up, and flew quickly through the tunnel to the chapel, up the stairwell, and out the nearest window. Once she had enough altitude, it was simple to find their house and go in through her bedroom window. She changed back to human, threw on some clothes, and went to tap softly on Colin's door.

Apparently he hadn't been sleeping well either, because he opened it almost immediately. "Zora!" he said in surprise. "Where have you *been*? What's going on? I've been worried sick!"

"Nobody told you?" she asked. "All I know is that I passed out during the Choosing and didn't wake up until the next day. I've been in a complex under the palace ever since—apparently the Goddess wants me to serve her *here*."

"No, nobody bothered to tell me," Colin said bitterly. "You just disappeared while everyone was distracted by Kyril's being Chosen. Did they tell you he's the new Year-King?"

"They didn't have to," Zora sighed. "Remember the venison? The Queen really *was* trying to keep him away from the city. When I woke up she was still having hysterics. It was almost as bad as being home with my mother. I haven't seen her since I first woke up underground, but I hear she's still crying."

"If you think the Goddess wants you here, I suppose you're going to stay here," Colin said with resignation.

"I don't want to find out what happens if I don't sneak back in before someone misses me," Zora said. "*Everyone* is upset right now. But I wanted to see you and make sure you were all right."

"I'm fine," Colin said, "but I feel suddenly superfluous."

"You haven't seen Kyril?" Zora asked in surprise. Colin shook his head. "Actually, there is something you could do to help me."

"Name it."

"Fly back to Eagle's Rest and talk to Aunt Akila and Uncle Ranulf. There's something very strange going on here."

"Aside from both you and Kyril being chosen?"

Zora nodded vigorously. "You can't tell anyone you know about this—especially my mother—but the Queen and I are half-sisters." Colin looked blank, and she didn't blame him. "She and I have the same father, and everyone here seems to think that he died *here*, that summer, not three years later at Eagle's Rest."

"But he wasn't a shape-changer, was he?"

"No. Aunt Akila says he wasn't, even though he was her twin and she's one." Zora shivered. "Somebody must have taken his place for the Sacrifice, and there was a famine here that year."

"And he died in an earthquake, didn't he?" Colin asked.

"He died, my mother—who was apparently the late Queen's

Heiress until the Queen was born—was crippled, and I didn't get a scratch on me. I don't know who did what, but something is very wrong. I'm floundering around in the dark, and I don't dare talk to anyone here about it!"

"I can see that," Colin agreed. "'Oh, by the way, my mother was the Heiress and my father was the Year-King everybody thinks died leaving only *one* daughter'..."

"Exactly," Zora nodded. "It's bad enough that they know Kyril's father was a Year-King without finding out that mine was as well, especially because my very existence proves that he didn't die when he was supposed to have."

"Are you sure they know that Kyril's father was a Year-King?"

"Has anyone called you 'Lord Colin' since you've been here?"

Colin shook his head. "Oh. Is *that* why they call him Lord Kyril?"

"Lord Kyril. Lady Esme. If a member of your family is the Year-King, you get called Lord or Lady for the rest of your life."

"So I get to go home and tell Lady Akila that, in addition to her husband and her brother, her son is the Year-King?"

"I wouldn't worry about Kyril's survival," Zora reassured him. "Apparently Lord Ranulf's swimming test is derived from the Sacrifice."

"Really?" Colin thought that over for several moments. Finally he said, "I always wondered why they drugged us."

Zora nodded. "That's why, all right. I got that out of the Queen, back when she and I were spending our afternoons in the chapel together." She sighed. "She was a lot calmer then. I have the impression that nobody has gotten a coherent sentence out of her since Kyril was Chosen, but they won't let me see her. They won't even let me go to the daily rituals."

"I'll go to the morning one before I leave," Colin said. "I'll find out as much as I can here tomorrow and then head north tomorrow night." He frowned. "How do I find you when I get back?"

"I don't know," Zora said. "Even when they do let me out of the temple complex, I'll be one of those women in the green robes and veils, not allowed to talk. But you can probably find Kyril and talk to him, at least. Maybe you can have him ask for you to be one of his Companions."

"Right. Maybe we could all pass notes." Colin didn't sound convinced.

"I've been winging it since we got here," Zora said. "Speaking of which, I need to change back to an owl and sneak back before I'm missed."

"Owl?"

She shrugged. "Quiet, blends into the dark, and really hard to catch if anyone happens to see me. Besides—"

"—most people don't look up," they finished in unison.

With Kyril occupied with the Queen and Colin away in search of something that would make sense of what was going on, Zora threw herself into learning to become a model young priestess.

The daily routine in the temple was simple. Zora spent the mornings in the book room reading, which was easily her favorite part of the day. In the afternoon she had lessons in the common room, taught by the priestesses not currently attending the Queen. *Too bad their teaching style comes from trying to teach Lina things she never wanted to learn. It's annoying to be treated the way they treat her, and it's not fair! I do want to learn. I just have to be careful what I say... If I agree with them that Druscilla was not a suitable Heiress, I'm going to have to explain where I met her.*

Then came supper, and bedtime. *Repeat. Day after day. After day. The worst part is being stuck in here. At least when I was a dog I was allowed outside!*

After a couple of weeks, however, Zora became accustomed to the rhythm of temple life. Meals became easier—and quieter—as she started eating at nearly the same pace as everyone else. She also learned to appreciate the silence. It no longer made her desperate for someone to talk to.

Zora sat at the table one morning, eyes lowered so that they fell on her empty bowl. *Even if I don't hear the Goddess, the silence gives me lots of time to think—especially about whether I really want to serve the Goddess. It was different at home. Serving her here means being part of having someone be killed each year—and I'm not sure I can do that. I want to serve her, but killing people doesn't seem like the act of a loving Mother. We all return to her in the fullness of time, so why do the people here think she needs human sacrifice?*

Zora woke up one morning and realized that she had completely forgotten about guard training. Was it time for swim training to resume? It was hard to keep track of time in the temple, where every day was the same.

"Eldest?" she asked, when the silence ended after breakfast. "Could you tell me what day it is, please?"

The First Priestess stared at Zora in astonishment. "Why in Earth would you need to know?"

"I'm supposed to go back for more guard training after the break for the festival is over."

"That's nonsense! Spring training ends before the Choosing."

"For most people, yes. But I'm one of the swimmers, and that training schedule goes all through the summer. I don't want to just not show up if I'm supposed to be there."

"I believe the Call of the Goddess supersedes anything else that might have been happening in your life," the Eldest said sternly. "But," she added, "it is good that you are mindful of your obligations. I shall speak to the Sword-Bearer."

"Thank you," Zora said meekly. She went to the book room, where her studies were still providing new and fascinating information. Today she found an explanation of the calendar used in Diadem, which wasn't at all like the one at home. The year started at dawn after the Longest Night, and was divided into eight parts, called eighths. The third and seventh eights started on the days in the spring and fall when the days and nights were the same length. The fourth eighth started the day of the Choosing. The fifth eighth started on the Longest Day, and there was something called "First Fruits" then. The Sacrifice took place around the middle of the sixth eighth, ten weeks after the Longest Day. Zora resolved to make a private calendar so she would know when the Sacrifice was coming up, but she would have to wait until the Longest Day to start counting because she didn't know how many days it had been since the Choosing.

The next morning the Eldest told Zora to put on her veil and reminded her that she was to remain silent while wearing it. She then put on her own veil and escorted Zora though yet another set of hallways Zora hadn't seen before until they reached the Sword-Bearer's office.

Catriona was already there, looking unusually grim. "Thank you, Eldest," she said. "I'll escort her back when I'm done with her."

"This is most irregular," the priestess complained.

"I know," Catriona said, "but I need to speak with her alone." The priestess left, shaking her head.

Catriona closed the door behind her, locked it, and then yanked the veil from Zora's head and glared at her.

"What were you thinking?" Catriona kept her voice low, but she sounded furious.

"What was I thinking when?" Zora asked blankly. She was pretty sure that only the fact that there could be people in the neighboring rooms kept Catriona from screaming, but she had no idea why. "I didn't want to just disappear from my assigned training with no explanation. Why are you so upset?"

Catriona slapped a hand on a pile of papers on her desk. "Do you know what these are?

Zora shook her head, still mystified. Catriona had always been kind to her, even when she was a dog. Now she was acting as if Zora had done something very wrong, but she had no idea what it could be.

"These are your training and injury reports." Catriona added grimly, "and I've talked to the swimmers. I gather that the very first day you nearly killed yourself by swimming upriver to the bottom of the waterfall—and then, in addition to the risks you were running in the water, you were training with live blades!"

"I didn't get 'nearly killed' by the waterfall," Zora said indignantly. "All I got were a few bruises! And everyone except absolute beginners trains with live blades for knife and sword work! I should think you'd be pleased that I made that much progress in a month, especially considering that I had no prior training with weapons."

"Did the Queen tell you anything about her training?"

"No," Zora said, bewildered by the sudden change of subject. "Kyril told me that all she did was archery, but she never talked to me about it at all."

"Yes, the Queen is restricted to archery. She's much too valuable to be risked in close combat. Did it *truly* not occur to you that the same restrictions would apply to the Heiress?"

"No. Why would it? Besides, what does that have to do with me?"

Catriona stared at Zora, her mouth hanging open. It was at least a minute before she managed to speak. "What, exactly, did your mother tell you about Diadem?"

"Nothing!" Zora suddenly flashed back to the helpless frustration she had felt when she was confined to her mother's rooms. "I'd never even *heard* of Diadem before I came here."

Catriona sighed. "Did you know that your mother was the Heiress until the present Queen was born?"

"I was beginning to suspect that she might be, after I heard enough people talk about her," Zora admitted, "but there really wasn't anyone I could ask about it. I didn't know anything when I came here, but I've heard people—mostly the priestesses—talk about Druscilla, and I saw the records..." She paused and then blurted out, "If my mother was the Heiress described in the records, was my father the Year-King?"

"Yes." It was a grim monosyllable.

"How did he survive?"

"I suspect that Akila and Druscilla contrived something between them, but I never asked. Remember that most people here don't know he survived, so *don't* tell anyone he's still alive."

Zora stared at her in surprise. "He's not. He died in an earthquake when I was a baby."

Catriona blinked. "Did he indeed? What about your mother—was she hurt?"

"Yes. The house we were living in collapsed, and her legs were crushed. She can't walk without help, even now. I was lucky—there wasn't a scratch on me when they dug us out. I don't even remember it."

"Do you get a lot of earthquakes at Eagle's Rest?"

"I don't think so. That was the only one I ever heard of."

Catriona sighed. "I don't know who took Briam's place for the Sacrifice, but, knowing your family, I'm sure someone did. Most people blame the disaster that ruined the harvest on your mother's behavior at the Choosing, but I think it's more likely the Goddess was angry that someone meddled so the Year-King who was Chosen was not the Sacrifice." She shook her head. "But that's old news. The thing that matters now is that *you* are the Heiress until the Queen has a daughter."

"But isn't my mother next after the Queen?"

"No. She renounced her claim after the present Queen was born. Even if she had not, do you really think she would be willing to come back here?"

"Well, no." *I think she'd rather throw herself out the tower window—and she can't fly.*

"Not counting your mother, you are the *only* one left after the Queen. This means that your life belongs to the Goddess and the people, and you are *not* free to take risks with it. Why do you think I spent so much time looking after you while you were a dog?"

Zora was still trying to take all of this in. "I was a *dog*. I wasn't thinking much. If anything, I figured that any member of Uncle Ranulf's family must like animals."

Catriona choked back a laugh. "I do admit it's a requirement. But you're a human now. *Think.* Be careful. Stay in the temple with the priestesses unless I'm with you or you're in attendance on the Queen. Do you understand?"

What you're saying, yes. Why you're saying it, no—not yet, anyway. "Stay in the temple unless I'm with either you or the Queen," Zora repeated back obediently. *At least that might give me a chance to sort all this out in my mind.*

"Good," Catriona said, more gently now. "Remember that I am officially your bodyguard, Zora."

"Yes, I know. They covered the rank structure in basic orientation. The Shield-Bearer is the head of the Guards and the Queen's bodyguard, and the Sword-Bearer is second in command and bodyguard to the Heiress. But with the Shield-Bearer being the Regent as well—and no Heiress to be guarded—you're currently in charge of the Guards." Zora considered the implications of that. "That means you're not exactly free to guard me, even if we wanted to admit that I'm here, which I don't think we do. If nobody knows I'm the Heiress, I should be safe enough—though I suppose you're going to pull me off the swimmers' roster." *And that takes care of any chance I might have to get outside and get any exercise.*

"You suppose correctly. But if you need anything, remember that looking after you is my job, and I do consider myself your ally and, I hope, your friend. Call on me if you need any help." Catriona rose and tossed the veil at her. "Put that on, and I'll take you back now."

Alone in the temple with books spread around her, Zora tried to come to grips with the changes of the last few weeks. *I thought my life was completely changed when the Goddess chose Kassie. I had to come here and be Chosen myself to discover that I never knew my own parents! In fact, one could say that I never even knew myself...*

The priestesses increased the range of Zora's training. They didn't tell her why, and she didn't ask. She didn't want to know. *I've had enough life-changing surprises in the last few months.*

Suddenly the priestesses really wanted Zora to know everything the Queen was *supposed* to know—as opposed to everything that Lina actually knew, which was much less than Zora was learning. *I still remember her saying of the anchor point, "It's a rock. With water on it."*

The other priestesses didn't have to memorize the Queen's public morning and evening rituals, but Zora was given a journal and told to copy the rituals into it. There were discussions with all four of the priestesses—and frequently with the Shield-Bearer as well—about the relationship between the Choosing, the Sacrifice, and the well-being of the land, with special emphasis on the harvest. Everyone told her at least twice that it was vital that the king who was Chosen be the Sacrifice.

Zora thought about what Catriona had *not* said. She was right. *We don't get earthquakes at Eagle's Rest.*

They may not know that Briam didn't die then, but they certainly seem to know that something *went wrong that year.*

"Zora," the Shield-Bearer asked one day, "do you understand why we're telling you this?" She had come down to the temple to sit in on the afternoon lessons. At the moment they were sitting on one of the couches, a bit apart from the priestesses.

"Because it's important?" *I did hear you the first five times. You really don't need to keep repeating it.*

"Yes, it's important," the Shield-Bearer said grimly, "and I want to be absolutely certain that you will *not* try to stop or interfere with the Sacrifice."

"Why would I do that?" Zora asked. "Kyril—" *No, don't tell her he's a shape-changer, just in case she hasn't figured it out.* "Kyril's father survived, so I don't see why Kyril shouldn't as well."

The Shield-Bearer lowered her voice so nobody besides Zora could hear her. "You're not planning to change your shape so you can take his place?"

Zora shook her head vigorously. *She knows I'm a shape-changer, but does she know about Kyril as well?* "Absolutely not! Even before I started training here I would never have done that. I know it would be wrong."

"Have you heard of sacrifice by willing substitution?" the Shield-Bearer asked.

"Of course," Zora said indignantly. "They did train me at home, you know. I didn't arrive here *totally* ignorant. It's a doctrine that says another person can choose to take the place of someone who is to be sacrificed. There is more power gained from a willing sacrifice than from someone who doesn't know what's happening and didn't consent. But isn't responding to the Call of the Goddess during the Choosing a type of consent?" Zora was interested enough in the question that she forgot to keep her voice down. "Pelar and Kyril both knew about the Sacrifice before they were chosen."

One of the younger priestesses frowned. "Are you certain Lord Kyril knew?"

"Oh, yes, he knew. Remember the fuss the Queen was making about venison the morning after the Choosing? She asked him to go hunting that day so he wouldn't be in the city during the ritual."

"She did *what?*" The Eldest sounded appalled. "Are you saying the Queen deliberately tried to circumvent the Goddess's choice?"

"I could be wrong, but that's what Kyril and I thought at the time. He asked if I really thought he was going to stand by and watch the Queen spend the summer with another man."

"How did you answer him?" The Shield-Bearer sounded somewhere between curious and appalled.

"I told him that if the Goddess willed it, he had better. And he said it was going to be the quickest hunt on record and that we'd see what the Goddess willed."

"So he would have chosen to be the Year-King if he had been given a free choice..."

"He *did* have a free choice, and he made it. He could easily have spent the whole day hunting instead of going out well before dawn so that he would be back in time for the Choosing." Zora considered the matter. "It's ironic, actually. *He* chose to be the Year-King, and the *Goddess* chose him to be the Year-King. It's only the Queen who didn't want him to do it."

"And what happens if he dies?" the Shield-Bearer asked.

Zora winced. "I think the Queen would take it very badly."

"What about you?"

"I'd miss him." Zora was appalled to find her eyes filling with tears. "We've lived in the same place all our lives, and I love him like a brother. But it is an honor to serve the Goddess." *And I've given the matter a great deal of thought—as well as being forced to consider the alternative.* "If Kyril dies in her service—or if I do—well, there are a lot of deaths with much less meaning."

"And are you willing to *live* in her service?" the Eldest asked sternly.

Zora regarded her with exasperation. "I'm here, aren't I? You asked me the first day if I was willing to serve the Goddess, and my answer hasn't changed since then."

The youngest priestess sighed. "Why do we have a trainee who understands this intuitively while we have a Queen who can't even be *taught* what's obvious to the rest of us?"

The question was presumably rhetorical, but Zora replied softly, "I don't think she wants to learn."

The next morning Zora discovered something in the book she was studying that made her much less certain that Kyril would survive being Year-King as easily as his father had. It was a list of tasks to be done at the start of a new reign: "...at the beginning of the reign of each new Queen, additional stones are placed beneath the waterfall, so that they may be shaped by the water into memorial stones for the Kings' Garden."

I was already at the bottom of the waterfall, and I wasn't drugged, and still I was black and blue for days from the stones I hit. If I'd been drugged, and then fallen down from the top *of the waterfall and been caught in that turbulence—* She shuddered. *I could have hit my head and drowned, or I could have broken my neck—and nobody ever did answer me when I asked about the rocks.*

She tried to convince herself there was no need to panic. *I need to find out exactly what the Kings' Garden is—although "memorial stones" does seem fairly clear. How many "additional" stones do they add? Lina has been Queen for about sixteen years, but she wasn't old enough to marry until last year, so however many rocks they added, most of them are still there. Only one would have been removed as a memorial, and there are a lot of them there, judging from the brief look I got. I have got to talk to Kyril!*

There were problems with that. Zora had not forgotten her promise to stay in the temple unless she was with the Queen or the Sword-Bearer. More importantly, however, she didn't know where to find Kyril. She didn't know if he was sleeping in the Queen's room at night. She didn't know how he spent his days. *For all I know, he could be spending the days with his Companions and his nights sleeping in a different wing of the palace. I'll have to trust the Goddess until I get a chance to see him—there's no point in trying to sneak out of here if I don't know where to look for him. But it's so much easier to trust the Goddess if you think someone you care about isn't in any real danger.*

Fortunately, the Goddess answered Zora's prayers before she even had a chance to frame them coherently. The priestesses decided she was ready to take her turn in attendance on the Queen.

"It's not particularly complicated," the Eldest explained. "You will sleep in the room between her bedchamber and the hallway, remain in the room behind the balcony during the morning and evening rituals, and stay near her in the daytime whenever she's outside her bedchamber."

"Except for meals," the Third Priestess added. "You either get a tray in the room you sleep in or come back to the temple, so you can take your veil off to eat. The Queen has at least one guard with her at mealtimes, in addition to the Shield-Bearer and usually the king. One of us who's not attending the Queen attends meals as well, although we don't eat then."

Zora remembered seeing veiled priestess sitting across the great hall from Lady Esme, and hoped whoever had that task was able to eat before everyone else, rather than after.

"The rest of us are around during the daytime, too," the Second Priestess said helpfully. "If there's court in the morning at least one of us will join you. We all try to keep track of what happens when she's hearing petitions or conducting business—even though the Shield-Bearer is still the one making the decisions."

"Thank the Lady she still has a Regent for a few more years," the Eldest muttered.

Zora wasn't sure whether she was supposed to respond to that, so she kept her mouth shut. Silence was rapidly becoming her default response to anything she wasn't absolutely sure about. *And they wonder why Lina acts as if she thinks nobody cares about her!*

"Go get the clothing you'll need," the Third Priestess said. "I'll take you upstairs and show you where everything is."

Oops! I'm glad she reminded me that I'm not supposed to know my way around the palace or to have been in the Queen's rooms. "Thank you, Elder Sister."

CHAPTER TEN

Zora was putting her clothes in the chest at the foot of the bed in the Queen's antechamber when Lady Esme walked out of the Queen's bedchamber, carrying a silver goblet on a tray. She ignored Zora, apparently considering her part of the furnishings.

Zora was perfectly happy to be ignored. She still didn't know much about Lady Esme, but being around her made Zora feel uneasy. The only thing more depressing than Lady Esme's black clothing was her temperament. She was gloomy on her good days and downright bitter the rest of the time. It made Zora wonder what she herself would have been like if her father had lived long enough for her to remember him. Zora could smell the scent of bitter herbs that clung to Esme's clothing, but it wasn't as bad as when she had been a dog. Being near Esme in dog-shape had always made Zora feel like sneezing.

The door to the Queen's room closed behind Lady Esme, and the guard stationed in the hallway said a courteous goodnight to her, which Esme ignored. *I guess I'm not the only person she treats like furniture.* Zora closed the door to the hallway that Esme had left ajar, noting the presence of two guards in sight of the door. *Do they keep others out, the Queen in, or both?* she wondered. *They could be a problem if I have to sneak out of here. Maybe I can go through the Queen's room. And no matter what the custom is, I really, really need to talk to Kyril.*

Zora laid out a clean gown for morning, peeled off the one she was wearing, blew out her candle, and slipped into bed. She listened carefully for any sound from the Queen's bedchamber and was relieved to hear both Lina's voice and Kyril's. *At least now I know where to find him at night.* They spoke briefly, and then there was silence. Zora decided to wait a night or two before trying to speak to Kyril. It would help to get some idea of how soundly the Queen slept.

The Queen slept very soundly indeed. The Shield-Bearer tapped on the outer door in the morning, passed through the anteroom without even looking at Zora, which was just as well because she wasn't dressed yet, knocked loudly on the inner door and entered a minute later, allowing just enough time for Kyril to dive under the covers if he wasn't still in bed.

Zora quickly pulled on the gown and veil she had set out the night before and moved to a spot where she could see into the bedchamber.

It was much more luxurious than she remembered from having seen it as a dog. Intricately patterned rugs covered most of the pale marble floor but didn't completely hide the veins of gold that glinted in it. The walls were painted with pastoral scenes, and the bed had a coverlet made of an intricately-textured woven fabric. There were three beautifully-carved wooden chests and two matching armoires, two chairs with embroidered cushions on either side of a small table, and a cushioned stool set in front of a table that held a mirror large enough to see not only one's face but at least half of one's body.

Kyril was awake but still in bed, propped on one elbow with his other arm curved protectively around the Queen's body. All that was visible of the Queen was the back of her head. Her face was turned toward Kyril, away from the door—and the Shield-Bearer.

"She's still asleep," the Shield-Bearer said. It should have been a question, but it wasn't. "I swear, it gets harder to wake her every morning."

Kyril nodded, looking concerned. "You might speak with Lady Esme about the strength of the drink she brings her at bedtime." He shook the Queen's shoulder gently. "Sweetheart, it's time to wake up." The only response was a mumbled protest. "Wake up," Kyril repeated more firmly. "It's time for the morning ritual." This time there was an audible groan in response. Kyril sat up, dragging the Queen with him.

The Shield-Bearer turned her head and saw Zora standing there. "Good, at least *you're* up. Help me get her dressed."

As she came forward and got a good look at the Queen, Zora thought, *She should be the one wearing a veil. She looks much worse than I do, and she got more sleep.* Lina had dark circles under her eyes, her hair was a tangled mess, and she moved as if she had forgotten how to use her body. The Shield-Bearer practically had to hold her up while Zora silently wrapped the gown around her—fortunately it tied at the shoulder instead of having to be slipped over her head. Zora winced in sympathy when the Shield-Bearer sat the Queen on a stool and ruthlessly combed her hair, but at least it did bring Lina to something approaching full consciousness.

Kyril's "I'll see you at breakfast after the ritual" actually evoked something that looked like a faint smile, which Zora considered the first positive sign from Lina since the Choosing. Zora hadn't actually seen her since then, but the priestesses had talked and they were *not* happy with her behavior.

As she followed the Queen and the Shield-Bearer to the balcony where the morning ritual was held, Zora prayed for help and guidance. *Somehow I feel certain I'm going to need it, and it looks as though Lina already needs all the help anyone can give her!*

Zora frowned as she listened to the ritual, glad that her face was hidden by the veil. *Is it my imagination, or is Lina just going through the motions? When I first came here, the power flowed between the Queen and the people during the rituals. It was noticeable even when I was on the far side of the plaza. And a dog. Now I'm almost close enough to touch her, and I can't feel more than the barest wisp of power.*

Other than that, the morning was fairly uneventful. The Queen had breakfast in the great hall with Kyril, did a short session hearing petitions, drank a bowl of broth that Lady Esme brought her at midmorning, and spent the rest of the morning playing a board game with Kyril.

After the midday meal the First Priestess came to escort the Queen to her meditation. When they were underground at the door to the Queen's chapel, she pushed back her veil. When she gave Zora a commanding look, she followed her example.

"You might remember Zora," the Eldest said in a tone that suggested she had no great hope of it. "We believe the Goddess has called her here to help you learn to be a good Queen, so she will enter the chapel with you, unless the Goddess wills otherwise." She opened the door to the chapel, waited for both of the girls to pass through, and closed it behind them.

"Does she really think you don't remember me?" Zora said in

disgust as they walked to the start of the labyrinth. "Just how stupid does she think you are?"

Lina burst into tears. Zora stared at her in horror, unsure what she had said to set her off like this. *Well, when in doubt, apologize.*

"I'm sorry," she said hastily. "I know it's been horrible for you, and I really don't want to make it worse." *Not that I know why what I just said was so horrible, but I'm on* your *side. Mostly. I think. Somebody needs to be.* "I just don't like hearing her talk to you like that."

Lina fled in a straight line across the labyrinth, completely ignoring the pattern in the floor, and flung herself facedown on the bench beyond the fountain. Zora tried to follow her but was still compelled to follow the path. She walked it as quickly as she could, not thinking about the pattern. *I contemplated this more deeply when I was a dog. But at least now I don't need to touch the water to change to human.*

Lina turned her head as Zora came out of the labyrinth. "Why did you walk the path?" she demanded bitterly. "Do you think the Goddess will grant your prayers if you do?"

"I don't know." Zora shrugged. "I can't *not* walk it—I had to follow the path even when I was a dog."

"When you were a dog?" Lina echoed, looking blank.

All right, now I'm scared. "Lina, I came in here with you every day for weeks. I was stuck as a dog, and this chapel was the only place I could change shape back to human. You were the only person I could talk to for over a month. I followed you around all day, I slept in your room at night..."

"The dog was Princess," Lina said softly, "but she had blonde hair like mine when she was human. Kyril took her away...but I don't remember why."

Zora changed back to her true shape, and Lina gasped. "I remember you now!" she said. "But what just happened to your hair?"

"I changed the color and made it longer, that's all. It's funny how such a small change makes me look so different, isn't it? I'm keeping it dark now because I don't want everyone in Diadem talking about how much alike we look."

"If the priestesses knew, they'd make you take my place in a heartbeat," Lina said. "They hate me!"

Unfortunately, there's a certain amount of truth in that. "Well, they can't make us change places—we're not interchangeable. You're the Queen, and I'm not."

"Lucky you." Lina was obviously still bitter about being Queen. Of course, now she was probably convinced that Kyril was going to die, which would make her even less happy with her role than she had been before the Choosing, and she hadn't been happy with it then.

"I'm starting to understand what you mean by that," Zora said ruefully. "I didn't really understand before what it means to serve the Goddess *here*. Where I grew up and was trained, we just did prayers and simple rituals—nothing that hurt anybody. Here, even if it's only one person a year, people *die*."

"I know that," Lina said bleakly. "I *hate* being Queen. Do you realize that every year for the rest of my life I have to marry some man in the spring and then kill him a few months later? And somewhere along the way I am supposed to produce a daughter to continue to do it after I die. She'll never even know her father. Doesn't that seem horrible to *you*?"

"When you look at it that way, yes, it does."

"How else *can* you look at it?" Lina demanded. "It was bad enough last year, but this year—" Her voice broke off.

"This year the king at least has a chance of surviving," Zora said bracingly. "Do you remember my telling you about Lord Ranulf's swimming test?"

"Is that Kyril's father?" Lina sounded uncertain.

I guess she really doesn't remember much of what we talked about before. "Lord Ranulf runs a school for shape-changers. He expects each of his students to be able to swim like a fish."

"Literally?"

"Actually, yes. He also expects us to fly. Anyway, for the final test for the swimming lessons, they drug your wine at the evening meal. Then they drag you out of bed in the middle of the night and throw you off a cliff above a river that runs into a lake. You don't pass the test until you can turn into a bird, make it safely into the water, change into a fish and swim down to the lake, and then get out of the water and change back to human."

"How many of his students get killed trying that?"

"None," Zora assured her. "There are several adult shape-changers, and they make sure that nobody dies. If a student is not awake enough to change into a bird, there are at least two people hovering halfway down the cliff to catch him. If you turn into a fish and forget how to change back, Lord Ranulf is really good at finding the shape-changer among the fish. Once you get dragged out of the water, believe me when I say that you turn into *something* that can breathe air really fast. And they don't give you the test until they're pretty sure you can do it. By the time I got it, I could practically change shape in my sleep. It's not so bad, really. The only thing I wondered about is why they drugged us."

Lina gulped. "The Year-King is drugged the morning of the Sacrifice. So is the Queen—it's supposed to make it easier. It still hurts, though."

Zora didn't understand that. "Are you saying that the Sacrifice hurts *you*?"

Lina nodded, hunching her shoulders forward as she clasped both arms across her stomach, apparently remembering the pain.

"How?" Zora asked. "And why?"

"If the priestesses are right," Lina said slowly, "and I think they might be about this, the Queen and the king are bound together during the Choosing. I never remember that part, so I don't know how it happens. During the Sacrifice ritual the Shield-Bearer cuts the bond between them with a sword right before the king goes," she gulped, "into the water. That's the part that hurts me, even though the sword is at least an arm's length away from me."

"I guess they wouldn't want you still bonded to him when he died."

Lina stared at her. "Do you think if they didn't break the bond, I'd die when he did?"

"I don't know. It would depend on the type of bond, and on its strength. I don't think it would be good for you in any case."

Lina frowned and concentrated on making pleats in her skirt with rigid fingers. "You passed this swimming test, right?"

"Years ago."

"What about Kyril?" Lina asked anxiously. "Can he do it?"

"Oh, yes. And I bet Lord Ranulf told him all about the Sacrifice as well. The main problem here is the waterfall and the rocks below it. Have you ever been in the water at the bottom of the waterfall?"

"Are you insane?" Lina looked at her in shock. "I'm not even allowed to do normal weapons training—do you really think anyone is going to allow me to go into the river?"

"Judging from the lecture the Sword-Bearer gave me when she found out what I did during training, probably not. But do you at least know *how* to swim?" Zora had never met anyone who didn't.

"No. I don't. My job is to do the rituals and to bear at least one daughter to keep on doing them when I can't anymore. I'm not permitted to do things that carry *any* risk of injury."

"I should think that falling into the water when you don't know how to swim carries a lot more risk than swimming lessons do."

"They don't let me anywhere near the water."

"Nobody stopped us from sitting next to the pool in the garden," Zora pointed out. "And you must be fairly close to the river during the Sacrifice."

"On the terrace above it, but there are guards and priestesses with me. And the pool in the garden isn't deep enough to drown in."

Zora gestured at the fountain in front of them. "*That* is deep enough to drown in. All you need to drown is enough water to cover your nose and mouth."

"Do you know how to swim? As a human, not just as a fish?"

"Yes." Zora deliberately didn't add 'of course'—Lina was hypersensitive, and Zora didn't want her in hysterics any more than anyone else did. "I was working with the swimmers during spring training."

Lina shuddered. "Maybe you're lucky to be a priestess instead. The swimmers are the ones who retrieve the king's body—if they can find it. If they can, it gets buried in the Kings' Garden. Otherwise they just put up a stone by itself."

"That explains why they put all the extra stones under the waterfall at the start of each reign. But Kyril needs to swim in that area before the Sacrifice so he knows where they are. If we can sneak out at night without being caught, he can practice, and I can teach you how to swim if you want to learn. But I warn you, the water will be cold."

"If you and he can stand it," Lina said, with a rare flash of determination, "I can learn to."

That sounded promising, but it didn't take Zora long to find a major problem with their plan: Lina was asleep long before the palace settled down for the night. After a couple of nights of this, Zora decided to talk to Kyril, regardless of whether Lina was awake or not.

She took the precaution of locking the door to the hall, and then slipped silently into the Queen's bedchamber and closed that door as well. Both Lina and Kyril were asleep, but Kyril woke up when she whispered his name.

"What's wrong, love?" He looked down at Lina, saw that she was still sleeping, and looked up at her. "Who are you, and what do you want?"

"I'm Zora, you idiot! Can't you see me?" *Given the fact that the night candle is shining on my face, you certainly* should *be able to!*

"Zora? What are you doing here, and what happened to your hair?"

"I changed it to brown when I stopped being a dog. Don't you remember? We *were* living in the same house at the time."

"Oh, yes, that's right. You did."

"As to why I'm here, at the moment I'm the priestess in attendance on the Queen. I sleep in the anteroom."

"That explains how you got in here, but it still doesn't tell me why you're disturbing us in the middle of the night."

"What 'us'? You know how hard it is to wake Lina in the morning—and it's getting worse every day! Do you really think we can wake her up now? That's the problem, actually. Did she tell you about the plan we came up with when we were in the Queen's chapel together? We were going to sneak out at night—the three of us—so you can practice swimming under the waterfall until you know where all the rocks are, while I teach her to swim."

"She doesn't know how to swim?" Kyril looked as surprised as Zora had been.

"No, but whether she learns or not, *you* have got to practice before the Sacrifice. There are a lot of stones directly underneath the waterfall, the turbulence is really rough and pulls you right under, and you do know, don't you, that you'll be drugged? This isn't being dropped of the cliff at home with people to catch you if you don't change in time, and the water is nothing like the river at home—aside from being wet, that is. And cold."

Kyril was unconcerned. "Father managed it. So did Mother."

Well that explains who took Briam's place. "That was later in the Queen's reign. They put in extra stones at the beginning of each new Queen's reign, and only *one* of them has been taken out so far. You need to know where they are and how to find a safe path through them, or you'll bash your brains in! I got horribly banged up and bruised, and I was coming at them from downstream, not falling through a waterfall."

"I'll bear that in mind," Kyril said, "but I'm not leaving Lina alone at night." He looked down protectively at Lina. "If you're supposed to be in the next room, why don't you go back there?"

Zora sighed. "I'll go. But think about it. I'll be staying with her, she's so deeply asleep she won't miss you, and if you get killed, she'll be *really* upset."

"Go back to bed, Zora."

Zora spun on her heel and stalked out. She was trying to help him, but he was acting like a total idiot! As she got into her own bed Zora resolved to talk to Lina again. Maybe *she* could persuade him.

Unfortunately, things didn't get any better. Lina seemed more tired and less interested in anything with each day that passed. Zora kept talking to her—or perhaps *at* her, given her lack of response—each day in the Chapel, but Lina didn't even remember what they had said from one day to the next, so Zora had no hope that she was persuading Kyril he needed to practice. It was as if Lina was sleepwalking through her own life.

Just before another priestess was due to take a turn in attendance on the Queen, and Zora would be stuck underground in the temple again, she made one more attempt to talk to Kyril. He got up and carried her forcibly back to the bed in the anteroom.

"Leave us alone," he snapped. "We get little enough privacy as it is."

You'll have plenty of privacy if you die, she thought resentfully. *I know you're supposed to love the Queen, but do you have to be so totally stupid about it? You and I have been friends for our entire lives. Doesn't that count for anything?*

Under the circumstances, Zora was not completely sorry when her time was up and it was somebody else's turn to follow the Queen around. She went to bed in her cell in the temple, glad to have some privacy of her own.

CHAPTER ELEVEN

Zora was wakened shortly before sunrise two days later by a cold canine nose poking the side of her neck. Between the pre-dawn light coming into her cell and the fact that she had excellent night vision even in human form, she was easily able to identify the dog as "Princess."

Zora sat up and reached for a tunic, but the dog's jaws closed over her wrist and gave a firm tug. Obviously she was wanted somewhere that she couldn't get to in human form. And given that *she* wasn't Princess and that Catriona was allowed to enter the temple quarters, Princess must be— "Kyril?" Zora asked softly.

He released her wrist and nodded. She flowed out of bed, changing to cat-shape. She didn't want to do multiple changes, and she was pretty sure that following Kyril was going to involve climbing.

It did. They slipped silently out of the temple, outside via an empty hallway, and across the garden to the wall below the Queen's rooms. There Kyril changed to cat-shape, and Zora followed him up the wall and over the windowsill.

Lina was flat on her back in bed. Zora jumped up and landed heavily beside her. That should have gotten some sort of response, but only Lina's shallow breathing showed that she was even alive. Her body was otherwise motionless, even when Zora nudged her. Hard. Kyril changed back to human and put his discarded nightshirt back on, then pulled one of the Queen's undertunics out of a chest at the foot of the bed and tossed it over a dressing screen in the corner.

"Change shape to match hers and put this on," he said softly, "and keep your voice down. One of the priestesses sleeps in the next room."

"I know that, Kyril," Zora said once she had changed to human and could talk. "Until two nights ago *I* was the priestess in the next room. Why did you sneak into someplace you totally should not have been instead of just sending her to get me?"

"She would have blamed Lina, and Lina's unhappy enough without having them scolding her all the time." Kyril scowled. "Even *I* can tell that they don't like her."

There was enough truth in that that Zora didn't argue.

"Besides, am I supposed to tell a priestess that we can't get the Queen to wake up and we need you to take her place for the morning ritual? They don't even know that you can take her place. You *can* do it, can't you?"

"Well, I guess that explains why you fetched me instead of Colin." Zora realized how completely she had lost track of time. "Is he back from Eagle's Rest yet?"

"Not as far as I know," Kyril replied. "Wait a minute, how did you know he was gone?"

"I asked him to go. There's something very strange going on here—and I don't mean your being the Year-King." Zora frowned. "Did you say anything to anybody about my parents?"

"No."

"Good. Don't."

"Now if we could get back to our *current* problem," Kyril said, "can you take the Queen's place for the ritual?"

Zora considered the problem. "I can look like her, and I know the right words..." *And if I'm the Heiress, it's probably my job to cover for her if she's sick.* "Why can't we wake her up? What's wrong with her? If she's sick, the priestesses can't really blame her..."

"They can and they do," Kyril said bitterly. "She's the sweetest, kindest, most gentle soul I've ever met, and they hate her for it. That's why she takes those damned potions."

"Which potions?"

"Lady Esme gives her something at night to help her sleep," Kyril said, "and it seemed to help her at first, but now it's getting harder and harder to wake her up in the morning."

I am such *an idiot! How many times did Lady Esme walk right past me with a goblet on a tray?* "Why is she drinking *anything* Lady Esme gives her?"

Kyril shrugged. "Why shouldn't she?"

"Kyril," Zora said with a sigh, "you *do* know that Lady Esme's father was last year's king, don't you?"

"What?" Kyril looked blankly at her. "That's crazy! Why would she stay here if her father died—did he die?"

"Yes, of course he died. And Esme blames the Queen. I once overheard her complaining that as soon as he was Chosen he stopped loving her and started loving the Queen instead."

"Well, she is very lovable."

It must be magic. "Is there any chance that we can wake this lovable person in time to do the morning ritual?"

Kyril shook his head. "I barely got her awake yesterday, and she must have sleepwalked through the ritual because she was still three-quarters asleep at breakfast. The Shield-Bearer even told her she should make more of an effort to look alert when everyone in the hall is watching her. And she's worse this morning. Much worse."

"Very well." There wasn't any real alternative. "I'll take her place for the ritual, but how do we hide her while she wakes up? It's not as if we can sneak her back into my room—and what they'll say when they miss *me* I don't know!"

"Maybe they won't miss you," Kyril said hopefully.

"I doubt that, but we can always hope for a miracle. Get back into bed, and lie on top of her or something—just make sure she can breathe *and* that nobody can tell she's still in the bed. If I'm up and dressed when they come for her, I can tell them not to disturb you while I'm doing the ritual, and that will give you time to wake her up while I'm gone."

"Sounds like a plan," Kyril said approvingly.

Just not a very good *plan. Unfortunately, it's all we've got.* Zora lifted the lid of the clothing chest. "Help me find her clothes for the morning ritual, will you?"

Kyril helped Zora dress, and then climbed back into bed, carefully hiding Lina's body with his own, just before the knock on the door.

Zora quickly opened the door and stepped into the anteroom before either the Shield-Bearer or the priestess—it was the Fourth this time—could get a good look into the room. As they moved into the main hallway and passed the Queen's guards, she repeated what she and Kyril had agreed on, ordering that Kyril be allowed to sleep undisturbed until she returned from the ritual.

Zora was very nervous as she walked down the hall, especially given how astonished the Shield-Bearer had looked when she saw the Queen out of bed and dressed. *What if she can tell us apart? I don't remember how Lina acts before she goes out to do the ritual! I should know. I've been following her around on and off for months, but I don't—I can't remember! And the priestesses may not know I'm a shape-changer, but the Shield-Bearer certainly does!*

As they approached the room that opened onto the balcony overlooking the square, Zora was positive she was doing something wrong. She was almost in a panic, and horribly self-conscious. *What if the Goddess doesn't want me to do this? What if I forget the words?*

Then they were there. Zora took a deep breath, said a quick prayer for understanding, forgiveness, help, and whatever else the Goddess might feel inclined to grant, and stepped out onto the balcony.

As she placed her hands on the waist-high marble railing in front of her and looked down at the crowd, Zora felt warm all over, as if the Goddess were sustaining her. The chant began to flow from her lips without conscious thought, and she relaxed into the ritual, feeling the energy growing between her and the people in the square. A small part of her mind noticed that there were fewer people than there had been when she first came to Diadem, but most of her mind and all of her body was caught up in the chant. She could feel it flowing through her from the soles of her feet to the top of her head.

The ritual seemed to take place outside of time, and then suddenly it was over. The people bowed and began to leave the plaza, and Zora stepped back from the balcony into the room behind it. The Shield-Bearer was staring at her as if she didn't believe what she had just seen and heard, and Zora suspected the veiled priestess was having the same reaction. *I know I did the ritual correctly—I hope that's not the problem.*

"What happened to you?" the Shield-Bearer demanded as they went back toward the Queen's rooms.

"I have no idea what you are talking about," Zora said, deliberately adopting Aunt Akila's most imperious 'and I do not want to hear another word about it' tone. It worked. The Shield-Bearer actually stopped talking. Zora concealed a sigh of relief and pondered how to buy more time. *I don't think breakfast in public is a good idea, even if Lina is awake by now—and she may not be.*

"I don't wish to be disturbed until it's time for morning court," Zora added as they reached the Queen's rooms. "Please send up breakfast for me and Lord Kyril, and leave us alone until then."

"Very well." The Shield-Bearer still looked puzzled, but she inclined her head and continued down the corridor toward the main part of the palace. The priestess stayed in the antechamber, and Zora closed and locked the bedroom door between them. The scene needed to be properly set when breakfast arrived.

"She's still not awake," Kyril said, hovering over the Queen in concern. He knelt on the bed beside Lina and continued to shake her. By now she at least bore more resemblance to a deeply sleeping human and less to a dead body. Eventually his effort produced something that sounded like a faint moan of protest.

Zora heard it, but she was listening more for sounds in the hallway and anteroom. "Breakfast is coming," she hissed. "Quick, hide her!"

Kyril quickly rearranged his body and the bedding to conceal Lina. Zora cast a quick glance over her shoulder to make certain that only Kyril was visible, then opened the door and had the maidservant put the breakfast tray on the table. She repeated the request to be left undisturbed until it was time for court and locked the door again when the girl left.

"How did you persuade them to send breakfast up here?" Kyril asked. "Usually they demand that we eat in the hall. We're supposed to be visible."

Zora shrugged. "I told the Shield-Bearer, and she ordered it. I think she suspects I'm up to something." *Time to change the subject.* "What does Lina usually eat for breakfast?" Zora asked as she looked hungrily at a tray full of food. She was starved from the changing she had done earlier, and she suspected that Kyril was pretty hungry as well. Depending on how much Lina ate, there might be enough for all three of them.

"She doesn't eat much in the morning," Kyril said, "though you have to admit that the cooks really try to tempt her." He gestured at the tray full of delicious-looking food. "I try to eat as much as I can at meals so they won't feel bad." He grinned. "At least this morning you can help with that."

"I'd better, or I'll fall over. We don't eat enough in the temple for me to be changing shape twice before breakfast."

"Lina usually just drinks that," Kyril said, indicating a mug of dark liquid.

"Is it some sort of stimulant?" Zora asked hopefully.

"What?" Kyril had grabbed a roll and stuffed the entire thing in his mouth. Now he was trying to talk around it.

Zora rolled her eyes. "Does it help her to wake up, make her more alert, anything like that?"

Kyril swallowed the roll in a single gulp. "I think so," he said, grabbing another roll, breaking it in half, and putting a slab of meat in the middle.

"Make one of those for me," Zora said. She grabbed a handful of dried fruit and started chewing on it while she propped Lina upright in bed and held the mug to her lips. Fortunately Lina appeared to be able to drink in her sleep, and the liquid—whatever it was—seemed to be bringing her closer to consciousness.

Zora was very glad, however, that *she* didn't have to drink it. The smell was sickening enough that she didn't want to know what it tasted like. Of course, two shape-changes on an empty stomach did not improve the way anyone felt. *It's a good thing the morning ritual is the kind that gives the participants energy instead of taking it from them.*

By the time Kyril had eaten enough that he was willing to stop stuffing *his* face and let Zora eat, she was starving.

"Get her out of bed and on her feet," she ordered him as she picked up the improvised meat roll he had fixed for her. "Walk her around the room until whatever she drank last night wears off."

Kyril obediently dragged Lina around the room, but her feet weren't really moving, even after he managed to get another cup of that revolting liquid into her. Zora finished the bread and meat and ate several more pieces of dried fruit. Then she took a piece of some sort of spice bread, added all the butter and jam it would hold, and shoved it into her mouth. This wasn't even close to acceptable table manners—most of the food went into her cheeks so more would fit in her mouth—but Kyril wasn't watching her, and the way he'd been eating wasn't acceptable in public either. Still chewing, Zora took Lina's other arm and helped Kyril hold her upright.

It seemed they spent forever dragging Lina around the room, but eventually her weight was more on her feet and less on their shoulders. When she was sufficiently awake to stay upright they sat her down next to the table, so Kyril could get the rest of the drink and at least a little food into her.

Zora quickly took off the gown she had worn for the morning ritual, leaving her in just an undertunic. She went back to the clothing chest, remembering that she had seen a bit of green near the bottom of it. *Yes! I thought she might have one of these—she was wearing it the day after the Choosing.* She put on the green overtunic that the priestesses wore and picked up the veil.

Lina finally noticed that she was in the room. "Zora?" she asked, squinting at her as if the light hurt her eyes. "What are you doing here, and shouldn't you have your veil on?"

"Yes, I should, but Kyril's my cousin, remember? It's not as if he doesn't know what I look like."

"I was having trouble getting you to wake up," Kyril explained, "so I got Zora to help me—I figured better her than any of the older priestesses."

"Umm," Lina made a half-awake sound of agreement. "What time is it, anyway?"

"Almost time for court," Kyril said. "What was in that drink Lady Esme gave you last night?"

Lina shrugged. "Just the usual herbs," she said absently. She looked at the gown Zora had dropped on the foot of the bed and frowned in bewilderment. "I don't even remember doing the morning ritual."

"It was fine," Zora said reassuringly, "but if I were you, I wouldn't mention to anyone else that you don't remember it."

"You're right," Lina sighed. "Most of the people here already think I'm crazy."

"Nonsense." Kyril stroked his hand over her shoulder. "You are *not* crazy."

Zora pulled an overgown suitable for court from the clothing chest. "Let's finish getting you dressed before the Shield-Bearer comes to fetch you." She helped Lina dress, which still bore a disquieting resemblance to dressing a doll, while Kyril hastily washed and threw on his own clothing.

Zora hid behind the dressing screen when the Shield-Bearer came to escort Lina to the audience chamber. Kyril and the priestess went with them. Once she was alone, Zora pulled the veil over her face and took the back hall to the stairs that went down to the Queen's chapel. From there she walked silently down the passage that led to the temple quarters. She managed to slip into the book room without being observed and resumed her reading, changing her hair back to brown before she took off the veil. She reminded herself to replace the Queen's set of robes later, preferably before they were missed. *And I'd better hide a spare set of my own clothing in with the Queen's things,* she thought grimly. *I'm very much afraid this is not the only time I'll have to do this.*

Zora decided to spend her morning study time in the temple's book room putting together a timeline of the last few decades. She began with a more detailed study of the Book of Kings. When she had looked at it before, she hadn't gone back further than Briam— the discovery that she and the Queen were half-sisters had completely distracted her.

Now she went back to Lord Ranulf, who had been king ten years before Briam. The notes for his year indicated that the harvest had been excellent.

She started to calculate the number of stones under the waterfall during those years. The reign instructions said to add twenty for each new Queen, but not all the Queens married that many times, so sometimes there would be extra, and a few of the Queens married more than twenty times. Lina's mother married twenty-three times, so there wouldn't have been too many stones the year that Briam was king, and there would have been ten more than that the year that Lord Ranulf was... So start with however many were there when Lina was born, subtract one for the king that year, add twenty, which have been slowly eroding for the past sixteen years, subtract one for last year—*that's eighteen extra rocks to dodge, nineteen of them fairly new, and they're right under the waterfall.*

Zora really was going to have to try talking to Kyril again. Or maybe she could get Lina to talk to him—he'd probably pay more attention to her. Without practice, he would have a fair chance of getting killed even though he could change shape. That wouldn't just be tragic. It would be stupid. *Of all the times for him to stop listening to sensible advice, this has to be the worst! And where is Colin? He should be back by now—I'm sure somebody at Eagle's Rest cares that Kyril is the Year-King. Lady Akila would care, all right—her husband, her brother, and now her son... I know she can't leave Eagle's Rest because she has to serve the Lady of Fire there. Still, I would expect her to send somebody, or at least send Colin back with instructions. I don't think I can cope with this mess all by myself!*

Zora decided that the best way to talk to Lina was to sneak into the chapel before the Queen arrived. The other way, sneaking into her room at night, would only get her thrown out by Kyril—and Lina would be asleep then anyway. Besides, Zora was finding that she missed the afternoon meditation in the Queen's chapel. Not that she thought Lina actually meditated—she had never even seen her walk the labyrinth.

Right after the midday meal, Zora slipped away and went to the Queen's chapel. If anyone had missed her at breakfast, they hadn't said anything. Yet. Of course, now she was disappearing again—at a time when she usually had lessons. They were probably going to notice that. Zora wondered how they punished erring priestesses— other than Lina, who apparently never got punished no matter what she did. Of course, punishment wouldn't help her or anyone else.

Zora had plenty of time to contemplate her misdeeds and the priestesses' possible reactions while she waited alone in complete darkness. When the door to the chapel finally opened, she was careful to stay hidden behind it. The priestess who lit the torch didn't even look in that direction. *Perhaps they think the Goddess keeps out anyone who doesn't belong here. They may even be right.*

Once the door was closed, Lina walked straight to the bench beyond the fountain, and slumped on it, leaning back against the wall and staring at her lap. She didn't even look up as Zora walked along the path of the labyrinth. Of course, bare feet didn't make any noise, and Lina wasn't expecting anyone to be here. As Zora reached the fountain, she grabbed a lock of her hair and pulled it where she could look to make certain she had remembered to change it back to brown.

"Lina?"

Lina looked up in surprise. "Zora! What are you doing here?"

"I wanted to talk to you."

"What for?"

"I'm worried about Kyril. I've been doing research on the stones for the Kings' Garden. According to my calculations, there are at least eighteen more of them under the waterfall than there were the last time a Year-King survived. I've tried to talk to him about it, but he wouldn't listen to me. I'm hoping he'll listen to you."

"What do you want me to tell him?"

"What we talked about before, remember? Tell him to sneak out at night and practice swimming under the waterfall until he knows where all the rocks are. Remember, he's going to have to jump in there from above and make his way through them, so he has to know them well enough that he can swim through them even when he's drugged."

"That sounds like a reasonable idea," Lina said slowly.

"*I* certainly thought so, but when I suggested it to him, he said he wouldn't leave you alone at night. I pointed out that you weren't going to miss him—the way you sleep, nothing wakes you up until morning, and we have a hard enough time waking you then. But he wouldn't listen to me. I'm hoping that if you tell him to do it, he will."

"I'll try to remember to tell him tonight."

"Thank you. I'd really appreciate it."

They sat side by side on the bench. Suddenly Lina said, "Zora? Why do you always walk the path through the labyrinth? I've never seen you just walk across the floor, even when you were a dog."

"It's a compulsion," Zora admitted. "I can't *not* do it. There's a sort of feeling as if I'm being pulled, and if I try to step off the path the floor gets cold and I feel that I'm going the wrong way. It's unpleasant. I don't understand how you can *not* follow the path."

Lina shrugged. "Probably because I don't feel anything."

"The floor doesn't feel warmer underfoot if you keep to the path?"

"The floor is cold in here, Zora. It's the same temperature no matter where you step. It's rock, in case you haven't noticed."

"Of course I've noticed it's rock, but most of it feels warm to me."

Lina slid her bare foot sideways to touch Zora's, and both of them gasped.

"Your feet are so cold!" Zora exclaimed.

Almost at the same time, Lina asked, "Why are your feet so warm?" She reached out and took Zora's hand. "Our hands are the same temperature."

"I guess my feet are warm because the floor is—at least for me." Zora frowned, trying to figure out yet another puzzle. *This is the strangest place.* "It's odd that you don't feel it. You're the Queen, so I would expect you to feel it more than I do, not less. Did you ever feel what I described?"

Lina was silent so long that Zora was about to repeat the question when she finally said softly, "I think I used to feel it. I remember when the priestesses first started sending me in here in the afternoons. It was about three years ago, and I remember walking the labyrinth like a game." She shook her head. "It's not a game anymore."

Zora supposed that Lina just stopped wanting to feel it—or anything else. They sat in silence for a long time before Lina spoke again.

"Zora? How are you going to get out of here without the priestess outside noticing?"

Zora winced. "That's a really good question. It's too bad I'm not still a dog."

"Can't you change back into one?"

"I can change back to Princess, but my clothes won't change with me..." *Actually, that could work.* "Can you take my clothing upstairs and hide it in the bottom of the chest at the foot of your bed?"

"I suppose so," Lina said. "Especially if the priestess is distracted wondering why Princess is here with me and how she got in."

"All right, then." Zora stripped off the clothing she was wearing. It was the Queen's anyway. She folded it into a neat little bundle, and changed to Princess.

The priestess was distracted all right, and nobody could blame her. The only entrance to the chapel was the door, and she had been right outside it the entire time the Queen had been inside. *Even I couldn't sneak in past her. The walls, floor and ceiling are all solid stone, and the door fits so well that I don't think I could change to a shape small enough to fit under it. Of course, the fact that the door is solid, thick wood and so well-fitted means that Lina and I can talk in here without being overheard as long as we don't start screaming at each other. It's too bad we can't get Kyril down here too. We really need someplace the three of us can talk, but he objects to using the Queen's bedchamber at night, which is the only other place nobody will bother us. During the day, there's always a risk that someone will insist on seeing the Queen for some reason.*

As a dog, Zora followed the Queen back to her room and watched her put the priestess robes in her clothing chest. Now Zora would know where they were if she needed to use them again.

The dog followed Lina around for most of the rest of the afternoon, and then split off and went back to the temple. She made it into her cell unobserved, which could only be attributed to the mercy of the Goddess. Zora changed to human, dressed in her green robe, and slipped silently into the bookroom. The night silence began with supper, so the priestesses could not scold her yet for not having been where she was supposed to be for most of the day. Zora figured she would probably get yelled at in the morning, when the silence ended.

As she fell asleep that night, she wondered if Lina would remember to talk to Kyril.

But it was Kyril, as Princess, who woke Zora up again the next morning. At least this time he had thought to stash extra food for them to eat as soon as they changed back to human shape. Zora was starving—she hadn't really gotten enough to eat the day before. She looked at Lina's unresponsive body and sighed. "Can't you get her to stop drinking whatever Lady Esme is giving her?"

"No," Kyril said. "I tried last night."

"Try again. If you can't stop her from drinking it, at least get it away from her long enough to dilute it."

Kyril shook his head. "Lady Esme gives her the goblet, and she drinks it straight down. There's no way to dilute it or switch it for anything else—I doubt I could even pry it out of her hands."

"Keep trying to wake her up," Zora said grimly, "while I go do the ritual. Again. Pretend you're asleep if anyone comes in, and for the Lady's sake keep her hidden." She dressed for the morning ritual and turned to face Kyril. "How do I look?"

"Your hair is wrong," Kyril said, turning briefly to look at her before going back to shaking Lina.

"You do realize, don't you," Zora said as she changed her hair to match Lina's, "that we can't get away with this for long. I know the Shield-Bearer is already suspicious."

"Don't worry about it," Kyril said, maddeningly oblivious to Zora's mixed feelings. "You wanted to serve the Goddess, didn't you?"

Not like this, I didn't! Zora realized she was grinding her teeth and made a conscious effort to relax as she left the room, met up with the Queen's escort, and headed toward the balcony.

The ritual went smoothly, but the Shield-Bearer and the priestess in attendance were apparently not the only ones who had noticed a difference between Zora and the real Queen. There were almost twice as many people in the square as there had been the day before. *There must be something obviously different in the way I'm doing this, but I don't know how else to do it.*

Zora thought she heard the Goddess whisper in her head, saying that she was doing well, but that wasn't going to be much comfort when the priestesses found out what was going on.

Zora returned to the Queen's rooms, and at least this morning she got enough to eat at breakfast, which helped. What didn't help, however, was that she and Kyril *couldn't* wake Lina. Apparently she had taken an even heavier dose of whatever-it-was last night. Zora finally had to leave Kyril hiding Lina and pretending to be half-asleep while she took the Queen's place at the morning hearings. She wondered if anyone would forgive her for *this* if they found out. This wasn't just the concern of the priestesses; this was the government of Diadem. At least the Shield-Bearer was the one who made the actual decisions, so maybe it wouldn't matter too much. Of course, that depended on how understanding the Shield-Bearer and the Sword-Bearer—and anyone else who found out—were likely to be.

Fortunately the few cases being heard that morning were not terribly complex, and the Shield-Bearer knew what they were about and what should be done, so all Zora had to do was ask her advice and then voice it as a royal decree. She tried to balance appearing awake and competent for the people with appearing drugged and disoriented for Lady Esme. The last thing she needed was for the woman to think her drug wasn't working. She would probably increase the dose...

No, she probably did *increase the dose. That would explain why we couldn't wake Lina this morning. If I don't do something, tonight's dose might be fatal.* Then Esme brought the Queen's usual midmorning bowl of broth.

Zora took one sip and nearly fell over. She did drop the bowl, which shattered, spilling the broth all over the floor and her—or rather, Lina's—skirts. She ignored the mess as she wrapped her arms tightly around her ribs and bowed her head, fighting to remain upright in the chair. *Beef broth*, she thought grimly. *I am* such *an idiot! I should have known.* One sip—and the loss of her bond with the Goddess—made just what was in that innocent-looking broth painfully clear. *Very* painfully clear. This was the *one* thing the Goddess had taught Zora before she left home, and she had forgotten it!

She focused on Esme's fingers as she fussed over her, playing the concerned lady-in-waiting. Zora recalled all the times she had seen Lady Esme stick herself while sewing and exclaim over her own clumsiness. But Esme hadn't been sewing that morning, and there was a fresh pinprick on her fourth finger. *She added a drop of her own blood right before she gave me the bowl.*

Zora wondered dimly, as she strove to remain conscious and upright, why Lina had never showed any response to the potion. If she was getting it often enough—*and I'll bet she is*—the potion wouldn't be changing anything for her. It would just be maintaining the status quo. No wonder she couldn't feel the presence of the Goddess! *And I'd thought it was just that she didn't want to... I'm as bad as the priestesses, blaming her for things that aren't her fault.*

"I'm not feeling well," Zora said when she finally got her body and voice back under at least *some* control. "I'm going back to bed until afternoon meditation." She forced herself to stand and walk as normally as she could back to Lina's rooms, ignoring the priestess who accompanied her.

It took Zora two tries to lock the door, and even Kyril, despite his absorption with Lina's condition, noticed there was something wrong.

"What is it?" he asked anxiously. "Did someone try to harm Lina?"

"What?" Zora stared at him blankly for a moment before realizing that, of course, Esme had thought that she was Lina. "Yes," she said grimly. "Someone has been trying to harm Lina for quite some time now."

Zora collapsed on the bed next to Lina without bothering to try to take off the court dress. "I'll explain later. I need to sleep now."

"What happened?" Kyril asked insistently.

"It's that gods-forsaken potion," Zora muttered, feeling herself slipping into welcome unconsciousness. "The one Kassie and I made at home." Then she blacked out completely.

The next thing Zora heard was Lina's voice saying, "Why is she wearing my court dress? She's going to get it horribly wrinkled sleeping in it—she should know enough to take it off before she lies down. And what happened to the skirt?"

"She didn't have time to take it off," Kyril said grimly. "She passed out almost as soon as she made it through the door."

"Are you worried about her?" Lina actually sounded jealous.

"I'm worried about *you*," Kyril said promptly. "How many people would look at her now and even *think* that she might not be you?"

Zora slitted her eyes open just enough to watch Lina counting on her fingers. "You, the Sword-Bearer, Zora, and me. Four."

And probably the Shield-Bearer. Five. Zora forced her eyes the rest of the way open. "What time is it?"

"Thank the gods you're awake!" Kyril said. "I can't explain what you're doing, and they'll be here any minute."

Zora's first attempt to get up landed her on her knees on the floor. She grabbed the lid of the clothes chest, shoved it open, and hastily pulled the green robe and veil out of it. "Lina, put these on, quickly!"

"What?" Lina looked at her in astonishment. "Why?"

"I'll explain everything in the chapel, but we have to get there first, and *I* don't have time to change clothes!"

"She's right," Kyril said. "She's fast, but not that fast."

"You *should* change," Lina protested. "You've spilled something on the skirt."

"Later," Zora said through clenched teeth. "For now, just get dressed!"

Footsteps sounded in the outer room, and someone knocked on the door. Kyril pulled the gown over Lina's undertunic and handed her the veil. "She'll have to keep pretending to be you for the minute."

"Listen to him, please," Zora begged, closing the chest and using it to shove herself to her feet. "We can change back in the chapel, but just put the veil on and don't say anything until we get there."

"You're going to tell me *everything*," Lina said as she pulled the veil over her face.

"And me, too," Kyril added.

"Later, Kyril, I promise. Open the door now, please."

Once again Zora blessed the fact that priestesses couldn't speak while veiled. Not only did Lina have to keep quiet, but the other priestess couldn't ask what Zora was doing in the Queen's bedchamber.

They made their way to the chapel in silence, and the two girls went in, leaving the priestess in the antechamber.

Then Zora discovered her next problem. Her sense of the Goddess's presence had not yet returned, and she couldn't walk the labyrinth. But distance from the door, and the priestess outside it, was the most important thing at the moment, so she walked straight across the chapel and collapsed on the bench next to the water-covered rock.

Lina sat next to her and pulled off the veil. "What's going on? Why don't I remember anything about this morning, why are you wearing my dress"—she frowned—"and why didn't you walk the labyrinth? You *always* walk the labyrinth."

"I can't right now," Zora said, "any more than you can—and probably for the same reason. I'm really sorry, Lina. I made a mistake, and I nearly got you killed."

"What in Earth are you talking about?" Lina wailed.

"Keep your voice down," Zora said urgently. "The door is thick, but remember that Catriona could hear you through it when you screamed the first time I changed shape in here."

Lina managed to lower her voice as she asked, "Could you get back to the 'nearly got me killed' part of the explanation?"

Zora took a deep breath. "Remember yesterday, when you said you couldn't remember doing the morning ritual?"

"Yes," Lina said, "and you told me not to tell anyone about it."

"The reason you don't remember doing the ritual is that you didn't do it. I did."

"Why?"

"Kyril couldn't get you to wake up, so he came and got me to take your place."

"He snuck into the priestesses' quarters?" Lina asked, obviously scandalized.

"Well, yes. Remember, he loves you very much, and he didn't want anyone to think badly of you, and he was afraid that people would be upset if you started missing rituals."

"He's right about *that*," Lina said. After a moment she added, "He doesn't *really* love me, you know. It's just because he's the king. Lady Esme says that at least I don't have to worry about whether men love me for my money, the way she does, because I already know they don't."

"Lady Esme is a poisonous bitch," Zora snapped, being careful to keep her voice down.

"How can you say that?" Lina protested. "She's my friend."

"Not if she says things like that she's not. Besides, it's nonsense. Kyril loved you before the Choosing, remember? He spent as much time as he could with you, even then."

"Yes," Lina said, looking at Zora wonderingly. "He did, and he really seemed to like me."

"And Lady Esme is the one who's been drugging you."

"What do you mean?"

"What's the drink she gives you at night?"

"Just some herbs to help me sleep. There's nothing wrong with that, is there?" Lina seemed honestly puzzled. "She takes them too."

"There wouldn't be much wrong with it if we could wake you up in the morning," Zora said, adding grimly, "but we *can't*, can we? It was a struggle to get you up in time for the morning ritual the entire time I was attending you. Then yesterday we *couldn't* wake you up in time for the ritual, and this morning we couldn't wake you in time for court. I think she's been increasing the dosage, to make you start missing rituals. And that's where Kyril and I made the mistake. We thought it was just an error, and so I did the ritual. But I wasn't drugged, so I'm afraid that it went a bit differently than it usually does..."

"You mean you didn't stumble through it half-asleep."

"I think there was enough talk—or maybe Esme was there— and she figured she hadn't made the potion strong enough. She watches you drink it, doesn't she?"

Lina nodded. "She brings it in on a tray, hands it to me, watches me drink the whole thing, and then takes the goblet away."

"So she knows you got the full dose of whatever she put in that cup. When it suddenly appeared not to work, she probably used more or stronger herbs. The problem is that it *did* work, and she could have killed you by doing that. As it was, I had to do the morning ritual *and* court today. So now we have two problems."

"Did you do something wrong at court?"

"No, I just did whatever the Shield-Bearer said to do. The first problem is that if Lady Esme thinks whatever she gave you *last* night isn't working, what is she going to give you *tonight?*"

"Oh, dear," Lina whispered. "She could kill me without even meaning to."

"Precisely. The other problem is the broth she gives you every morning. How long has she been doing that?"

Lina smiled. "She started making it for me as a morning treat when she first came to court, back when her father was king..." Her voice trailed off. "There's something wrong with the broth?"

"Remember you asked why I suddenly can't walk the labyrinth?" Lina nodded. "That 'broth' is a potion, and it's a really nasty one. When did you wake up today?"

"A few minutes before you did," Lina admitted.

"Then you didn't see the effect it had on me."

"Not really. Kyril said something about letting you sleep it off."

"What that potion does is sever our bond with the Goddess."

"It what?" Lina looked at Zora as if she were crazy.

Zora almost wished she were.

"You said it yourself," she reminded Lina. "You told me that you could walk the labyrinth before Esme came to court."

"I didn't say that!" Lina protested.

"Yes, you did. Think about it. Remember."

Lina looked down at her lap and then up at Zora. The look on her face was a combination of horror and incredulity. "Yes," she admitted, "I could still walk the labyrinth at the beginning of last year—before the...king was Chosen. Soon after he was Chosen I stopped being able to do it, so I haven't tried since then."

"When did Esme come to court?" I asked.

"A few days after her father did," Lina said. "She was really a bother at first, demanding his attention—it made the Shield-Bearer very cross with her. But after a few weeks she settled down, and that's when I offered her a position as my lady-in-waiting, so that she could...be with her father as long as possible."

"Year-King idiocy." Zora could see what had happened as if she had been there.

"What are you talking about?"

"One of the things that happens at the Choosing—Kyril's parents told him about it, and he told me—is that a bond is established between the Queen and the Year-King that supersedes all other relationships in his life. I'm guessing Esme was her father's only child and her mother died a long time ago?"

"She's certainly his only child—the Year-King's children are freed from all tax obligations for life, so I'd know if she had siblings—and I've never heard her mention her mother. Why does it matter?" Lina asked.

"The temple records say she was thirty-one last year, and apparently she never married," Zora went on, "so I'm guessing that she lived with her father, and it was just the two of them."

"And—?"

"So one day she's his beloved daughter and the most important person in his life, and a single day later, *you* are the focus of his life."

"Are you saying she blames me for that?" Lina said. "I really had nothing to do with it. I don't know how he was Chosen. I don't even remember most of the ceremony." After a moment she added. "Either time."

"That doesn't matter; I don't think the Queen ever remembers much of it. Apparently the Goddess simply works through you." Casting her mind back, Zora added, "I don't remember it either, and I wasn't even the one doing it. I remember going to the plaza for the ceremony, and the next thing I knew I woke up in the crypt, and it was the next day!"

"So I'm not a bad Queen if I don't remember it?" Lina blurted out.

Zora suddenly felt very much like the older sister instead of the younger. "No," she said. "Not at all."

Lina started crying. "You don't know how awful it is," she sobbed. "I've tried, but I *hate* being Queen! I don't want to be the reason people die, and I don't want people to hate me." Lina sniffed. "Do you think Esme hates me? It's not as if I *wanted* her father to die!"

"I think Esme hates the whole world by now," Zora said, "but yes, I'm fairly sure she hates you. The last ingredient in the broth potion is 'a drop of blood from someone who hates you'—and from the way one sip of it affected me, I think there was a lot of hatred in it."

"But she doesn't hate *you*," Lina protested. "She doesn't even know you exist."

"I don't think she hates you as a *person*, Lina. She hates you as the Queen, and she thought I was the Queen, so..." Zora sighed. "I think mostly she hates you because you stole her father's love from her even before he died."

"I didn't!" Lina protested.

"Not by anything you could have changed, but she lost his love and you gained it." Zora giggled, suddenly remembering something. "When I'm in my true shape, we look identical, right?"

"Yes..."

"Kyril is firmly convinced that you are much more beautiful

than I am."

"Really?" Lina started giggling too. "Maybe he's the one who's crazy."

"In a limited way, mostly where you're concerned, he is," Zora admitted. "I think it's a sort of *geas*—the king will love the Queen, and he'll refuse to even think of leaving either her or the land. It *does* insure that he'll still be here when he's needed, and that he won't make much of a fuss."

Lina shuddered. "How can you be so cold-blooded about it? I don't want Kyril to die!"

"I don't either," Zora assured her, "but we don't have to worry about *that* now. At the moment what we have to worry about is making certain that *you* don't die. Tonight."

"I don't think I can stop her," Lina said slowly. "There's something about her..." Her voice trailed off.

Zora looked at the green gown the Queen was still wearing. "I guess I could keep pretending to be you—as long as you pretend to be me."

"Won't the priestesses notice?"

"They don't know that we *can* change places," Zora pointed out. "At least I hope they don't know, so it probably won't occur to them. They may think you're different, but that's a long way from thinking that you aren't you."

"That *you* aren't me, you mean."

"Either way, I don't think it will be their first guess. The other thing we need to do to make this work is to change the schedule so my time to attend you and sleep in the next room starts again tonight. As long as you wear my clothes, keep the veil on and don't talk, which you're not supposed to do anyway, I don't see any reason why they should suspect."

"All right," Lina said. "Can you stand up to Lady Esme if she tries to make you drink the potion? I don't want you to get killed."

"I'll manage somehow." *Just don't ask me how.*

Lina subsided into silence, while Zora tried to meditate. Given the effects of the potion, it was much harder than usual. *When the Goddess said there was danger to our lives, she really meant it. I wonder what the danger to our souls is? Loss of faith? I think Lina's already lost any faith she ever had. And I admit that finding out about the Sacrifice has shaken my faith. I wonder...*

"Lina?"

Lina shook her head as if waking from a nap. "What?"

"Do you remember what the First Priestess said during your lesson, when she was talking about attempts to end the Sacrifice? It sounds as though the people require it more than the Goddess does. Maybe the Goddess is working to stop it, and you just can't see it yet."

"That sounds like the most incredible wishful thinking I've ever heard," Lina snapped.

Maybe it is wishful thinking. On the other hand... "Maybe that's why I'm here."

Lina shook her head in disbelief. "What?"

Zora said slowly, "I know this sounds crazy, but I think the Goddess may be trying to do away with the Sacrifice, to make it— what did the priestess call it?—an empty ritual. I think that whenever there is someone who can survive the waterfall, the rocks, and the river, *that's* the person who gets Chosen. Kyril is perfectly capable of changing shape to something that can breathe underwater—as long as he doesn't break his neck or hit his head on the rocks."

Lina frowned. "Can't you and Colin do the same thing?"

Zora nodded. "I'm probably the one who would do best at the moment, because I'm the only one who has actually seen the rocks, but all of us have the ability."

"I can understand that the Goddess wouldn't choose you for the Year-King, but why Kyril and not Colin?"

"I suspect it's because Kyril was already in love with you."

CHAPTER TWELVE

When they left the chapel, the First Priestess finally got her chance to ask where Zora had been. Zora, still pretending to be Lina, told the priestess that Zora had been with her and that she wanted to keep Zora with her. Then she drew on Lina's status as Queen and High Priestess to refuse to answer further questions. *At least I'm probably not going to get into trouble now. They can't blame me for the Queen's behavior when they can't control it themselves.* They retrieved Zora's clothing from the priestesses' quarters and moved it to the Queen's rooms, allowing the priestess who had been on duty there to return to the temple and rejoin the others.

Unfortunately, they didn't get a chance to explain to Kyril what was happening before he and Zora had to sit down for the evening meal, at the high table in the great hall, in public view. The way he was eyeing her made Zora certain *he* could tell they hadn't switched back.

"Kyril," she said softly to him from behind her goblet, "if you don't stop staring at me like that and start treating me the way you treat Lina, she could be in serious trouble. I know it's a stretch, but try to look besotted!"

"Where is she?"

"Having supper alone in her rooms. It's really hard to eat when you've got a veil covering your face. We'll retire soon, and we can all talk then." She took a sip of wine. "Now smile, if only for her sake!" She put the goblet back on the table.

Of course, if I want him to talk softly in my ear... "Kyril, exactly what did your father tell you about Diadem? Did he tell you *everything* about the Sacrifice?"

As she expected, Kyril leaned closer to her and lowered his voice. "Yes, he did. He said that the Sacrifice was the reason he set up the swimming test the way he did. He warned me that they drug the king the morning of the ritual. He told me how the ritual goes and what it feels like—they sever the bond between the king and the Queen, and he says that makes the king feel very cold and empty inside, so it's important to concentrate as you go down the waterfall. He said some interesting things about the Choosing, too—did you know that your father was a Year-King?"

"I found out when I read the temple records," Zora replied softly. "It was quite a surprise. Your mother took his place, didn't she?"

"Yes. Father said it made the Goddess angry—or at least the crops failed afterward, so everyone thinks the Goddess was angry. But what's really interesting is that when Briam was Chosen, my father was there in wolf-shape—and he said that he *still* heard the Calling. In fact, he followed Briam right up to the Queen, but because everyone thought he was Briam's pet, they ignored him. He thinks the Goddess will choose a shape-shifter if one is present—and she chose me, so I think he's right—but he also thinks the same person can be chosen more than once. That means I can come back and marry the Queen again next year." He smiled at her. "Isn't that great news?"

Zora blinked in astonishment and then remembered she was supposed to be Lina and forced herself to smile fondly at him. "It certainly could be." *If the same person was chosen repeatedly, he'd know where the rocks are—and there would be fewer of them each year. With enough practice he could just swim to King's Cove and walk out of the water. And that matches what I was telling Lina in the chapel this afternoon. Maybe I'm actually right about what the Goddess is doing.*

As soon as the meal was over, Zora sent Kyril back to the Queen's room, while she waylaid the Shield-Bearer.

"Shield-Bearer, could you give me any documents relating to the petitions being heard in the near future? I would like to know what to expect when I hear them in court." *And I need a good excuse for staying up later tonight.*

The Shield-Bearer stared suspiciously at her. "Why are you suddenly interested in this?"

Zora had no difficulty looking worried. "I thought it might help if I paid more attention to the aspects of my duties that *don't* involve killing people..."

"Very well," the Shield-Bearer replied. "When would you like them?"

"Could someone bring them to my room this evening? I'd like to read at least the most urgent ones before I go to bed tonight."

"You'll have them within the hour."

"Thank you." Zora inclined her head, then turned and headed for the Queen's rooms.

As she expected, she found Kyril and Lina sitting side by side, talking in low voices. At least Lina still had the veil on, which was a very good thing, considering that the door was unlocked.

"We're going to have company soon," Zora warned them. "I asked the Shield-Bearer for the documents related to the petitions we'll be hearing, and she said they'd be here within the hour."

"Why do you want those?" Lina asked.

Zora grinned at her. "The need to read at least some of them before I go to sleep gives me a good excuse to tell Esme to leave the potion with me. That way I won't have to drink it in front of her."

"That's brilliant," Lina said.

"Thank you," Zora said. "But it means at least two people will be coming here before we can shut the doors for the night and really talk, so we need to make sure things look proper. Lina, you need to sit in the anteroom and pretend to be meditating or something. Just sit still, keep your veil over your face and don't say anything, and you'll be fine." Lina nodded and moved to the antechamber, while Zora turned to Kyril. "If you can't do a convincing job of pretending I'm your wife, at least do something that keeps your back to the door."

Kyril glared at her. "You're getting really bossy," he complained, but he took his dagger and whetstone and went to sit by the fire.

I'm trying to keep you alive, and Lina moderately sane. Since you presumably share the same goals, a little more cooperation and a little less attitude would be helpful. Why do I have to do everything? I shouldn't have to do the thinking for all three of us!

The Shield-Bearer brought the papers herself, which enabled Zora to find out which cases were being heard first. She piled the documents neatly in order, and picked up the first one. "If I have any questions, I'll ask them tomorrow—if that's acceptable to you?"

"That will be fine," the Shield-Bearer replied bemusedly. She left the room, obviously wondering what had happened to the Queen, but there wasn't much Zora could do about that.

When Esme arrived with the nightly goblet of sleeping herbs, Zora smiled, thanked her, and told her to leave it on the table.

"But you should drink it now, while it's freshly brewed," Esme protested. "The herbs lose their potency if they sit too long."

"I won't be long." Zora gestured with the scroll she was holding. "I just want to finish this before I go to sleep."

"I'll be happy to take this away and bring you another one later," Lady Esme said quickly.

"Nonsense," Zora said briskly. "I wouldn't dream of putting you to so much trouble. Just put the goblet on the table. The servants will return it in the morning." Lady Esme opened her mouth to say something else, and Zora smiled and cut her off. "Thank you, Lady Esme. You may go now. I wish you a pleasant night and a peaceful rest."

With Kyril in the same room and a priestess in the next room, both listening to every word, there wasn't much Esme could do. She bowed and left, silent and tight-lipped.

Lina closed the door to the hall, and joined them in the bedroom, locking the door behind her and shedding her veil. "I don't think I've ever seen her look so angry," she said. "I don't know how you can stand up to her like that."

"I think it's mostly that we were raised differently. I spent my childhood around Kyril's mother, and she's very assertive. She ran her father's estates whenever he was away, and she was even younger than we are now when she started doing that."

"She sounds like a really strong woman," Lina said wistfully. "I'll bet the Shield-Bearer would like her."

"Probably," Zora said, "but the people who serve the gods at home can't leave. They have to be there for rituals every day."

"Kyril," Lina said hesitantly, "do you remember any of the Choosing Ritual?"

"Yes, of course I remember it," Kyril said. "Why wouldn't I?" He frowned. "Did Lady Esme drug you before it, so you don't remember?"

Zora shook her head before Lina could answer. "No. I don't remember it either, and we know I wasn't drugged."

"Maybe that's why the Queen doesn't remember," Lina said slowly. "Not just because the Goddess is using her body, but so the Queen won't try to change the outcome. I swear, Kyril, I would *never* have picked you for the Sacrifice!"

"I know." Kyril actually chuckled. "You tried to get me out of the city for the day, remember? You asked me to hunt venison for you."

"Yes, that's right," Lina said, remembering. "And you did bring in a deer that day, didn't you?"

"He certainly did," Zora said. "He took Colin and me with him to catch it and we left before dawn. I think it was the fastest deer hunt in history. He said he wasn't going to spend the summer watching you with another man."

"Well, you did get *that*," Lina said bleakly. Kyril patted her hand.

Zora hastily dragged the conversation back to practicalities. "Are you going to do the ritual and court tomorrow, Lina?"

Lina looked appalled. "No, you do it," she said quickly. "You do much better than I do anyway."

"But *I'm* not the Queen," Zora pointed out. "You are."

"I still don't think we want to change who does the morning ritual for the second time in three days," Lina said.

"You're probably right about that." Zora chewed on her bottom lip. "I'm afraid people can definitely tell the difference. I'll do the ritual if you'll take morning court." She handed her the top parchment. "You'll need to read this—after the Shield-Bearer went to the trouble of bringing all of this up here, she'll expect you to know what it says."

Lina took it, but nodded to the rest of the pile. "We'd better both read these. If we keep changing back and forth, we'd better *both* know anything one of us is supposed to know."

"True." Zora picked up the second item in the pile. For the next hour the girls read, switching documents as they finished them, until both of them had finished about a third of the pile.

Zora found herself yawning. "I don't know about you two, but I'm tired. It's been a long day. I didn't know there were so many cases being heard soon."

Lina nodded. "There are more during the summer. It's when the people who spend the winter in the countryside come to Diadem for the social season."

Zora laughed. "Judging from some of these documents, they spend the winter starting stupid quarrels in the country, and the summer picking fights in the city."

"I think you find these more interesting than I do." Lina yawned. "I don't think I'll need Lady Esme's potion to sleep tonight."

"I can't believe I almost forgot that." Zora picked up the potion and took a cautious sip. Her eyes widened. "How long have you been drinking this?" she asked urgently.

"Lady Esme started making it for me after she came to court last year," Lina replied. "She takes it too. Why? Is there something wrong with it?"

"You really don't know?" Zora asked. "Can't you tell from the taste?"

"You are the one who studied herbs," Lina pointed out. "I was being taught to be Queen, not an herbalist."

"It has Queen's Lace in it," Zora said, "and you've been drinking this every night for a year!"

"What's Queen's Lace?" Kyril asked. At Zora's incredulous look he added, "I didn't study herbs either. Is it going to hurt her?" he added anxiously.

"If she stops now," Zora said, chewing on her lower lip as she thought, "probably not." She took the goblet into the outer room and shoved it under her bed. "It could be worse," she said as she returned. "She could have used tansy or pennyroyal."

Lina's gasp showed that she had heard of at least one of those.

"What do they do?" Kyril asked as Lina started crying.

"If a woman is with child," Zora explained, "they'll make her miscarry—assuming they don't kill her first. Queen's Lace isn't as strong, but it would keep her from conceiving a child."

"Ever?" Lina raised a tear-stained face and looked imploringly at Zora.

"I doubt it," Zora said, trying to be reassuring. "The effects will probably wear off in a few months after a year's exposure, but you should be fine once they do. If you'd been taking this for decades…"

Kyril was starting to look seriously angry. "So what you are saying is that *Lady*"—he sneered the word—"Esme has been feeding Lina harmful potions. On a daily basis. The intended effects are to cut her ties to the Goddess, to make her too tired to fulfill her duties, and to ensure that she is unable to bear a child. Is that it, or have we missed anything?"

"Lady of Earth, I hope we haven't missed anything!" Zora said fervently. "What we do know is bad enough."

"More than bad enough," Kyril said grimly. "Zora, take Lina's place until we can do something about this mess. I don't want Lina to be put at risk anymore."

"But what about the risk to Zora?" Lina asked timidly.

"Oh, Zora can take care of herself," Kyril said blithely.

"I am more likely to notice if someone tries to poison me," Zora said thoughtfully, "and the Goddess doesn't seem to mind my doing the morning rituals." She frowned. "Actually, I can pretend to be the Queen indefinitely. The problem is more that *she* has to pretend to be me."

"I'll just stay veiled and make sure I'm always with you," Lina said hastily.

"We'll have to stay away from the temple. We'd be expected to remove our veils there." Zora looked from Lina to Kyril. "What about the sleeping arrangements?" she asked. "I imagine that you two want to continue sleeping together."

"Yes," Lina and Kyril said in unison.

Lina added, "Can you sleep in the antechamber, and then we'll both get dressed in here in the morning?"

"We'll try that tonight," Zora said, "but we'd better make very certain that we're both awake before anyone comes looking for you."

They all woke in time to get dressed in the morning, and Kyril disposed of Lady Esme's "sleeping herbs" while the girls were at the morning ritual. Zora was relieved that the effects of the broth-and-blood potion had worn off and her link to the Goddess was back. *I couldn't do the ritual properly if it hadn't worn off—not to mention how horrible I'd feel in general.*

There were even more people in the square during the morning ritual than there had been the day before. Zora could feel power from the crowd in front of her, but none from Lina, who was standing in the room behind her. *I hope Lina will recover soon—she really can't be a good Queen without a link to the Goddess, which probably explains why Lady Esme did this to her.* Zora suddenly realized this was why the Goddess made her take the potion while she was still safe at Eagle's Rest. *Nobody would ever have figured this out otherwise.*

She ate breakfast in the hall with Kyril at her side. Now that he realized Lina was in danger, he was doing a much more convincing job of pretending that Zora was Lina. He went off with his Companions after breakfast, while Zora went to morning court. Lina trailed just behind her, a silent green shadow, and Zora silently blessed her for having insisted that both of them read the documents for today's hearings. She was actually able to make a few intelligent remarks on the cases when she discussed them with the Shield-Bearer, rather than having to just echo what the older woman said.

Lady Esme handed her a cup of "beef broth" after the hearings were done. Zora looked under her eyelashes at Esme's hands. Sure enough, there was a fresh pinprick on one of the fingers. She thanked Lady Esme, pretended to take a sip from the cup, and then asked the Shield-Bearer a question about one of the morning's cases. By the time their discussion was done, the broth sitting untouched at her side was cold enough that no one could realistically expect her to drink it.

Zora was rapidly coming to realize that the only place she could truly relax was the Queen's chapel. She went through the maze and collapsed on the bench at the end with a sigh of relief.

"You can walk the maze again," Lina remarked as she removed her veil.

"Yes, thank the Lady," Zora agreed.

"So do you think that I'll be able to again someday?" Lina asked. "If I don't get dosed with that potion again?"

"You should be able to," Zora said. "Nothing I've learned suggests the effects are permanent."

Lina shivered. "Lady Esme scares me," she admitted.

"She should scare you," Zora pointed out. "After all, she *is* trying to harm you."

"That's not what I mean," Lina said. "I can't stand up to her the way you do. Can't you just keep being me?" She took a deep breath. "I know you said you could be me indefinitely, but I couldn't be you. But if I just disappeared—how long would they even look for a missing junior priestess?"

Zora gaped at her. "You're the *Queen*—you can't just run away!"

"You don't know that," Lina said. "Maybe I can."

"Cheer up. Things aren't that bad. I can cover for you for a while and cope with Lady Esme. As soon as you want your life back, just tell me."

"I don't want it back at all!"

Zora hid her dismay and said lightly, "Well, I draw the line at pretending to be married to Kyril—it would be like being married to my brother!"

"You don't have a brother."

"No, but Kyril and Kassie and I were all raised together, so he feels like my brother. Besides, isn't the Festival of the First Fruits coming up soon?"

Lina winced. "Yes, it's..."

"The day after tomorrow." *I can't believe I lost track of time that much.* "You'll have to do that. I don't know the ceremony."

"And Kyril does it with me," Lina agreed, "so he'd have to pretend to be in love with you in front of the whole city."

"We had better not put that much of a strain on his acting abilities," Zora said. "He's doing better, but he's not that good, and *he* can tell us apart."

That actually got a faint smile from Lina.

CHAPTER THIRTEEN

The ritual for the Festival of the First Fruits involved elaborate costumes, a stone crown for Lina that was so heavy Zora was thankful she wasn't the Queen that morning, and a procession from the palace to a dais at each of the gates to the city. At each gate the Queen and the Year-King sat there long enough for everyone who had come in from the surrounding countryside to see the Year-King. Then the Queen blessed the people, and she and the king proceeded to the next gate to repeat the performance, ending back at the palace, where the Queen stood on a platform in the plaza and received the first fruits from the farmers.

Fortunately nothing the Queen had to eat passed through Lady Esme's hands, but as the presentations went on, Zora, standing near Lina with the other priestesses, noticed that she looked more and more tired. Even through the green cloth of her veil, Zora was sure that Lina was turning pale and starting to tremble.

After receiving the first fruits, the Queen presented awards to the craftsmen. This would be followed by a public feast—already tables had been set up along the sides of the plaza, and the food was just inside the palace waiting to be set out as soon as the awards were finished.

The Queen had just presented the last award, and the goldsmith who had won was descending the steps to the ground. Suddenly, to Zora's horror, Lina stiffened, her muscles started twitching, and she fell to the floor of the platform. Zora unfroze enough to grab the crown, which was rolling toward the edge of the platform, before it bashed her ankle, while Kyril and the Shield-Bearer grabbed Lina.

Kyril looked across Lina's body and glared at Zora. "Do something!" he demanded.

Fortunately the First Priestess thought he was speaking to all of them. She took the Shield-Bearer's place at Zora's side, leaving the

Shield-Bearer free to grab the nearest guard and order a litter to take the Queen inside the palace. By the time it arrived most of Lina's muscles seemed to be going into spasm, one after another, and she was only semi-conscious. Zora followed the litter back inside the palace and into the temple quarters, so concerned for Lina that she scarcely realized she was still carrying the crown. She noticed she was holding it while the other priestesses were putting Lina to bed, and then she simply set it down on the nearest table. There were obviously more important things to worry about.

The First Priestess had pried Kyril loose from Lina at the entrance to the temple. Until that point he had been walking beside the litter and holding her hand. He was obviously unhappy about it, but he went without any verbal protest.

It seemed to Zora that only a few minutes had passed before he was back at the doorway, holding a glass bottle containing a dark liquid. "I think you might want this," he said to her as she hastily moved to the doorway to block his entrance. "It's the potion Lady Esme was giving her at night. I saved it in case we needed it." He gave Zora an anguished look. "Let me know how she is as soon as you can. I'll be in her room."

Zora nodded silently, taking the bottle. *I can't believe I forgot about this stuff. Good thing he remembered it.*

Zora listened to Kyril's footsteps leaving as she let the hanging that covered the doorway drop back into place. Making sure that her hair was brown rather than blonde, she dropped her veil on the table next to the crown and headed toward her cell, which was where they had put Lina.

"—up on the platform, in front of all those people," one of the priestesses was saying. "They'll be talking about bad omens already."

"It's not as if they weren't before," another one muttered.

"Lina," the First Priestess was saying insistently. "Can you hear me?" Zora was relieved to hear a response from Lina, even if it was only a soft moan. "Can you tell us what's wrong, what happened to you?"

Zora arrived in the doorway in time to see Lina's exhausted and bewildered face as she shook her head.

"It might be this," Zora said, holding out the bottle. "The king brought it. It's the potion Lady Esme was giving the Queen each night. She stopped taking it two days ago, but if it has poppy or aqua vita or something like that, that might be at least part of the problem." *And given what Lady Esme's been preparing, it probably has both*, she thought grimly.

"Why did you stop taking it?" the Eldest asked Lina. Lina did not respond.

"It was making it too hard for her to wake up in the morning," Zora said. "You all know that's true. I'm pretty sure it has Queen's Lace in it, too."

That produced a unanimous gasp of horror. The Third Priestess took the bottle from Zora. She poured a small amount into a cup and took a cautious sip. "I'm afraid she's right about the Queen's Lace," she told the other priestesses. "I'll take it to our stillroom and see if I can determine the rest of the ingredients."

"Does Lady Esme have access to our stillroom?" Zora asked. *I didn't even know we had a stillroom. I can't believe there is something around here they haven't started teaching me. Or maybe they don't think I need to know; Goddess knows the Queen doesn't. Of course, that made it possible for Esme to poison her in the first place, so maybe the Queen should know about herbs.*

"Don't be silly, Zora," the Second Priestess said. "Of course she doesn't. Lady Esme is not a priestess."

"Maybe somebody should check the stillroom she uses," Zora suggested, "and see what is in it that she might be using. Is she using one in the palace, or does she have a house in the city? She obviously got the ingredients from someplace."

"The palace stillroom would have Queen's Lace," the Third Priestess said.

"So does the Guards' stillroom," the Shield-Bearer said as she entered the room. "The feast has started—I had the food put out and told several of the Guards to start a rumor that the Queen simply fainted. Why are we talking about Queen's Lace?"

"Lady Esme has been putting it into the Queen's nightly glass of wine," the First Priestess said grimly, "apparently along with several other things."

"Are we sure of that?" the Shield-Bearer demanded. "And can

we prove it to legal standards?"

"Yes to the first," the Third Priestess replied, "but unfortunately not to the second."

"So we'll need to find some way to protect the Queen until we can prove what Lady Esme's up to," the Shield-Bearer said. "It's too bad we can't just keep her down here until the Sacrifice."

"I'm very sure that the king would object," Zora said. "When he brought the bottle down he told me that he wanted to know how she was as soon as possible."

"Did you talk to him?" the First Priestess asked sharply, turning her attention from Lina to glare at Zora.

"No," Zora shook her head, annoyed at being unfairly accused. Again. "I did nod when I took the bottle from him, but I didn't say anything."

"Have you *ever* spoken to him?" The First Priestess didn't seem satisfied with Zora's answer.

Zora had to force herself not to start shouting at the woman. "Isn't Lina's condition more important?" she snapped. "Of course I've spoken to Kyril. We grew up together!"

"Lina's condition is definitely more important," the Shield-Bearer said quickly. "Can you have her in shape for the evening ritual? This is rapidly turning into a political disaster as well as a spiritual one."

The Third Priestess shook her head. "Even if we gave her enough of the potion to take the edge off the muscle spasms, it would just make her sleep."

The Shield-Bearer sighed. "I'm almost desperate enough to have Kyril impersonate her, but he doesn't know the ritual, and it would likely bring the wrath of the Goddess down upon us again even if he could do it."

"Let *who* impersonate the Queen?" the First Priestess asked incredulously.

"The king," the Shield-Bearer sighed. "I'm pretty sure he's a shape-changer. But obviously he can't lead rituals for her." She sank into a chair and leaned forward, crossing both forearms on the table in front of her as if she couldn't support her own weight otherwise. "We should never have let Druscilla leave—or at least we should have fetched her back when Queen Zoradah died."

"Druscilla?" The First Priestess sounded incredulous. "Can you imagine what the Queen would be like if *she* had been around to influence her?"

"Probably no different than she is now," Zora snapped. "They're incredibly alike for two people who never met." *Oops! Let's hope they're too distracted to ask how I know what Druscilla is like. But as long as the subject has come up...* "Is Druscilla the Queen's Heiress?"

"No," the First Priestess said firmly. "She was completely unsuitable. After Lina was born, Druscilla formally gave up all rights to the crown in her favor. It's written in the Book of Oaths in Druscilla's own hand and signed with her blood."

"That sounds binding, all right," Zora said. "So who is the Heiress now?"

"That would be Druscilla's daughter," the Shield-Bearer said.

"If she has one," the Second Priestess said.

"She does," the Shield-Bearer assured them. "One of Lord Ranulf's kinswomen is in the Guard, and she's seen the girl."

Despite the fact that the Shield-Bearer was not looking at her, Zora shivered. *She knows. She knows about Kyril, and she knows about me. I was pretty sure she knew I was a shape-changer, but I didn't know she knew I was the Heiress. I guess Catriona did tell her.*

"For the moment," the Shield-Bearer said, pushing herself upright, "we'll have to cope as best we can. Is Lina able to go back to her room?"

"As long as that's *all* you want me to do," Lina said weakly, propping herself up on one elbow with an obvious effort.

"I'll give you a hand myself," the Shield-Bearer said, "and I'll sit with you until you're feeling better. Zora can come with us, while the rest of you find out what was in that potion." She turned to Zora. "Put your veil on." As Zora hastily obeyed, the Shield-Bearer said to the rest of the priestesses, "Send someone to the Queen's room when it's time for the evening ritual."

The three of them made it to Lina's rooms without incident—as long as one ignored the unusually large number of people who were pretending to have legitimate business in the hallways. The Shield-Bearer posted an extra guard outside the door to the anteroom, while both girls joined Kyril in the bedroom. Kyril

169

practically carried Lina to the bed; she had started shaking again as soon as they were out of public view.

"Don't worry, love," he said. "It will be all right. We'll take care of you."

Lina promptly started crying again. Considering the mess they were in, Zora wished she had the luxury of doing likewise.

The Shield-Bearer sat on the clothing chest at the foot of the bed and waited until Lina had cried herself to sleep in Kyril's arms. Once the Queen was sleeping normally, the Shield-Bearer rose to her feet and said casually, "I'll wait in the anteroom until it's time for the evening ritual. The Queen can join me there when she's ready."

Kyril stared at her incredulously as she left the room without even glancing at Zora, who sat, still silent and veiled, on the stool in front of the Queen's cosmetics table.

Zora was thankful that Kyril at least waited until the door closed behind the Shield-Bearer before he blurted out, "Is she *insane*? She can't possibly think the Queen will be awake and in shape to do the evening ritual!"

"She doesn't think that," Zora said, "but she needs someone to do it so badly that she told the priestesses she was tempted to have *you* do it!"

"But I can't!" Kyril protested.

"She knows that, Kyril. They all know that." Zora sighed. "I'm afraid she knows what we are—and who I am."

"Are you certain?"

"You didn't hear the discussion downstairs. She said she was pretty sure you were a shape-changer, and she knows Druscilla has a daughter." She looked him squarely in the eyes. "Druscilla renounced her claim on the throne, so her daughter is the Heiress."

"Oh."

"Yes. Oh. The only thing the Shield-Bearer *didn't* say was that she knew where Druscilla's daughter was, but you might have noticed that she's left the room now. She expects to see someone who can pass for the Queen and lead the evening ritual very soon."

Kyril looked down at Lina's peacefully sleeping face. "It's going to have to be you."

"Oh, yes," Zora sighed. "It certainly is."

She rose from her seat and pulled out Lina's clothing for the ritual, dressing while Kyril looked down at Lina as though only his concentration was keeping her breathing.

As Zora changed back to her normal shape—and hair color—she remarked, "I feel as though I'm spending more time as her than I am as me." She ran a brush through her hair. "How do I look?"

Kyril looked from her to Lina, comparing them. "Fine. Do you know the ritual?"

"Yes, but I haven't done it much. I hope I remember all the right words." Zora went into the anteroom, closing the door softly behind her. "The king is tired," she told the Shield-Bearer. "He's going to rest for a while."

The Shield-Bearer nodded approvingly. "I think that's an excellent idea. I'll make sure he isn't disturbed." She closed the door to the anteroom and paused briefly to murmur instructions to one of the guards before following Zora to the front of the palace.

Zora had done the evening ritual only a few times, and Lina had been in the room behind her, which had given Zora a feeling of security, however small. Tonight she was alone, and she was willing to swear that at least half the population of Diadem had turned up in the plaza, swelling the crowd of people who had already been there for the ceremony and the feast. *Of course, after this afternoon, they all want to see what condition the Queen is in.*

She said a quick, silent prayer to the Goddess and prepared to start the ritual. That was when she remembered that there was a different hymn at the beginning because today was a feast day. *I would forget about that until I'm standing here in front of a crowd of people who probably know the hymn better than I do.* Her mind went blank with sudden panic. *How does that hymn start? If I could just remember the beginning of it...*

After an agonizing moment, the first lines came to her. "She bade the soil herbage yield, And blossoms fair to deck the field, And golden fruit and harvest bear..."

The ritual took over her mind and body. Once again she felt strong and powerful, and energy flowed between her and the people. She felt connected to every single person in the plaza, and the feeling was almost overwhelming, but it also filled her with warmth and peace. Then the ritual was over, and she was joining the Shield-Bearer and one of the priestesses in the room behind the balcony.

"Well?" the Shield-Bearer asked the priestess.

No one else was in the room, but even so the priestess's voice was barely above a whisper. "The ritual went well, if that's what you're asking."

"Good." The Shield-Bearer sounded relieved. "At the very least it should help quiet the rumors."

"Goddess grant it," the priestess said softly.

"Amen," Zora whispered. *I just hope it doesn't start any new rumors. And may the Goddess give me the strength and knowledge to get through all of this. I'm very much afraid I'm going to be the Queen for the foreseeable future.*

The next morning, Zora was still *de facto* Queen. Kyril was pretending to be ill so he could stay in Lina's room with her, and Lina, while apparently through the worst effects of suddenly stopping taking the potion, was too exhausted to get out of bed.

Zora did the morning ritual, ate breakfast in the hall, told the king's Companions that he did not require their attendance until afternoon, and went back to the Queen's rooms—ostensibly to fetch a document she wanted for the morning hearings—but actually to make sure there was still a guard on the door who would let no one but her into the room. Satisfied on that point, she went back to join the Shield-Bearer for morning court.

After court, Lady Esme joined her, bringing the daily cup of "broth." The Shield-Bearer took it from her, saying casually, "That looks good. May I try it?"

"Certainly," Zora replied, hoping the Shield-Bearer didn't have a close personal relationship with the Goddess. Apparently she didn't, for she drained the cup with no change of expression, and complimented Lady Esme on her cooking skills when she finished it.

Lady Esme thanked her politely and said she'd get another cup for the Queen at once, but Zora hastily said, "Don't concern yourself. I'm not particularly hungry this morning."

Lady Esme stalked off, obviously offended. The Shield-Bearer looked after her with narrowed eyes. "I'm beginning to get a bad feeling about any food she makes." She looked sharply at Zora. "She's angry you didn't drink that. What does she put in it?"

Zora sighed. "I'm pretty sure one of the ingredients is her own blood—she always appears to have a fresh pinprick on her finger when she gives it to me." The Shield-Bearer stared at her in disbelief, and Zora shrugged. "She's not as clumsy at sewing as she wants people to believe. She doesn't want anyone to see anything about her fingers she can't explain away."

"Why her blood?" the Shield-Bearer asked.

"I think it's some sort of spell," Zora said. "Do you feel any different?"

The Shield-Bearer frowned in thought. "I feel as if the world is suddenly just a little bit further away from me than normal," she replied in a low voice.

"Don't worry," Zora reassured her. "The effects should wear off completely by tomorrow morning, if not sooner."

"For just one dose, or for long-term daily consumption?"

"One dose. You'll be fine."

The Shield-Bearer shook her head, smiling faintly in spite of the situation. "For a moment there you sounded just like Akila." At Zora's horrified look, she added, "Don't worry, nobody else around here knew her well enough to notice." She sobered again. "If you've been taking this potion for months, as I gather the Queen has...?"

"I don't know how long *that* will take to wear off," Zora admitted.

"From this moment on," the Shield-Bearer said firmly, "you are not to eat or drink *anything* unless it is either from the same dish that everyone else at the table is eating from or it is handed to you by me or one of the priestesses." She frowned. "You can identify all of the priestesses, even when they're veiled, can you not?"

"Yes," Zora assured her, making a mental note to be sure that Lina could too. "I'd notice if Lady Esme put on a robe and veil and tried to pass herself off as one of them." She added, "I'm pretty sure the other priestesses would notice, too."

"Good." The Shield-Bearer rose to her feet. "Why don't you go eat with the king in your room? I'll bring you a tray from the kitchen."

"Thank you," Zora said gratefully. *It's time I got back to my—I mean the Queen's—room and checked on Lina, anyway.*

As she went down the hallway, trailed by a silent priestess as well as a guard, she realized that taking Lina's place was a bit like taking an animal shape for a long period of time. *I don't need to worry about freezing in the wrong shape, because this actually* is *my true shape, but the mental effects are similar. If I'm already starting to think of the Queen's room as mine, how long before I forget that I'm not really the Queen? That could happen all too easily, and I'm afraid everyone wants me to be the Queen anyway—including Lina.*

Fortunately Lina was well enough to dress in Zora's clothing and accompany Zora to the Queen's chapel, even though she lay down on the bench and napped rather than meditating. Zora wished she could call what she was doing meditating, but she was afraid that 'fretting' was the more accurate term. *At least Kyril went out with his Companions when we came down here,* she thought. *We don't need rumors about* his *health on top of rumors about the Queen's. We'll have people thinking the entire land is cursed if things don't improve soon.*

CHAPTER FOURTEEN

As she expected she would have to, Zora did the evening ritual that day and the morning ritual the next day. *Lina is still sick,* she tried to reassure herself, *and she's been drugged the entire time I've known her. She can't have really meant what she said about not wanting her life back...*

There was no formal court that morning, so Zora took Lina's sewing and went to sit with her ladies. Kyril was out with his Companions again, working on dispelling the various rumors, and Lina was still pretending to be Zora.

Lady Esme had apparently realized that her days as a poisoner were at an end—at least for the moment—and was trying another tactic. Seating herself at Zora's elbow, where she could speak without being overheard by the attendant priestesses, who included Lina, she began by expressing concern for the king's health. "It would be a bad omen if the Year-King were to sicken before the Sacrifice," she said with false concern.

You'd probably be thrilled if he dropped dead before the Sacrifice, Zora thought, carefully keeping her face blank and her stitches even. *And you shouldn't be talking about the Sacrifice at all, even—or especially—to me.* Aloud she said calmly. "Lord Kyril is well, thank you. He was merely tired by the long ritual two days ago."

"And concerned for *your* health, no doubt," Lady Esme said archly.

"He loves me," Zora said simply.

"You know that's not really true." Lady Esme's voice dropped lower, even as she forced a smile onto her face as if she were making pleasant conversation. "He doesn't love you any more than my father did. It's just part of the spell."

Zora considered smiling back, but decided it was too out of character for Lina. "I truly am sorry for your father's death," she said gently. "As for Kyril, he sought out my company from the day he arrived in the city, and he cared for me even before the

Choosing."

"And in a couple of months, you'll be killing him," Lady Esme snapped, still keeping her voice down. "A fine return *that* is for his love!"

"It's the will of the Goddess."

"And it will be someone else next year, and the year after that, and the year after that—for the rest of your life! How long can you live with yourself as you repeatedly betray every man who loves you? How can you live with yourself *now*?"

After a morning like that, Zora was perfectly content to sit silently in the Queen's chapel with Lina. She really didn't want to think about Lady Esme's questions. *The problem is that she's right about some things. Not many, but some. Why should* anyone *have to kill someone who loves her every year? Can the Goddess really want that? And could I do it if she did?*

Lady Esme started in again the next morning after court. Lina still showed no signs of wanting her life back—or of being able to cope with it if she had it—and Zora didn't want her exposed to Lady Esme's malice. *It's easier for me to deal with Lady Esme than with Lina having hysterics because of her, and if Lady Esme is getting to* me, *Lina can't begin to cope. I'm just going to have to pretend to be the Queen for a while longer. It's a good thing I'm her Heiress; nobody else could get away with this.*

"I miss my father," Esme said, in what Zora suspected was one of the few really honest statements the woman had made in the past year. "But at least I knew him before he died. You didn't even have that."

Zora didn't know what Lina would have said to that, so she kept her eyes on the embroidery in her lap and didn't reply.

"What was the Queen thinking of when she had you so late in her life, knowing that you would never have a father, and that you wouldn't have a mother for long?"

"I don't think she expected to die as young as she did," Zora said, allowing her voice to tremble slightly. "And how can I miss a father I never knew?"

"You could stop this, you know." Lady Esme's voice was even lower, but still firm.

"What do you mean?" Zora knew that Lady Esme had to be

plotting something, but not what it was. *Surely she can't hope to end the Sacrifice forever. Can she?*

"You're the last of the royal line, as long as you don't bear a daughter," Lady Esme explained condescendingly, as if to a small and not-very-bright child. "If you're not here, there's nobody else they can force to do the Sacrifice."

"There must be somebody in line after me," Zora said, hoping Lady Esme really believed that there wasn't. *She actually* does *think the Sacrifice can be ended.*

"No," Lady Esme shook her head. "The Heiress before you were born was disinherited and sent away. They said she was unsuitable." Her lips thinned. "Do you know why they said that?"

I can make a few really good guesses, Zora thought. "Why?" she asked, curious as to what Lady Esme knew or would admit to.

"The only reason they didn't want her to be Queen was that she didn't want to do the Sacrifice. *She* didn't want your father to be killed."

Well, that's *certainly true—if incomplete.*

"That's the only reason they banished her, because she didn't want to kill someone every year or raise fatherless children."

"But she can't be the only relative I have," Zora protested weakly.

"If you had any *suitable* relatives," Lady Esme said scathingly, "would your Regent have come from your mother's guardswomen?"

Zora had never been so glad to be called to a meal in her entire life.

Apparently, however, the Goddess didn't feel she had enough problems to deal with. Lina slept through the afternoon's meditation again, and when Zora joined Lina and Kyril that night at bedtime she discovered that Kyril had turned his mind to their problems and decided to help.

"Zora, remember when you said that you could be Lina indefinitely, but the problem was that she couldn't be you?"

Zora nodded, vaguely remembering having said something like that. What she couldn't remember was when she had said it. *Was it a long time ago, or does it just feel that way?*

"Well, actually," Kyril corrected himself, "she could replace *you* easily enough—she looks just like you, after all—but she needs to be able to act like Zora."

Zora decided that he didn't mean to insult her, but if he thought that Lina could come anywhere close to handling Zora's life, he had to be suffering the worst case of 'Year-King idiocy' in history.

"Unless one of us can teach her to shape-change," she pointed out, "there's no way she can impersonate Zora. And there *is* more to Zora than the physical appearance—I've spent months being tutored by the priestesses, on top of what I'd already learned from Marfa and Akila. Furthermore, even if she is a shape-changer—and I believe she is—she can't learn to shape-change when she can't even stay awake all day! Look how long I was stuck as a dog, and I wasn't nearly as sick as she's been."

"She doesn't have to shape-change," Kyril said. "We can dye her hair brown."

"Are you insane?" Zora demanded. "First, that would prevent her from taking her rightful place when she recovers, and second, hair grows. As soon as she has brown hair with blonde roots, it's going to be very obvious. And she'd have to dye her hair without anybody noticing, which would be impossible because dye stains things it touches, like towels, which the maids would notice. And skin, which everyone would notice."

"But if I can pretend to be you, you won't have to try to be both of us," Lina said. "I want to help, even if I can't be Queen. Which I can't," she added hastily. "I don't understand why you aren't falling asleep in the middle of the day, too."

Zora looked at her in surprise. "I get strength from the morning and evening rituals," she said. "Don't you, when you do them?"

Lina frowned. "I think I used to," she said, "but I can't really remember. My mind's all fuzzy."

"That's probably just from the potion," Kyril said reassuringly.

"It probably is," Zora agreed. "Between the potion at night, which turned out to have poppy juice in addition to everything else that was in it, and the broth Esme was giving you in the morning, which severed your connection to the Goddess—"

"What?" Kyril interrupted, surprised and horrified.

"I *told* you," Zora said impatiently, "the morning I got a dose by mistake—don't you remember?"

"If you mean the day you staggered in here after court, collapsed, and slept for the rest of the morning," Kyril retorted, "you weren't very coherent—and besides, that was ages ago!"

"Fine! I'll be coherent now. Do you remember the potion your sister used your blood for?"

"Gods and Goddesses," Kyril whispered. "Esme is making *that?*"

"She was," Zora said. "At least until a few days ago, when the Shield-Bearer drank it."

Lina gasped. "Is the Shield-Bearer all right?"

"She's fine," Zora assured her. "She barely noticed the effects."

"It didn't affect my sister much either," Kyril said, "and *she* had just been chosen to be the Earth Mother's priestess. But it made Zora really sick."

Zora shivered at the memory. "I thought I was dying, alone and cut off from the Goddess. At least when Lady Esme gave it to me I recognized it and knew it wasn't fatal—just very, very unpleasant."

"But it didn't make me sick like that," Lina said, obviously trying to reason it out. "Does that mean I'm not supposed to have a bond with the Goddess?"

"Of course you're supposed to have a bond with the Goddess," Zora snapped. "You're the Queen!" She forced herself to get a grip on her temper and looked steadily at Lina. "What I suspect happened is that she started giving you the evening potion first. That way you wouldn't notice when she gave you the second one. She must have started giving it to you last summer, when you lost the ability to"—she choked back 'walk the labyrinth' in view of the fact that Kyril was listening—"sense the presence of the Goddess. At some point this winter, she must have removed at least one of the potion ingredients from the beef broth."

"Why?" Kyril asked.

"It had to wear off before the Choosing, because Lina would need the link to the Goddess for that," Zora explained. "After the Choosing, however, Lady Esme could put the full potion back into Lina's midmorning cup of broth, and her link to the Goddess would go away again. Actually, this is good news, because it means the effects aren't permanent, even with daily use over several months."

"I think you're right," Lina said thoughtfully. "I started taking the evening potion over a year ago, soon after last year's Choosing. I was nervous about the...rituals...and I was having trouble sleeping, so Lady Esme made it for me."

"Were you nervous about the rituals before or after she started talking to you about them all the time?" Zora asked.

Lina stared at her. "How did you know?"

"That her tongue is as poisonous as her potions?" Zora shrugged. "She's been trying it on me."

Kyril chuckled, "I'll bet she's not getting far."

"With me, no. But with Lina..."

Kyril's grin vanished instantly. "Can't we get rid of her?"

Lina shook her head sadly. "No, we can't. It was the King's Boon."

"The what?" Kyril asked.

"When the king comes from Diadem," Lina explained, "he gets to ask for a favor for his family. Esme's father asked that she be given a position and a home at Court for as long she wanted it."

"And she's still here," Zora said. "Lucky us."

"But does that apply *after* his death?" Kyril still seemed confused.

Lina gaped at him in astonishment, so Zora explained. "That's precisely when it *does* apply, Kyril. When the king comes from here, he knows he's going to be dead in a few months. The King's Boon allows him to provide for any family he leaves behind."

"Oh," Kyril said, "of course. I'm so used to knowing and pretending that I don't that I forget that someone who's lived here all his life wouldn't be expected to pretend."

"And would probably have family here." Lina was recovering from her surprise at Kyril's obtuseness. "I didn't expect Esme to stay here after his death. I thought he just wanted her to be able to stay with him during the last months of his life, and perhaps have a guarantee that she would always have a place to live if she needed one. She certainly can afford to live elsewhere, and," she frowned thoughtfully, "I think it's painful for her to remain here. She must be reminded of his death every time she looks at me." She shivered. "I sometimes think she hates me."

"It's not personal," Zora assured her. "If it was just you she hated, the potion wouldn't have worked on me. And she can certainly afford to live elsewhere. The records say all taxes are forgiven for the rest of her life."

"That's right," Lina said. "I'd forgotten that bit. She doesn't even have to do training with the Guard now.

"So is she staying here to punish herself?" Kyril asked.

Zora shook her head. "I think she's trying to destroy—it's hard to say. She's not *exactly* trying to kill Lina, although I'm pretty sure she wouldn't mind the Queen's death. It's more that she's trying to get rid of the entire royal line—or something like that."

"Can she get rid of it?" Kyril asked.

"She believes she can—as long as she thinks Lina has no possible successor. That would explain the Queen's Lace in the potion. As soon as Lina has a daughter, there's one more generation to get rid of."

"But how would that help *her*?" Lina asked, obviously bewildered.

"It wouldn't help her personally—aside from any satisfaction she might gain from getting rid of us." Zora thought about it. It really was a good question. She would have sworn Esme didn't have an altruistic bone in her body... "Lina, what was Lady Esme like *before* her father was chosen?"

Lina shrugged. "I don't know. I never met her until her father chose his Boon, and she's so much older than I am that I never really got to know her—not that it would have helped much at that point. She was over thirty, so why would she pay any attention to a seventeen-year-old?"

Zora mentally reviewed everything Esme had said to her. "I think she's trying to end the Sacrifice, once and for all."

Lina gaped at her. "Can she do that?" She sounded hopeful.

"Not while you live," Zora pointed out, "but her plan may be 'no Queen equals no Sacrifice'—which makes a certain amount of sense, given that there weren't any while you were a child."

"But that still doesn't gain *her* anything," Kyril pointed out.

"It ensures that no other girl loses her father the way she did," Lina said slowly, "or the way that I did."

Kyril looked sharply at Zora over Lina's bowed head.

Uh-oh. Lord Ranulf must have told him that Briam was Lina's father. Zora shook her head. *She's got enough to deal with without our telling her that her father survived long enough to have me.* "Let's just get some sleep."

She went to her bed in the anteroom, and fell asleep almost immediately, dimly aware that Kyril and Lina were still talking in the next room.

"Another day, and I'm still the Queen," Zora sighed to herself two weeks later. Despite the fact that she was getting energy from the rituals, she was tired. And worried: about Lina's health and mental state; about whatever Kyril was planning now; about what Esme would try next; about what would happen when it was time for somebody other than Zora to attend the Queen. At least she could do something about the last problem. As Queen, she could order Zora to continue in attendance on her. The priestesses would accept it because they thought having a priestess her own age was a good influence on the Queen and because they didn't really want to spend time with Lina themselves. As for the rest, she would just have to watch and listen to Esme and Kyril as much as possible and hope for the best. Prayer would be good, too.

When she returned to the Queen's room after breakfast to change for the morning's petition hearings, it appeared as if her prayers were at least beginning to be answered. Both Kyril *and* Lina were out of bed and dressed. Even though Lina was dressed in Zora's clothing, it was a definite improvement to have her out of bed so early in the day.

"Feeling better?" Zora asked hopefully.

"A little bit," Lina said. "I don't feel up to being Queen, but I'm beginning to feel like I can manage youngest priestess—as long as nobody ever sees me unveiled!"

"It's a start," Zora said. "Come sit in on the petition hearings, and Kyril can go out with his Companions. Even though I don't hear it directly, I can tell there's gossip about the amount of time he's supposedly alone in your room."

"It would be better if we started acting normal again," Kyril agreed. "I'll spend more time in public view."

"And I'll spend more time in attendance on you, Zora," Lina

said. "But what are we going to do when they want another priestess to replace you?"

"Maybe you'll be able to be Queen yourself by then," Zora said hopefully.

Lina shook her head emphatically. "No!" she said firmly.

"If you can't be Queen by the time someone suggests switching priestesses, I'll just have to say that I want to keep you with me. Given that they think I'm a good influence on you, they'll probably agree readily enough."

"They think *you're* a good influence on her?" Kyril asked incredulously.

"Yes, but they won't keep thinking that if we're late for the morning hearings." Zora grabbed the green veil and tossed it at Lina. "Here, put this on and hurry!"

"You shouldn't be giving orders to the Queen," Kyril said.

"When she's willing to be the Queen again, I'll be delighted to stop!" She stalked out of the room with Lina, now veiled, following her.

CHAPTER FIFTEEN

The morning hearings went well. Over the weeks that Zora had been acting as Queen, she had learned a great deal about the day-to-day working of the realm. She still didn't announce any decision without consulting with the Shield-Bearer, but more and more often she was making the decisions rather than asking the Shield-Bearer what she should do. She was glad to have Lina with her, because she still had hopes that Lina would be resuming her own duties soon. *And when that happens, she had better know how I have been acting while I've been taking her place.*

But when Lina's ready to be Queen again, what happens to me? I'm used to making decisions now, and I think I'm good at it. Can I sit in silence and watch Lina be Queen?

When they were in the Queen's chapel that afternoon, Lina still stayed on the bench while Zora walked the labyrinth, but at least now she was sitting up and awake instead of sleeping though the entire meditation period. Zora even dared to hope, when they sat side by side on the bench, that both of them were meditating.

There were no petitions to be heard the next morning, so they embroidered in the garden. Lina sat in silence with the other priestesses, and Lady Esme was at Zora's side.

Esme had obviously decided to resume her campaign. "Have you thought about what you're going to do when it's time to kill the king?" she asked, speaking softly enough that nobody but Zora could hear her.

Left to her own devices, Zora would have simply assured Lady Esme that she would do her duty, but after Lina's semi-public hysterics when Kyril was chosen, that response would be implausible. Besides, if Lady Esme thought her verbal poison was working, she'd be less likely to try anything more physical. "I don't know," Zora said, allowing her voice to quaver. "I don't think I can bear it..."

"At least my father knew what to expect..." The wobble in Lady Esme's voice sounded genuine.

It probably is. True, she is manipulative, but she appears to have really loved her father.

"Kyril doesn't know," Zora lied, adding slowly, "and if the potion we give him is strong enough, maybe he won't notice—"

"Won't notice your betrayal of his love?" Esme said almost sarcastically. "I don't think you can drug him that much and still have him on his feet during the ritual."

You should know, Zora thought, biting back a verbal reply. There was nothing she could say that wouldn't make the situation worse.

But Esme appeared to have a new idea. "Maybe you don't have to kill him," she said slowly.

"How can I save him?" Zora asked. "There will be guards all around us, not to mention the priestesses and the Shield-Bearer!"

"Maybe we can think of a way to save him before then," Lady Esme said hopefully. "If we can't think of anything else, I'm afraid that you're right. The people around you at the ritual would stop any attempt you made to save him. But you don't have to leave him. If you step into the water with him, they won't have time to stop you—and besides, they won't expect that."

Zora stared at her in awe. She hoped that Lady Esme would think she was struck by her suggestion, which she was—just not in the way Lady Esme intended. *"Step into the water"—now there's a gentle description of stepping off a cliff into a waterfall with rocks at the bottom of it!* She made a mental note to nag Kyril again about finding out where the rocks were before the ritual. "You're right," she finally managed to choke out the words. "Nobody would be expecting that!"

"And you wouldn't be sending Kyril to his death alone," Lady Esme said gently, "and it would be over—you wouldn't have to grieve for him."

"And I wouldn't ever have to do this again," Zora said. She added what Lina had said. "And no other girl would lose her father the way you and I did..."

Lady Esme nodded, blinking back tears.

"Maybe," Zora said softly. "Maybe it *is* time to end the Sacrifice. Maybe it's what the Goddess wants."

"Maybe it is," Esme agreed. "I can't help thinking that enough men have died…"

She could actually be right about that, Zora thought, staring down at the embroidery lying forgotten in her lap. *Maybe that's why Kyril and I are here. Maybe that's why I had to come to Diadem. I doubt that we can end the Sacrifice just yet, but we can certainly increase the survival rate. Goddess knows there are enough male students at Lord Ranulf's that we could provide Year-Kings for decades!* She suddenly realized that could actually work, assuming that Lord Ranulf was correct in his belief that a shape-changer would be chosen if one was present.

She realized that she had nodded only when Lady Esme patted her hand, and said softly, "Think about it."

"I will," Zora said. It came out sounding like a vow, and Esme suddenly looked extremely satisfied. Zora knew they had been talking almost at cross purposes, but she didn't enlighten Lady Esme. *Let her think what she likes…*

After the midday meal, when Zora and Lina went down to the Queen's chapel, the First Priestess joined them in the antechamber and unveiled her face. "It's past time for the priestess attending you to change, Lady," she said formally.

"I know it is," Zora said, forcing her voice to remain calm. This would be the worst possible time to seem even slightly hysterical. "But I have found having Zora in attendance such a comfort that I would like to keep her with me as long as she feels able to remain."

The Eldest raised her eyebrows in surprise. She looked from Zora's face to Lina's veiled figure and bowed head. "It is rather unconventional," she said dubiously, but her voice trailed off. Both girls stood quietly, allowing her to consider past fits of hysteria, episodes of apparent laziness and indifference, and the change over the last few weeks. It didn't take her long to reach a decision. "If Zora is willing to remain in attendance, I see no reason why it should not be so."

Lina nodded silently, and Zora said, "Thank you. I appreciate the support that all of you have been giving me." She opened the door to the chapel, and she and Lina entered and closed it behind them before the First Priestess could raise her dropped jaw.

Once they were on the far side of the chapel, she dragged Lina onto the bench beside her and said, "We have to talk about Kyril."

"What about him?" Lina asked fearfully.

"It's nothing bad," Zora assured her. "You do know that his father survived being Year-King, don't you?"

"He did?"

"You really *were* drugged when we first got here," Zora said. "The Sword-Bearer told you, remember? It's why he was *Lord* Kyril even before the Choosing."

"She did tell me..." Lina was obviously struggling to remember.

"Yes, that's right," Zora said, striving for patience, "but the point is that Kyril's father survived being Year-King, married Kyril's mother, and had more children."

"How did he survive?"

"He's a shape-changer; he turned into a fish and swam downstream."

"And you're a shape-changer, too." Lina remembered that much, which wasn't too surprising because Zora had been a dog when they met and was currently taking her place. "Could you survive the Sacrifice? Could you take Kyril's place?"

"Yes to the first, and absolutely no to the second," Zora said firmly. "The Sacrifice *must* be male and must be the person who was chosen." She looked Lina firmly in the eye. "Don't *ever* forget that. But it's not a problem in this case, because Kyril is a shape-changer too, remember?"

"Are you sure?" Lina asked. "I've never seen him change."

"I grew up with him," Zora said. "I'm sure. We talked about this after the Choosing. Don't you remember?"

Lina shook her head, looking blank. Zora sighed.

"Then you probably don't remember my telling you that there is something he needs to do so he'll survive the Sacrifice. So far I haven't been able to persuade him to do it."

"What is it?" Lina asked.

"He needs to practice."

"Jumping off the terrace into the waterfall?" Lina gasped and looked at her in horror.

"Not that part," Zora said quickly. "First, somebody would probably see him, and second, that way is too dangerous." Lina started breathing normally again, and Zora continued. "What he needs to do is sneak out at night, go downriver from the waterfall, and swim up to it so he can see where the rocks are underneath it. He needs to practice swimming around the rocks and getting safely downstream while he's not drugged, and he needs to do it repeatedly, because the day of the Sacrifice he will be drugged. He has to practice enough times that he can *literally* do this in his sleep."

"What do you want me to do?"

"Tell him to go out at night and practice," Zora said. "The Sacrifice is less than eight weeks away. He really needs to start soon. Tell him it's all right for him to leave you at night, and that it's important to *you* for him to do this." She gave Lina a rueful grin. "He'll listen to you much better than he does to me."

"I'll do it," Lina said. "But can he really sneak out of my room without being caught?"

Zora laughed. "That part he can already do in his sleep," she said. "You'll see."

Zora was right; once Lina remembered what Zora told her, she had only to ask. That night, after they had all ostensibly gone to bed, both girls sat in the Queen's darkened bedroom and watched a large mottled gray bird launch himself off the windowsill, fly silently across the garden, and head downriver. Then Zora sat and held Lina's hands for two hours until he returned. He changed back to human and promptly collapsed into bed and fell asleep.

"He's fine," Zora assured a worried Lina. "Changing uses a lot of energy. Tomorrow we'll make sure he eats a big breakfast, and we'll get some fruit bars and keep them here so he'll have them when he gets back from practicing at night. He won't be so tired next time. It gets easier."

Lina looked somewhat reassured, but when she climbed into bed next to Kyril, she put her arms around him as if to prevent him from going anywhere.

Zora, knowing that no force on earth was going to get Kyril out of bed before morning, smiled to herself as she went to her bed in the antechamber.

"So, how did it go last night?" Zora inquired the next morning.

The three of them were eating breakfast in the Queen's room, unbeknownst to the priestesses, who thought Zora was eating by herself in the anteroom, Kyril wasn't feeling well, and the Queen had decided to breakfast with them. *I can get away with this for one day, but I'll have to be back in the hall tomorrow.* The truth would have horrified them—and probably the entire court—so Zora didn't plan to tell them.

"The current is pretty strong," Kyril admitted, "and there were a lot more rocks than I expected. It's practically a rock garden under the waterfall!"

"Beginning of the Queen's reign, remember," Zora said. "I told you that two months ago!"

"You don't need to say 'I told you so,'" Kyril grumbled. *Especially when I did.*

"So will you be all right the day of the Sacrifice?" Lina asked anxiously.

"I should be fine," Kyril assured her, "but I will need more practice." He glared at Zora. "Don't say it!"

"Have some more eggs," Zora said instead, extending her plate to him.

"Thanks," Kyril took half of her portion and continued shoveling food into his mouth. "I can't believe how hungry I am," he said between bites.

"I'll get some fruit bars and hide them in here," Zora promised him. "Skip tonight, and do another session tomorrow. If you can stay awake long enough to eat something when you come back, you won't be quite as starved in the morning."

"Says the voice of experience," Kyril muttered.

"Your father taught me the same things he taught you," Zora pointed out.

"Is it hard to learn?" Lina asked.

"Is what hard to learn?" Zora asked, because Kyril had his mouth full.

"Shape-changing."

"I'm not sure," Zora said. "I can't remember the first time I did it—I'm told I changed into a cat while I was still an infant."

"Why a cat?" Lina asked.

"We had one that slept in my cradle with me."

"So," Lina said slowly, "did you learn how to be a cat from being next to one?"

Zora stared at her. "I never thought of it that way, but that would make sense."

"What about you?" Lina turned to Kyril. "Do you remember the first time you changed?"

Kyril swallowed his food. "Oh, yes," he said fervently. "I was about five, and I fell out of a tree. I turned into a bird."

"So what did your father teach you—if you both already knew how to change?"

"Lots of things," Kyril said. "How to change into other shapes..."

"What shapes shouldn't be used for long periods of time," Zora contributed. "Cat isn't a good one to use once you grow up—they go into heat too often."

"And it's a good idea to turn into a female animal rather than a male one," Kyril added, "so that you don't go mindlessly running after a female in heat."

"That it's a bad idea to turn into a fish when you're upset..."

"How to turn into a wolf and still be able to talk," Kyril said, "but that's pretty advanced."

"It sounds like it," Lina said. "But the simple things..." She took a deep breath and blurted out, "Do you think I could learn?"

"That's a good question," Kyril said.

"I've been wondering about it for a while," Zora admitted, "Your half-brother is a shape-changer, which means that your mother could give birth to one—"

"Half-brother? What are you talking about?"

"Lina, didn't the priestesses give you the same books to read that they gave me? The ones about the Queens and the kings?"

"They gave me a whole lot of books," Lina admitted, "but I didn't read most of them. Why would I care about a bunch of people who died before I was born?"

"Well, not all of them died," Zora pointed out. "Kyril's father was married to your mother, and they had a son named Rias, who lives at Eagle's Rest, where we grew up. Then Lord Ranulf married Kyril's mother and they had six children together."

"A son? But the Queen's children are always daughters," Lina protested.

"Apparently not," Kyril said. "Rias is the priest of the Sky Father at home, so he can't leave there, but he is still alive."

"And your father's twin sister is a shape-changer," Zora said quickly before Kyril could describe any more of his family. "It's possible that you are a shape-changer who just never learned to change because you didn't know it was possible. You do have the right type of body for it."

"My father's twin sister?" Lina looked at her in astonishment. "How do you know about his family?"

Zora rolled her eyes. "I read the records in the temple book room."

Kyril looked appraisingly at Lina. "You're right about the body type. She's got the small frame that makes bird-shapes easier."

"So if I jumped off the balcony..."

"Bad idea, Lina," Zora said. "Really, *really* bad idea. It's too close to the ground. Your clothes don't change with you, so you have to either start without them or get out of them while you're changing. And if you're using panic to force yourself into a bird-shape, you need to have enough time to panic, change, and get control of the new shape, which mean you'd need a *lot* more height. All you'd do if you jumped off the balcony is break both legs."

"I'll try to teach you," Kyril said, "if you promise you won't do anything when I'm not with you. And," he added, "we will *not* start with birds. There are plenty of things to learn before you try to fly."

"I promise," Lina said. "I want to learn."

"It would certainly be helpful if you could learn to change your hair," Zora said. "And staying in human shape means you don't have to get in and out of your clothes all the time."

"Good point," Kyril agreed. "That sounds like a place to start."

Life continued in its usual pattern for the next couple of weeks. Zora remained the acting Queen, Lina wore Zora's robes and veil anytime someone else was around, and Kyril spent a portion of his nights doing practice sessions in the river, and most of his days in public with his Companions being ostentatiously healthy, which finally dispelled the rumors about *his* health that had begun circulating after the disastrous First Fruits festival.

As far as Zora was concerned there were two major problems with this seeming normalcy. Lina still refused to take her place as Queen, and she was upset and frustrated because she couldn't seem to learn how to shape-change. Feeling that the second problem was in the hands of the Goddess, Zora tried to tackle the first.

"Lina," she said one afternoon as they sat in the chapel together, "you really need to return to your own identity. The longer you wait, the harder it's going to be." *For both of us.* Lina was sitting on the bench at the end of the labyrinth, while Zora sat on the floor next to the fountain. "If we don't change back very soon," she added, "people are going to notice the difference. The Shield-Bearer would notice the difference if we changed back today." She didn't tell Lina that she was certain the Shield-Bearer could already tell the difference between them. She trusted "their" Regent to keep quiet about whatever it was she knew.

"Why do we have to change back at all?" Lina asked, leaning forward and running her fingertips idly through the water on the top surface of the fountain. Wherever her fingers touched, the smooth flow of the water was disturbed, and its movement became visible.

"Because *you* are the Queen, and *I* am not."

"But you do a much better job of it than I do." Lina traced a circle in the water with one fingertip.

"That's because *I'm* trying to do a good job," Zora snapped.

"That's precisely it," Lina said with infuriating calm. "You *care* about being a good Queen. I don't."

"You will have to be the Queen for the Sacrifice," Zora pointed out.

Lina shook her head vigorously. "I can't," she said, in a voice that threatened to become hysterical. "And do you really think the Goddess *cares* which one of us does the ritual?"

Yes.

Lina jumped, and then snapped, "You don't need to shout at me!"

"I didn't say anything," Zora said, conscious of a sense of relief so immense that she thought she might melt into the floor. She smiled radiantly. "Lina, you can hear the Goddess again!"

"No," Lina shook her head adamantly. "You're just playing a

joke on me."

"Lina." Zora reached out and grabbed her face with both hands. "I am, however reluctantly, impersonating the Queen. There is *no* way I would *ever* impersonate the Goddess!"

"So you're saying that I have to do the ritual?"

"The Goddess says that," Zora replied. "And it does make sense from the religious point of view. You were the one he married, so you have to be the one at the ritual. Beginning and end, both have to be the same people. It has to be you and Kyril."

Lina sighed. "Very well," she said reluctantly. "I'll start being you—"

"Being *yourself*—"

"—but slowly," Lina said. "I'll be the Queen *after* the ritual in the morning on days when there are no petition hearings. We can change back when we get here and there's no one to see us."

It's not much, Zora thought resignedly, *but it's a start.* "All right," she agreed.

But when Zora returned to the Queen's rooms after the morning ritual the next day, she discovered that Lina had finally learned to change her shape. When tapping on the door to the bedroom produced no response, Zora went in, prepared to wake up Kyril and Lina. What she saw in the bed, however, was two copies of Kyril.

CHAPTER SIXTEEN

Her horrified gasp woke one of them. "What's wrong?" Kyril asked sleepily. "You look as though you've seen a ghost."

Zora pointed with a trembling hand at the second body in the bed.

"Lord of the Sky!" Kyril tilted his head and frowned. "Do I really look like that?"

"Yes," Zora said, "but that's hardly the problem right now. Wake her up and make her change back!"

Kyril leaned over Lina and gently shook her shoulder. "Lina, wake up." The eyes of the second copy of Kyril opened and looked up at him. "Congratulations. You've learned how to change shape."

"I have?" Lina said excitedly, then stopped and put a hand to her throat. "Does my voice sound funny to you?"

"Yes," Kyril said.

"No," Zora said. "You sound just like Kyril. You look just like him, too. Now would you please change back before someone comes to ask why we're not at breakfast?"

Lina looked down at her body and shook her head. "I don't know how to change back," she said in a small voice. "I don't even know how I finally managed to change in the first place—I was asleep when it happened!"

"We'll sort it out later," Kyril said soothingly. "Just put on my clothes and pretend to be me during breakfast."

"But if I'm you," Lina said, "who will you be? We can't both be you."

"I'll have to be Zora, I guess." Before either of the girls could say anything, he changed to Zora's shape, complete with long brown hair, got out of bed, dressed in the green robes, and tossed his own clothing to Lina. "Get dressed so we can eat breakfast. Aren't you hungry?"

Lina began to dress, fumbling with the unfamiliar clothing. Kyril moved to help her. "Yes. I'm starving!"

Zora tossed the green veil to Kyril as soon as he finished helping Lina. "Put this on. I hope *you're* not starving, because you won't be able to eat in public. We'll get a tray for you afterwards. We don't want anyone to notice us behaving differently."

"You're right." Kyril pinned the long brown hair and fastened the veil to it with a fair amount of dexterity, considering his gender. He draped the veil over his face, hiding it from view.

It wasn't perfect, but Zora doubted that anyone would be looking closely at *him*. She shook her head. "It's like a shell game," she sighed. "Now *none* of us is who we're supposed to be."

As far as Zora was concerned, breakfast was a nightmare. Kyril sat silently at the side table, where he was no help at all. But at least *he* wasn't making things worse. Lina had thrown herself enthusiastically into Kyril's role, and she spent the meal alternating between eating more food than Kyril normally did and flirting outrageously with Zora. Given that anything Zora wanted to say to Lina had to be said softly into her ear so that they wouldn't be overheard, she was afraid they were giving a horribly convincing portrayal of a pair of lovers.

Zora intended to drag 'Kyril' back to their rooms the minute that breakfast was over. Unfortunately, the king's Companions were in the hall, and at the end of the meal Lina joined them. They all went off together before Zora could stop them.

Zora's mouth dropped open, and she hastily forced it shut. *I can't believe she just did that...*

She rose to her feet and headed rapidly back to the Queen's bedchamber. Tempted as she was to start breaking every dish on the table, *she* had more self-respect than to throw a tantrum in public. 'Zora' followed close on her heels, and anyone they passed moved quickly out of their way. This included both the Shield-Bearer and Lady Esme, but Zora was too annoyed to care. She managed not to slam the door, but it was a near thing. When they were in the Queen's bedchamber with two doors between them and the guards in the hallway, she put a pillow over her face to muffle the sound and screamed.

"Don't be so hard on her," Kyril said. "All she wants is a day off—it's hard being Queen all the time."

"I know it is," Zora said through clenched teeth. "I've been Queen more than she has lately! But you don't see *me* running off and leaving everyone else to cover for me!"

"I guess that means you're the Queen again today." Kyril appeared to take that for granted.

And I'm getting very tired of being taken for granted. Kyril just assumes I'll do whatever Lina wants, and Lina thinks that because I can take her place, she can ignore her duties and the people who depend on her! Zora knew it was petty of her, but she was happy to tell him that *she* wasn't the only one stuck playing a part today.

"Well, *you* can't be the Queen," she said sweetly. "That would be blasphemy."

Kyril nodded, suddenly looking wary.

"That means you'll have to keep being Zora," she continued.

"*What?*"

"You can't be yourself," Zora pointed out, "because your wife has taken your place. There are three of us, and three people we're supposed to be. There can't be two of *you*, and if Zora suddenly goes missing, the priestesses will notice and make a fuss, especially because she's supposed to be attending the Queen all day. So, until your loving wife deigns to return your life, you'll have to be Zora." She smiled sweetly at him. "And you need to fix your veil. It's crooked."

Kyril stood unmoving in the middle of the room.

Zora sighed. "They'll be here for us in a few minutes. Don't panic. All you have to do is keep your mouth shut and follow me around all morning. With luck, she'll be back in time for the afternoon meditation."

Kyril opened his mouth, then closed it again. Zora turned away to put on the Queen's gown for the morning's court session. Behind her she could hear the rustling of cloth as Kyril struggled with his veil.

"Cheer up," she said consolingly. "You can do this. It's easier than being a wolf, and much easier than being an eagle."

"But I don't know how to act like a girl," Kyril said desperately. "Are you sure this is going to work?"

"It's not as if you really have to *convince* anyone you're a girl,"

Zora said. "Just copy the body language of the other priestesses, and don't make any unnecessary movements. As long as you don't try to talk, which you're not allowed to do anyway, you'll be just fine. No one pays much attention to Zora, anyway. As long as there's a person the right size and shape under the veils, nobody will notice anything."

"I hope you're right," Kyril said. "How do I look?"

Zora turned and surveyed him critically. "The shape is pretty good. I didn't know you'd paid that much attention to the shape."

"It's my wife's body," Kyril pointed out, still struggling to get the veil straight. "I *have* spent a certain amount of time looking at it."

"Here, let me give you a hand with that." Zora twisted a lock of hair just above Kyril's—Zora's—face around her finger, and pinned the veil firmly to the resultant loop of hair. "There. You'll do fine—probably better than I will. I've spent so much time switching back and forth that half the time I can't even remember what I'm supposed to answer to." She sighed. "I just want to be *one* person."

"Me too," Kyril said.

"Talk to your wife!" Zora snapped. "I *still* can't believe she did that! Does she even know the names of your Companions?"

Kyril shrugged. "I have no idea." He smiled fondly, and said, "I'm sure she'll manage. She's really very smart." Zora was reminded once again of why his mother called his condition 'Year-King idiocy.'

"At least she can't go beyond the boundary stones," Zora reminded herself. It was some consolation.

That consolation failed in the late afternoon. Zora was sitting in the garden with her usual assortment of attendants when a group of white-faced young men returned with the 'king.' Noting Lady Esme's rabidly curious expression, Zora dismissed all of her attendants except 'Zora.' Unfortunately, there was nothing she could do about the cat that had followed the Companions and was now curled up under a nearby bench. It wasn't one she had seen before, and as far as she knew none of the Companions had a cat. *I hope that's Catriona, rather than some shape-changer I don't know about.*

"What happened?" she asked quietly once everyone else was out of earshot. Lina was sitting unconcernedly on the bench next to Zora, but the king's Companions were still standing stiffly in front of them.

The Companions all looked at one another, obviously wishing that someone else would tell her. Finally one of them blurted out, "He crossed the border."

Zora heard a gasp from the veiled form standing behind her and wasn't surprised. This was bad, and Kyril knew it. If a Year-King could cross the border and leave the land, it meant—or at least strongly implied—that he wasn't a proper Year-King.

But an even more dismaying question passed through Zora's mind. *What does it mean when the* Queen *can leave the land?* At least the grim-faced group around her wasn't considering that question— unless Lina was...

"I don't see what you're making such a fuss about," Lina/Kyril said. "All I did was ride a little bit beyond a rock, and the whole lot of you pitched a fit."

"Ride?" Zora grabbed at the word. "Is it simply that the horse crossed the border, or did the king actually dismount?"

"Considering the way they all charged after me, surrounded my horse, and forced us straight back past the boundary stone," the 'king' replied in disgust, "I couldn't have dismounted if I'd tried! Which I didn't. I just wanted to enjoy a ride and not have to be on display all the time!"

I may be able to salvage this after all. "So," she said aloud, "it was actually the *horse* that crossed the border, rather than the king. Given that the horse is not bound to the land, I cannot see that any blame attaches to it. Of course, the king should have had it under better control, but I don't see that any actual wrong was done."

The Companions looked torn between relief that the Queen was not blaming them—or having hysterics—and dismay that the king had come so close to leaving the land.

"In the future," Zora commanded, "don't ride that close to the border."

"We won't, Lady," the Companions assured her fervently, in ragged unison.

"And I see no reason to mention this to anyone else," Zora

added.

"No, Lady." The unison was perfect this time.

"Very well," Zora said. "You may leave us now."

The young men bowed and departed hastily, leaving Zora, Kyril, and Lina. The cat followed them, perhaps to foster the illusion that it belonged to one of them.

"Do you realize," Kyril/Zora's voice came softly from under the veil, "that none of us are in our proper bodies?"

Zora found that only mildly annoying at the moment. She had more serious concerns. "You did that deliberately, didn't you?" she demanded of Lina.

"Yes." Lina glared at her from behind Kyril's face. "I wanted to see if I could leave the land—and I can! You can't stop me! You can't keep me here—and you make a better Queen than I do, anyway."

"You're forgetting your husband," Zora pointed out, glad that Kyril was veiled and had lapsed back into silence. *He'd probably support the wretched girl!* "What you did today reflected on *him*, not on you. Now his Companions not only don't trust him but they're also afraid he's not a proper king. *And* he got stuck with being Zora all day!" She glared right back at Lina. "I think that's a rotten thing to do to somebody who loves you as much as he does."

"It's not as if he *really* loves me," Lina said sulkily. "It's just the spell—you know that. Lady Esme says that *she* may have to worry about whether a suitor loves her or her money, but I don't have to worry about that because I know nobody really loves me."

With everything she forgets, she still remembers that, Zora thought in disgust. *To be fair, however, Lady Esme probably repeated that until a rock would be unable to forget it.*

"And Lady Esme has been such a good friend—and so concerned for your well-being," Zora said sarcastically. "She was poisoning you—physically, and apparently mentally as well! If you'll just cast your mind back to when Kyril first came to court, you can see for yourself that he loved you long before he was chosen."

"Did you really?" Lina looked longingly up at Kyril's veiled form.

Zora rose quickly to her feet. "Let's move this indoors to your room," she said. "People may not be able to hear us, but this is starting to look strange to anyone watching, and there's bound to be more than one person looking out a window." *And anyone who saw this thinks they just saw the Queen fighting with the Year-King, which is probably considered a bad omen.*

They reconvened in the Queen's bedchamber, having locked the doors to both the antechamber and the bedroom.

"This is getting completely out of hand," Zora said. "It's past time we all change back to our own bodies and start dealing with our respective lives."

"No," Lina said firmly. "I don't want to change back! Do you have any idea what it's like to be stuck sitting in court, day after day, listening to people complain?"

"Of course I do," Zora shot back. "I've been doing it for you for *how* long now?"

"But you can't make me change back, can you?" Lina challenged her.

"Technically, no, she can't." The answer came from Kyril, who was still in Zora's shape, although he had dropped the green veil on the cosmetics table as soon as they had entered the bedchamber.

"He's right," Zora said calmly. "As far as we know, in order to force anyone *into* a particular shape you have to be a shape-changer *and* have magic. But there are certainly ways to encourage someone to change out of the shape they're presently in."

"Like what?"

"Well," Zora said, hoping that this would be a good example, "when Kassie was chosen instead of me to be priestess of the Earth Mother, I thought the Goddess didn't want me, and I was really upset." She realized as she spoke that she still found the memory upsetting, particularly the sense of desolation she had felt then and was suddenly feeling again now.

Do they also serve who do nothing but listen to the ones who serve the Goddess whine about being chosen? First Kassie and now Lina—don't they realize how lucky they are? Why in Earth did the Goddess choose them instead of me? I wanted to be chosen! What is so wrong with me? Am I really so much less fit for her service than they are?

"I couldn't deal with what was happening, and I didn't want to think about it, so I turned into a fish."

"A real fish?" Lina asked incredulously.

Kyril laughed. "It's not quite as crazy as it sounds. There's a big lake at Eagle's Rest, and sometimes a group of us change into fish and play hide and seek. The biggest problem is that fish are cold-blooded, so you can get very cold if you're not careful or you stay in the water too long."

"Also, if you take the shape of an animal with a small brain," Zora added, "you lose some of your reasoning ability. That's why I did it then—I didn't *want* to think."

"That sounds stupid," Lina remarked. "If you stayed a fish long enough, would you forget that you weren't supposed to be one?"

"Actually, yes," Kyril said. "That happened to my mother once. She spent six days as a fish before my father found her."

"What did he do?"

"The same thing he did to me when he found me," Zora replied. "All you have to do with a changer in fish-shape is take her out of the water. I can assure you that not being able to breathe will make you change shape in a hurry!"

"But that won't work on a human shape," Lina said smugly.

"There are things you can do to a changer in human shape," Zora pointed out. "Push one off a cliff and he'll change to something that can fly. Dump him in the water and he'll change to something that can swim..."

"But those are drastic measures," Kyril assured her hastily. "We don't do that to beginners like you."

"Kyril," Zora said, "you are not helping. Do you really want to try to convince the priestesses that you're Zora? And how long do you think the Goddess is going to put up with this? I definitely got the impression she was not happy about your being in the Queen's chapel this afternoon."

Lina gasped. "You took a *man* into the Queen's chapel?"

"I thought the Goddess might be more understanding than the priestesses," Zora replied. "And it's not as if you left me with much choice. Zora and the Queen *always* spend the meditation period in the chapel together."

Lina shrugged. "So start leaving her outside with the other priestesses."

Zora looked her straight in the eyes. "*You* start going to the chapel alone. You're the one who's supposed to be there."

"Not in this shape, I'm not," Lina said smugly.

"I've never told you about my mother, have I?"

"Zora, no!" Kyril said urgently.

"I was just thinking of the first time I changed shape," Zora said, regarding him with mock innocence. "Surely you know the story." *Does he really think I'm going to tell Lina that my mother is her cousin and I'm her Heiress? I don't trust her enough for that.* It was a sobering realization.

"Of course," Kyril said quickly. "You turned into a cat, and she dipped you in the fountain. Cats hate water, so you turned back into a baby again."

"Precisely," Zora said. "All one has to do is convince the recalcitrant changer that there are disadvantages to her current shape." She let her eyes drop from Kyril's face to trace a line down the center of his body.

Kyril shifted uneasily, crossing his legs. "Lina. Please change back. For me? Please?"

Lina sighed. "It was so wonderful to be free..."

"I'll teach you more shapes," Kyril said hastily. "I'll teach you to fly—"

"Very well," Lina said. "Teach me how to be Zora."

"I will," Kyril said.

"No, I mean teach me to do it *now.*"

Kyril looked frustrated. "I don't know how to teach you that one right now," he said. "Zora is a created shape, not a natural one, so it's much harder to learn—and I'm not even sure how you learned *my* shape."

"Lady of Earth!" Zora gasped, suddenly realizing what had happened. "She learned it the same way I learned cat-shape. She slept next to you."

"But that's not normal." Kyril frowned, and Lina started laughing.

"You mean there's a *normal* way to learn shape-changing?"

"Yes," Kyril said when Zora remained silent, still stunned by what she had just realized. "Normally, a changer learns a bird-shape first, usually by falling off something during childhood. "You two are the only ones I've ever met who learned to change differently."

"And we both learned the same way," Zora whispered. "Just the two of us, out of all the students your father has trained..."

"Well," Kyril said, starting to look uneasy himself. "Your true shapes are identical."

"How identical?" Zora asked urgently.

"Right down to the last freckle identical," Kyril said. "You don't see it because you only see yourself as a reflection, but you two are more identical than Kyrina and Kyrilla."

"Who are they?" Lina asked.

"My two youngest sisters. They're identical twins."

"That's more identical than we should be." Zora frowned. "I wonder what was happening here when we were babies."

"You were born almost four months apart," Kyril said impatiently. "It's not as if they could have confused you then!"

"Too bad," Lina said. "If we'd been switched at birth, then you really would be Queen!"

I don't want to think about that right now. I'm afraid I know how they could have switched us.

"Lina, just change back," Kyril said. "Please."

"I don't want to." Lina wasn't shouting, but she did sound determined. Very determined.

"We don't have much time before you have to appear for the evening meal," Zora pointed out. "And Kyril's not all that good at pretending to be a girl. For that matter, you don't quite have the right body language for the king—and they'll be watching *him* very closely after today!" She glared at Lina. "You need to change back now and let him be himself, because *he* needs to repair the damage to his reputation."

"But the Companions won't talk," Lina protested. "They said so."

Even Kyril gave her a pitying look at that. "This is a court, Lina. People always talk. And even if the Companions don't say anything, they're going to be uneasy around me for a while. The sooner I can go back to acting normal, the sooner they'll think what happened today was the horse's fault. It's important to convince them that I'm a proper Year-King."

"Do you really think anyone cares?" Lina snapped.

"The people care," Zora said. "It's important to them that he be a good king and that you be a good Queen. Things go well when you are—and they can go catastrophically bad when you're not! Haven't you *read* any of the histories in the temple?" she snapped at Lina. "I don't care how you do it, but you change back *now!*"

"I'm sure she's doing her best," Kyril said soothingly. "Just calm down."

"Don't tell me to calm down!" Zora snarled between gritted teeth. "And while you're at it, give me my clothes back!" She changed to the brunette Zora shape and began to shed Lina's clothes. "And change back to your own shape!"

"She can't force you to, can she?" Lina asked anxiously.

"I don't know of any way she can physically force me to change," Kyril said, peeling off the green over-robe, "but believe me when I say she can make our lives a living hell if I don't. What she didn't learn about being bossy from her mother, she learned from mine." He went to the corner where the chest that held his clothing was, changed to his own shape, and began to dress.

"There are always ways to encourage someone to change back to their natural shape," Zora said. "Remember what my mother did to me." She grabbed the green overtunic she wore as Zora and pulled it on. Was it loose enough for what she had in mind? Yes, this should work.

"I think that was cruel of her," Lina said pettishly.

"Well, it's not as if I was old enough to understand words at the time," Zora pointed out, "so talking to me wouldn't have helped." She looked at Lina, still in the shape of the Year-King. "You really need to change back," she said, moving around the bed to stand right in front of her.

"But I can't—I don't know how," Lina protested, "and you know that dunking me in a pool wouldn't work."

"Not at all," Zora agreed. "We don't need something that will make you not want to be a cat. What we need is something that will make you not want to be male." Out of the corner of her eye she could see Kyril wince even before she started to move. Lina, being new to the male shape, didn't even notice as Zora's knee came up, much less block or twist away before it hit her squarely between the legs. She dropped to the floor, screaming.

Zora fled to the antechamber, making sure her veil was in place, as one of the guards pounded frantically on the door. She unlocked and opened the door before the guard could kick it in. The woman ran past her, ignoring the veiled green figure, as everyone did, and paused in the bedroom doorway, hand on her sword hilt, and looked about, presumably for an intruder. Kyril stood quietly, keeping his hands in plain sight, but Lina was hidden from view behind the bed.

"Lady, are you all right?" the guard asked anxiously. "I heard a scream. What happened?"

To Zora's relief, the head that appeared from behind the bed was Lina's, and she had sense enough to keep her body, still dressed in Kyril's clothes, out of sight.

"It's nothing," she said quickly. "Just a muscle spasm. It surprised me, that's all." When the guard still stood there, she added, "You may return to your post."

The guard bowed and returned to the hallway. Zora closed both doors behind her and returned to the bedroom.

"Well, *that* worked," Lina said, dragging herself up with the aid of the bed. "I hurt in places I don't even *have* anymore."

"I hope you can remember how you changed back," Zora said, "because I really don't want to do that again."

"I don't think any of us does," Kyril remarked. "Is it time for supper yet? I'm starving."

"Me too," Lina admitted. "I probably got more exercise today than I have for the past year."

"Changing shape makes you hungry, too," Kyril explained. "You'll feel better once you've eaten something."

CHAPTER SEVENTEEN

Zora couldn't eat with them, due to the fact that she had to stay veiled in public. She considered going down to the temple to eat with the priestesses but decided not to. She was afraid they might have heard about the boundary incident, and she didn't want to be questioned about it. By the time she got a chance to eat, alone in the antechamber after the Queen and king had retired for the night, she was both extremely hungry and almost too anxious to eat. She forced the food down, knowing that she would need the strength for what she planned to do next.

After locking the door to the hall, she slipped quietly into the bedchamber. Lina and Kyril were both sound asleep, which didn't surprise her at all, given the day they'd had. Slipping out of her clothes and laying them out on the chest nearest the window so she could dress in a hurry if she had to, she perched on the windowsill, changed into bird-shape, flew across the garden and then followed the river north. Just inside the boundary, near the stone marker she remembered from her journey here in the late winter, she checked for any signs of people who might see her. Finding none, she changed back into human shape and walked up to the boundary stone.

This is it, she thought. *Time to see if I can cross the boundary now.* She took a deep breath for courage and stepped forward.

It was like walking into a wall of semi-solid water, except it wasn't wet and she could still breathe. It was cold, however, much colder than the air on her bare skin had been a second before, and while it—whatever it was—had enough flexibility not to hurt her, it was too solid for her to proceed. She looked down at her bare feet and discovered that they were planted firmly inside Diadem.

I guess I still can't cross the boundary, she thought, easing back. *In fact, this is worse than when I first got here. The wall may not be as hard—or maybe it's just that I'm not running at it—but it feels much colder. Lina can cross it, while I haven't been able to since the moment I arrived here. I think that's probably a bad sign. For Lina, at least. I just hope Kyril can't cross now. Of course, he probably isn't going to try.*

The air now held only the usual night chill, but Zora still felt cold. She considered changing to wolf-shape to warm up, but remembered in time that wolves were not native to this area. Fortunately, foxes were, and they also had warm fur, so she changed into a fox.

I can't cross the boundary in human shape. Can I cross it as an animal? She walked up to the stone again. Standing next to it, she leaned her head forward. Whatever had stopped her before was still there, and she recoiled, sneezing violently. Her nose was cold, and running her tongue over it failed to warm it.

I guess the Goddess really *wants me here. What scares me is that she doesn't seem to care whether* Lina *is here or not.*

Before the chill could take over her entire body, fur and all, she turned and ran back toward the palace as fast as her four legs could carry her, trying not to think about the questions that circled relentlessly through her mind. *If I can't cross the boundary, and Lina can, which of us is really supposed to be Queen? What is happening to me? Am I changing, or was I always like this? I remember not being able to cross back over the boundary when I first got here, but I expected that to be temporary, until I found out what the Goddess wanted. So what is it that the Goddess wants from me?* She was so caught up in her thoughts that she didn't notice the cat until it knocked her over and pinned her down on her side.

As Zora struggled to catch the breath that had been knocked out of her, she studied the cat. Aside from its initial attack, it was not being aggressive, and she was pretty sure that it was a larger version of the one she had seen follow the Companions into the garden that afternoon. It was also heavier than a natural cat its size should be. Zora was much more solid than she looked in fox-shape, and it had used the precise amount of force needed to knock her over without hurting her. Not only was the cat obviously a changer, but whoever it was, it knew that Zora was one as well.

The cat let her up and gave her a nudge in the direction of the city, and Zora allowed herself to be herded to the city walls. At the walls, the cat stopped, shrunk to normal size for a housecat, and waited for Zora to match her shape. They went up the wall together and across the roofs to the compound that held the training yard and the guards' barracks. Zora wasn't surprised to find herself following the cat first into Catriona's office, and then into her quarters behind the office.

"You promised me that you would stay safely with the rest of the priestesses," Catriona reproved her as she returned to human shape.

"You were there this afternoon," Zora replied, returning to human shape and wrapping herself in the blanket Catriona handed her.

Catriona dressed quickly, then pulled bread and cheese out of a cupboard and cut some for both of them. Zora was so hungry she had to remind herself to chew the food before swallowing it.

"I heard the Companions say that the king crossed the boundary," Catriona said, "but that doesn't explain why you decided that you had to try it."

"It wasn't the king," Zora said bleakly. "It was the Queen."

Catriona gaped at her. "That's impossible!"

"Obviously not." Zora sighed. "I did what I could to minimize the incident, and Kyril says he'll spend more time with the Companions and try to act normal and reassure them. But Lina shouldn't have been able to cross the boundary—even on horseback. So I went out to see if I could cross it—and I can't, not even in animal shape."

Catriona was momentarily speechless, so Zora took another helping of bread and cheese. She needed the food now, and she suspected that what was to come would be even worse. She thought of various things she had heard during the past months. Lina's "If we'd been switched at birth, then you really would be Queen!" contrasted with Kyril's comment that nobody would confuse a newborn with a baby almost four months old. *But was I born in Diadem?* Zora wondered. *Druscilla was here at least part of the time she was pregnant with me, not at Eagle's Rest as I thought when I was growing up. And she vowed me—or her daughter?—to the Goddess when she was afraid she was going to lose the baby. Akila told me once that it was one of those 'please, let my baby live' bargains.* And Zora suddenly remembered something that she had known for years but never really thought about.

"Druscilla spent the last four months of her pregnancy flat on her back in bed," she said aloud. "Akila told me that. But the temple records say that she was present to witness the birth of the new Heiress." She looked up and met Catriona's eyes. "Who took her place?"

Catriona winced. "I did," she admitted. "I was in Diadem with my mother when she was arranging the grain shipment from Lord Ranulf's lands." She stirred up the fire and stared at it, as if looking into the past. "I was thirteen and the family failure. I wasn't as good a changer as everyone else, and, despite my family's best efforts to teach me, I had virtually none of our father's magical ability."

Another memory flashed through Zora's mind. *I may not have much of my family's magical ability, but I have enough to see your true shape no matter what you shift into.* Catriona had said that to her last spring.

"My sister Ertha and I were put into guard training that spring," Catriona continued. "She hated it—she was a mage. I liked it, and I was actually *good* at it. It was the first time in my life I'd been good at something, and it made it easier for me to change shapes, too— Uncle Ranulf had been training me in that."

"Did you know that Druscilla was pregnant?" Zora asked.

"Yes. Mother, Ertha, and I all knew. Ertha and I were still at Eagle's Rest when Briam came home after Druscilla was dragged back to Diadem. Because the Queen was so sick with her pregnancy, Mother was working with Druscilla to coordinate the food shipments and storage. It was going well at first. Druscilla was over the worst of the morning sickness and not really showing, and she was very good at dressing to hide the changes to her figure. Also, she was spending most of her time at the house Lord Ranulf bought for us, because that's where the work was being done. Then one day she started bleeding, and my mother put her to bed. We could have worked around that, but the Queen went into labor that evening and they sent for Druscilla."

"And Druscilla couldn't get up and witness the birth without the risk of losing her baby."

"Not to mention having everyone find out she was with child," Catriona added. "I wasn't very good at copying a human shape, and

I didn't have time to learn. My mother and sister had to stay and take care of Druscilla, so my sister did a force-change spell on me."

"Like the one you did to get rid of my collar?"

"I'm surprised you remember that."

"It was excruciatingly painful," Zora pointed out. "That's probably why the memory stuck."

"You're right about its being painful." Catriona winced at the memory. "Ertha changed my shape to match Druscilla's. I was the one who witnessed the birth of the Queen's child, and I was the one who took her out on the balcony and presented her to the people." She smiled at the memory. "I thought we'd both go deaf from the cheering. She was such a beautiful baby, and so good..."

"What happened next?" Zora asked when Catriona had been silent for several minutes, apparently lost in her memories.

Catriona sighed. "I spent the next few months changing from body to body—Druscilla when she had to be at court, myself for guard training, and Druscilla for morning and evening rituals."

"But you can't do the rituals," Zora protested.

"True," Catriona agreed, "but the Queen was still too ill to do them, so I learned the words and did them with the baby in my arms. Nothing *else* went wrong, so I figured the Goddess found that acceptable. After about six weeks the Queen recovered enough to take over the rituals again, and two weeks after that was the Choosing." She frowned. "The king that year was a prince, a younger son. There was speculation that he made the choice, not the Goddess."

"You mean he thought he could marry the Queen and take over?" Zora asked incredulously.

"If you don't know about the Sacrifice," Catriona pointed out, "it's not that crazy an idea. And while he was publicly devoted to the Queen, none of us liked the way he treated the Heiress. He kept bringing her playthings small enough that she choked on them, and he fed her food that was fine for him but made her sick because she was too young for it. So 'Druscilla' and the Shield-Bearer got together and persuaded the Queen to let Druscilla and the baby stay at Lord Ranulf's house, where the king would have no reason to go. The Queen was still doing the rituals, so we finally had something approaching peace—all we had to do was keep the guards and the baby's wet nurse confused and away from Druscilla."

"So you had to be Druscilla in front of everyone else and make sure they didn't see the real Druscilla."

"It wasn't as easy as you're making it sound," Catriona protested.

"I *know* it's not easy," Zora sighed. "I've been switching bodies like a pea in a shell game, and this morning Kyril got dragged into the mess as well."

"What?" Catriona looked appalled.

Zora sighed. "I was the Queen, the Queen was the king, so he had to be me—there really wasn't any choice."

Catriona shook her head. "If anyone but the king impersonated one of the priestesses, the Goddess would probably strike him dead."

"Probably," Zora agreed. "I'll have to point that out to Lina before she tries this again. But getting back to when we were born, *what happened?*"

"I've got to give Druscilla credit. It's not easy to give birth without making any noise, but she managed it. My mother was a competent midwife, and my sister had healing abilities, but Druscilla lost a lot of blood and was sick for weeks after the birth. And her milk didn't come in properly, so she couldn't feed the baby."

"And you couldn't bring in another wet nurse or expect the one you had not to notice the difference between a newborn and a baby who was nearly four months old..." Zora shuddered. *I was one of those babies.* "Another force-change spell?"

Catriona nodded. "Ertha did it, but nobody had ever done the spell on such young children before. As far as we could tell, it permanently changed the true shape of the newborn."

"Kyril said that Lina and I are absolutely identical, even more identical than his twin sisters. That's why, isn't it?"

Catriona nodded. "Once Ertha did the force-change, the only way to tell you two apart was by temperament."

Temperament? Oh. "The infant would be physically fragile and would need extra food to catch up with her older sister. Didn't the wet nurse notice?"

"She said that some babies went through fussy periods," Catriona said. "You know how people tend to see what they expect to see."

Zora nodded. "But once the babies were identical, how did you keep from mixing them up?"

After a long pause, Catriona admitted, "We don't know that we *didn't* mix them up."

Zora was silent, trying to absorb the implications. *I was one of those babies, and nobody knows which one. For all we know, I could be the Queen—it would certainly explain why I can't cross the border and Lina can. But I wasn't the Queen at the Choosing and I am not the one the Year-King married... Goddess, what do I do now?*

What she actually did was to dress in a spare guard uniform, put on the hooded cloak that Catriona handed her, and allow Catriona to escort her back to the garden below the Queen's window. She changed briefly to cat-shape to climb up the wall and through the window, then changed back to human and collapsed into her bed.

Lina was still herself the next morning, but she seemed to sleepwalk through the morning ritual. Zora wasn't in much better shape. Even a large breakfast was no substitute for several shape-changes and not enough sleep. Fortunately there was no court that morning, so the Queen went to the garden to mope over her needlework, attended by her ladies, and, of course, Zora.

Less than an hour later, Lina rose from her seat next to Lady Esme, dropped her needlework unheeded to the ground, and fled the garden, sobbing hysterically. Zora hurried after her, but Lina had enough of a head start that Zora heard the comments of the people she had passed.

"Not again!"

"I thought she was over this..."

"She was doing so well for a while..."

By the time Zora reached Lina's bedroom, Lina was facedown on the bed, sobbing into a pillow. She raised her head to glare at Zora. "Do you know what Lady Esme said to me?"

"Something nasty, I'm sure," Zora said, "but she has a wide variety of nasty things to say. Which one was it this time?"

"She said that I shouldn't be cross with the king for going off with his Companions...that he'd be dead soon enough, anyway, so I should try not to be so attached to him." Lina gulped. "And she added that I should make sure not to get with child, because if I had a child, the Sacrifice would go on for another generation. And then she said that if I was with child, she could make me a potion to get rid of it!'"

"Well, we know she can do that easily enough," Zora agreed. "That's why neither of us eats or drinks anything she could have drugged."

"She says I should die with Kyril," Lina sobbed. "She says it's the only way to end the Sacrifice."

"I have heard her say *that* before," Zora said. "I should have warned you—I think she's trying to persuade you to commit suicide."

"During the ritual?" Lina looked shocked. "Is she insane?"

"Yes," Zora said sadly. "I really think she is."

And I'm really scared, but I don't dare confide in Lina. She'd love the idea that she might not be the Queen's daughter.

By flatly refusing to change back to her true shape, Zora managed to persuade Lina to remain Queen. She also warned Kyril that the Goddess was likely to be angry if *he* imitated the Queen again, and had seemingly casual conversations with Lina about how Kyril would need all his energy for the shape-changing practice necessary to survive the coming Sacrifice. But her efforts were successful, and Zora started to feel things might work out after all.

Kyril reported that he had progressed upstream to the area right under the waterfall and was choosing the best place to go into the water beneath it. Lina was still nervous, even though Zora repeatedly told her that no, Kyril was not just saying that to reassure her.

"He really *can* survive this," Zora said firmly one afternoon as they sat together in the chapel. "His father did, after all."

"What if the Goddess wants him to die?" Lina asked. "Lady Esme talks as if his death is a certainty."

"Lady Esme is trying to persuade you to join him," Zora pointed out, "which you are not at all likely to do if you actually expect him to live. *I* expect him to live, and I've known him longer than you have."

"Could *you* survive it?" Lina asked intently.

"If I had the chance to practice the way he has been doing, yes, I could," Zora said. She hoped this would be enough reassurance so that Lina would stop her near-constant fussing over the matter.

"So you could take his place, and he could pretend to be you."

Oh, Lady, not again. "You've forgotten that we discussed this before. And Kyril would never agree to it, even if I did," Zora said firmly.

"Why not?" Lina asked. "Do you think he doesn't love me enough?"

"Lina, you have *got* to stop listening to Lady Esme!" Zora said in exasperation. "He loves you, and he loved you even before the Choosing, which means it's not just part of his being the Year-King. He went to the ritual that morning deliberately, despite your attempt to keep him away—he wanted the Goddess to choose him so he wouldn't have to watch you with another man all summer! He knew what he was getting into. His father told him about the Choosing and the Sacrifice before he came here. Kyril knows what to do, and he has to be the one to do it."

"Is it really that important?" Lina asked desperately.

"Yes. It is *absolutely* that important," Zora replied firmly. "He is the Year-King, you are the Queen, and you both must do what the Goddess wishes." She patted Lina's arm. "Don't worry so much. I think the Goddess really is trying to end the Sacrifice—or at least the deaths. Kyril's father says that any time there's a shape-changer at the Spring ritual, the Goddess will choose him. He even says a man can be chosen more than once—he came back again years later, and he said he could still hear the Calling, even though he was a wolf at the time."

That got a giggle from Lina. "That would have been an interesting marriage."

"Probably a bit more than the people here could accept," Zora agreed.

To her great relief, Lina appeared to give up the idea of having Zora take Kyril's place. *Not that I would do it, but not being nagged about it gives me one less thing to deal with.*

CHAPTER EIGHTEEN

The morning of the Sacrifice was a nightmare. Zora woke up convinced that she had forgotten something vitally important, but she couldn't think of what it was.

Lina was hysterical with fear that Kyril would die. Kyril was the calmest of the three of them, but that wasn't saying much. When his attempts to soothe Lina failed, he dragged Zora into the bedchamber to help him.

Zora collapsed onto the clothing chest at the foot of the bed and put her face in her hands. *It's too early for this*, she thought. *The sun is barely at the horizon and my eyes are hardly open.*

"Zora," Kyril insisted, "do something!"

"*You* do something," Zora shot back. "She's *your* wife, and I'm tired of having to cope with *everything!*" Then she considered Kyril's past efforts to fix things. "On second thought," she told him, "go away. Get some breakfast—you'll need the energy, and having food in your stomach will make the drug less effective. Your father warned you about being drugged for the Sacrifice, remember?"

Kyril glared at her. "You might have some faith in me!" he said before he slammed out of the room.

"Great." Zora sighed. "Lina, I know it's impossible to *be* calm, but at least try to *pretend* you are. Right now everyone who sees the king will think you had a fight with him—on the morning of the Sacrifice..."

Lina sighed. "I didn't think of that..."

Do you ever *think?* Zora wondered, but managed to bite back the words. "We just have to get through the ritual today," she said aloud. "Everything else can wait until after the Sacrifice."

"But as soon as the Sacrifice is over, they'll shut me up in the temple for a week!" Lina protested. "That's why there's a cell for me down there, so I can be in seclusion for my first week of mourning." She frowned. "I wonder where they're going to put you."

The crypt where I woke up that first day sounds really good right now. At least I'd finally get a chance to rest!

"I have no idea," Zora said aloud. "We'll have to wait and see."

Several hours later Zora was still waiting, but she was waiting on the dais where the Sacrifice was about to take place. It was located next to the wall on the north terrace, above the waterfall. The floor of the dais was level with the top of the wall, making it easy for the king to step off it. Zora stood at the end of a diagonal line of priestesses, all of them robed and veiled. Lady Esme, who stood next to the eldest priestess, was wearing an ornate dress of black velvet so long it dragged on the ground, and she was sniffling into a handkerchief, while everyone else made a point of ignoring her. Zora was annoyed with Esme's behavior—not to mention the ridiculous affectation of wearing black velvet in the summer heat. *I hope she faints.* Across from the priestesses the Year-King's Companions stood in a line. Like the priestesses, they were arrayed by age, with the youngest nearest the water. The guards on the platform all wore dress uniforms, and they were lined up behind the priestesses and the Companions.

Kyril and Lina arrived, escorted by the Shield-Bearer. Today she was in her role as Head of the Queen's Guard, and she carried an ornate ceremonial sword. She wore a dress uniform even fancier than those of the rest of the guards, while Kyril and Lina had been dressed for the ritual in long, loose wheat-colored robes and small matching crowns. They had presumably been drugged, although Zora didn't know that for certain because the other priestesses had taken her away to change into a different gown for the ceremony while the Queen was dressing. Zora hoped Kyril wasn't drugged too heavily, but she thanked the Goddess that Lina, for whatever reason, was subdued instead of hysterical.

The three of them walked through the assembled people, ascended the dais, and faced the crowd. The Queen drew in a deep breath and began to speak, addressing Kyril. "For answering our call, we thank thee. For thy service to us and ours, we thank thee. Thou hast done well."

Her voice should really be louder, Zora thought, *if the people are supposed to hear her. But at least she's saying the right words. And she's not sobbing hysterically, which I'll bet most of the priestesses expected. They probably gave her as much of the drug as she could take without passing out during the ritual.*

A young girl came up the steps of the dais and handed Kyril a large sheaf of wheat. "Receive the fruits thy life provides," the girl said, bowing low to him before returning to her place in the crowd.

Kyril stood there, clutching the wheat, as the Queen continued to speak. "Now thy time is come. Now do we release thee. We loose our claim upon thee and yield thee to Water, the Blood of Earth, Mother of us all, from whence we come and to which we return. Let that which binds thee to us be severed." Zora heard a quaver in the Queen's voice and hoped that nobody else noticed it.

The Shield-Bearer unsheathed the sword, raised the blade high and then whipped it downward in an arc between Kyril and Lina. It didn't touch either of them—it didn't even pass close to either of them—but Zora could feel it sever the bond which tied Kyril to Lina. *And to me? Why in Earth am I feeling this?*

Lina obviously felt it. She looked pale and she was starting to shiver. The Shield-Bearer's sword was still held out so that it blocked Kyril from everyone else. She murmured something in Kyril's ear, too softly for Zora to catch the words, but it must have been instructions, for Kyril bowed to the Queen, and took three steps backward.

The third step carried him over the edge of the wall and out of sight. Zora listened for a splash over the noise of the waterfall, even knowing that she wouldn't be able to hear it. *Goddess, please, let him be all right.*

Everyone on the dais, however, could hear what happened next. "No!" Lady Esme cried out. "You promised!" Before anyone else could move, she darted forward, holding her skirts with one hand and grabbing Lina's arm with the other. She pulled her to the edge of the dais and tried to shove her over the edge. Lina struggled to break free, but both of them went over.

Zora didn't hesitate to dive after them. She pushed downward off the edge of the wall to give her extra speed so she could reach them before they hit the water—and the rocks. She knew she had to knock Lina clear of the worst of the rocks if the girl was to have any chance of surviving.

She went straight down, through the air beside the waterfall, splashed by the spray, and caught them only a few yards above the water. She struck Esme's arm, breaking her grip on Lina, and pushed Lina away from the waterfall as hard as she could. This had the effect of pushing Esme into it, but Zora didn't much care.

The water closed over her head. Lina had been knocked clear of the rocks, but Zora landed among them, collecting scrapes and bruises as she worked her way clear. *It's a good thing I was here the first day of swimming practice. At least I remember how I got out of the rocks before.*

She suppressed her instinctive desire to turn into a fish. Lina didn't know any water-breathing shapes, so Zora needed to be something that could get Lina's head out of the water and keep it there. She blew out her breath to get further below the surface so nobody watching from above could possibly see her, made herself small enough to get out of her clothing, and then changed into a dolphin.

It wasn't a shape that she'd had much practice with, given that the lake at home was fresh water and dolphins lived in the ocean, but she had seen pictures in a bestiary, and both she and Kyril had experimented briefly with the shape. It had some interesting abilities.

In the water below the waterfall, the shape's hearing made finding the human thrashing about easy. *That's the good thing about this shape. Nothing else would be able to tell the difference between human motion and turbulent water.* She positioned her body underneath Lina's and pushed up to the surface. Once there she supported Lina while they both gasped for breath. When she twisted to see how Lina was doing, however, she was astonished to see Kyril clinging to her.

For a moment she simply floated, letting the current take them both downstream, and then she realized what had happened. Lina had changed shape, but she had changed to the only other shape she knew. Kyril's.

They were not alone in the river. Something larger than a fish was coming downriver from the waterfall, and another dolphin was leaping upriver toward them.

The dolphin, who had to be Kyril, reached them first, and Lina promptly launched herself from Zora to him. As soon as she flung her arms around him, the dolphin turned and swam rapidly downstream, while Zora stared after them in horror. *I can't catch up with them in time, and I can't force Lina to change to back even if I could catch them!* If people saw 'Kyril' being borne downstream by a dolphin, however, they would take it as a sign of divine favor. *At least I hope so.*

But the Goddess needs her High Priestess, and the people of Diadem need their Queen. I really hope you want me, Lady, because I'm all you have left. Zora dove to the bottom of the river and shifted back to her true shape, completing the change just before something grabbed her and dragged her up to the surface and onto the land. At least now she looked like Lina, and she silently prayed that was what the Goddess wanted.

She lay prone on the ground, trying to get her breathing back to normal. It helped that dolphins were air breathers, so she didn't have to cough up water out of her lungs. She didn't have the energy to lift her head yet, but she was able to breathe, and nothing seemed to be broken. She felt cloth being draped over her body. It was wet and cold, but at least it kept her from being naked. She opened her eyes and saw that it was a guard's dress cape, and that the person who had dragged her out of the water was Catriona, who was still wearing the rest of her dress uniform. As Zora became aware of her surroundings, she realized she was on the beach at the edge of King's Cove, the very place she had been the first day of spring training. *Talk about going full circle...*

"Did you jump in after me?" It came out as a whisper, but Catriona heard.

"Yes, of course I did," she replied promptly.

That's right. Catriona is supposed to be my bodyguard—or maybe my sister's, depending on which one I am. By now, even I don't know.

"I'm amazed you came through this as well as you did." Catriona sounded relieved, rather than suspicious.

Zora hoped to keep it that way. "Do you know what happened to the others?" she asked anxiously, wondering how much Catriona had seen.

Catriona shook her head. "It all happened so fast it's hard to tell. Apparently Esme suddenly decided to kill you—she was screaming something. Do you know what happened? Or why?"

Good. Catriona thinks I'm Lina. "I don't remember much—the part on the terrace was confusing, and after I hit the water...I don't remember any of that part. All I remember is that Esme was trying to push me into the water, and she fell in with me when I struggled. I thought I saw Kyril?" she added hopefully.

"I saw him, too," Catriona said. "I think it's safe to say he survived."

"Thank the Goddess," Zora said fervently. She sat up, pulling the cloak together around her. "I need to go back, to let the people see that I'm alive and well."

Catriona looked sharply at her. "You'll need some clothing, too," she said after a moment. "What happened to what you were wearing?"

Zora shrugged. "I have no idea," she lied. "I was still wearing it when I went into the water." *Well, that part is true.*

The sound of hoofbeats heralded the arrival of several guards on horseback. Zora recognized some of them from swimming training, and she was startled to realize that her training with the guards had been only four months ago. It seemed to her as if most of her life had happened since then. *Of course, it was more like parts of several people's lives. And I'm not sure I'm thinking straight—did I hit my head on a rock? I was getting tossed around pretty badly for a couple of minutes.*

Fortunately the guards were carrying dry blankets with them, and they made quick work of drying Zora off, wrapping her in enough blankets to make a cocoon, and putting her up in the saddle before one of them.

They had a spare horse and dry clothes for Catriona as well, but—

"Sword-Bearer?" Zora asked before the woman could reach for the clothing.

"My Queen?" Catriona bowed formally.

"I was wondering," Zora said. "Is there any chance of finding bodies? I'd like to know if I'm going to have to worry about Lady Esme in the future."

Catriona nodded. "I'll see what I can do," she said.

"She'll find them if anyone can," one of the other guards

remarked. "Swims like a fish, that one does."

Zora found herself smiling faintly as they rode back to the palace.

The priestesses surrounded her as soon as she arrived and hustled her down to their quarters, ignoring her protests. Not that she objected to a warm bath and dry clothing, but she felt very strongly that this was *not* a good time for her to disappear for a week. *Goddess knows what the rumors will be like by then!*

Fortunately, the Shield-Bearer arrived as she was getting out of the bath, carrying one of the gowns she wore to do the evening rituals.

"Are you mad?" the Eldest demanded. "You know she is supposed to be in seclusion!"

"Under normal circumstances that would be so," the Shield-Bearer agreed. "But these are *not* normal circumstances. A good portion of the city's population saw her go into the water, the rest of them have certainly heard a garbled version of the story, and very few people have seen her alive since. It is vital that she be *seen* to be alive and well."

"I've been trying to tell them that since they brought me down here," Zora agreed, reaching for the gown. "I'll do the evening ritual tonight—I know it's not the usual custom, but it will allow the maximum number of people to see me. *Then* I can afford to spend a week in seclusion."

The Fourth Priestess suddenly burst into tears, and everyone turned to stare at her. "I was so afraid when the Goddess chose Zora," she sobbed. "I thought it meant that one of us was going to die. And just this morning we were wondering how we'd manage with six of us in quarters designed for only five."

"Zora and I were wondering the same thing," Zora said. "We were talking about it when we were alone this morning. She said we'd have to wait and see." Zora stopped, astonished to find herself fighting the urge to cry. As far as she knew, the only casualty of the day was Lady Esme... But would she ever see Kyril or Lina again?

She followed the Shield-Bearer up the stairs to the terrace where she did the evening ritual. The cries of joy that greeted her appearance made her think that she was doing the right thing, and feeling the presence of the Goddess made her certain of it.

Then she returned to the priestesses' quarters to spend her week of seclusion. She hoped she'd be allowed to spend a lot of that time sleeping. She was just now realizing how very, very tired she was.

When Zora awoke, at midday the next day, she barely remembered how she had ended up in her cell in the underground temple. In fact, it had been so long since she'd been in her cell that it took her several moments to recognize where she was.

The priestesses had not wakened her for either prayers or breakfast, but Zora didn't know whether that was the custom or their reaction to her obvious exhaustion after the chaotic ordeal of the Sacrifice. Her biggest worry now was that she didn't know how the Queen was supposed to behave during her period of mourning. *At least I'll know next year*, she consoled herself. *Somehow, I don't think Lina is going to come back.*

For the moment, she put on the clothing laid out for her—black robes and veil, instead of the usual green. She ate the food they had saved for her, and then used the passage from the temple to the Queen's chapel that allowed her to make her way there without going through the public areas of the palace, politely declining the Third Priestess's offer to attend her. Apparently being followed everywhere was optional at the moment.

She entered the chapel, lit the torch next to the door, crossed to the start of the labyrinth, and walked along its path to the bench behind the fountain. She was glad to be able to sit down. For some reason she felt as if her body had been almost completely drained of power. She hadn't felt much of anything inside the labyrinth, and even the short walk from her cell to the chapel had tired her. She slumped on the bench, leaning back against the stone wall.

"So here I am, Lady. Your sole remaining Queen. Lina and look so much alike—and I've spent so much time learning to be her—that nobody knows which one of us I am. And nobody cares. The really sad part is that I don't believe that anyone ever *did* care. We're interchangeable. The only one who knows which of us is which is you."

It doesn't matter.

"How can it not matter? It's the difference between being the Queen and not being the Queen!"

Zora had never heard the Goddess really laugh before.

My dear child, do you truly believe that all of this was a series of accidents? Just consider all the events and decisions that have brought you to this place. You haven't learned to be your sister. What you've learned is to be Queen. The Queen I wanted all along. The Queen only you can be. You are the one who is the true Queen. It doesn't matter whether you are the child of Queen Zoradah's body. You are the child of her soul.

Zora remembered the dreams she'd had back at Eagle's Rest, and the vision of the Goddess she had seen in the fire. *Not here... You must choose...* "You said I had to choose freely. Was this a free choice? What about Lina? Did she ever get a choice?"

When a person refuses a choice it creates a space—a hole—and the people who have chosen to serve fill it as best they can. Zoradah chose to bear a daughter, knowing that it might well cost her life. You chose to leave behind everything you had ever known to serve me here, and when your sister refused her duties, you took them up. Not because you wanted the glory of being Queen, but because you knew the work was more important than the person doing it. You came here, knowing that it was dangerous—remember how many times you were attacked or poisoned. Do you not realize that if you had not been here, your sister would be dead?

Zora thought about that for a moment. It was true.

Druscilla and your sister were raised to be royal and chose not to be. You, despite every discouragement, made the opposite choice. You are my High Priestess and the Queen of Diadem because I chose you and you chose this. Every decision and every action brought you to this place.

And don't tell me you don't know who bore you. I know you do.

"Yes," Zora admitted. "I'm not Druscilla's daughter, which means I never knew my mother." She wasn't sure how she felt about that. There was regret and a sense of loss, but there was also relief. *If I'm not her daughter, it doesn't matter so much that I'm not the type of daughter she wanted. I suspect that she and Lina will get along very well.*

Speaking of which...

"Lady, should I change my name? If I'm really Lina." *Zalina Miradah, if we want to be really accurate.*

The Goddess sounded amused. *Do you think your sister can convince anyone at Eagle's Rest that she is you?*

"No."

You don't need to swap places or pretend to be what you are not. The few people who use your name will call you Lina, anyway. Simply be yourself and let the priestesses think what they will. As for your true parentage, you are my beloved daughter and have served me faithfully through difficult circumstances. I am well pleased with you.

Zora felt the Goddess's hands on her shoulders, and a soft kiss on her brow.

Welcome home.

Zora didn't know why feeling so completely loved should make her cry, but it did. These tears, however, didn't hurt; they washed away all the doubts and insecurities of her old life. And the presence of the Goddess filled up all the empty places inside her.

She fell asleep on the bench, and nobody came to check on what she was doing, to wake her up, or to make demands on her.

CHAPTER NINETEEN

After a week in seclusion, Zora had finally caught up on her sleep. Life was much easier now. Trying to remember what she should know as Zora and what she should know as Lina had been exhausting and confusing. At least now if she slipped up, she could claim Zora had told her whatever it was she suddenly knew. And she no longer had to worry about which name she was supposed to respond to, because nobody was calling her Zora anymore.

As she returned to court, she watched the Shield-Bearer and the priestesses for clues to the behavior expected of her. As far as she could tell, she was behaving as they expected—or perhaps as they desired, given what they had apparently expected from Lina.

The only thing she watched more carefully than the people around her were the reports on the harvest. She was thankful beyond words that it was a good one.

As soon as she was released from seclusion, Catriona had come to her with the results of the search for bodies. "The only one we found was Lady Esme's," she said. "The others appear to have gone downstream. Hers was caught in the rocks behind the waterfall. Oddly enough, it was right next to her father's. Do you want us to retrieve it—or them?"

Zora turned to the Shield-Bearer, who was sitting with her, as usual. It seemed that her Regent was reluctant to let her out of her sight. *Nobody is trying to kill me now, but she's still as protective as ever—or maybe even a bit worse.* "Is there a precedent for removing the body of the Year-King from the river?"

The Shield-Bearer nodded. "Sometimes they wash up on the shore. That's how King's Cove got its name. We bury them in the Kings' Garden when that happens."

Zora nodded, turning an idea over in her head. "What was the public reaction to Lady Esme's behavior?"

"If she hadn't fallen into the river with you," the Shield-Bearer said, "I expect she would have been torn to pieces on the spot. But given that you survived and she didn't..."

Catriona shrugged. "From what I've seen and heard, the general reaction appears to be 'good riddance.' There's no family left to mourn her, and no one else seems to care about her either—except those of us who are relieved she's gone."

"I'm certainly relieved—especially after all her attempts to drug or poison the Queen," the Shield-Bearer said. "Her property escheats to the crown, but I'd be glad of her death if we weren't getting a single copper from it."

"I can see why," Zora agreed. "Especially after the morning *you* got a dose of her special broth. But it's still sad. In a way, she's another sacrifice—she never recovered from her father's death." She looked down at her lap. "She tried to persuade me to kill myself along with the king so that no other girl would ever lose her father the way she and I did."

"Persuade!" Catriona choked out.

"I didn't promise, but I did let her think I was considering it," Zora said. "I thought that as long as she was expecting me to sacrifice myself, she'd stop trying to kill me."

"Obviously *that* worked only up to a point," the Shield-Bearer said dryly.

"True, but it did get me a period of relative peace at a time when I badly needed it," Zora pointed out. "Anyway, what I would like to do with her body, if it's possible, is to bury her with her father."

"In the Kings' Garden?" Catriona said in horror. "After what she did?"

"The Sacrifice of her father caused her death," Zora said sadly. "I spent enough time in her company to be very sure of that. If he had not been Chosen, she would still be alive—and perhaps even happy."

"If you claim his death caused hers," the Shield-Bearer protested, "you are saying it almost caused *your* death as well!"

"Yes, I am. What's really sad is that in a way Lady Esme was right. The time for a yearly death is coming to an end—you don't think Kyril is dead, do you?"

Neither the Shield-Bearer nor Catriona said anything, but the looks they exchanged were eloquent.

"That's why laying her to rest with her father seems fitting to me," Zora concluded.

"As the Queen wishes," the Shield-Bearer finally said. "It's not as if the burial of a Year-King is a public event." She turned to Catriona. "Have the grave dug for him, and then choose a couple of very discreet guards, shroud the bodies together, and bury them quietly at night. That's when kings are traditionally buried, anyway."

"I want to help with the burial," Zora said. "It's all I can do for her now."

"Why should you do anything for her?" Catriona asked. "She nearly killed you!"

"And I *did* kill her. I pushed her back into the rocks when we fell. Look at where we each landed." *Not that she had a good chance of survival* before *I shoved her into the rocks...but she had none at all after that.* "Someone at her burial should mourn her—or at least be sorry she died the way she did."

"Very well," Catriona sighed. "I'll round up a detail to dig the grave while I retrieve the bodies."

The burial was done very quietly, with only Zora, the Shield-Bearer, Catriona, and Genia participating. Apparently the Goddess did not disapprove, because the harvest continued to go well.

Zora could feel the presence of the Goddess even more strongly now during the morning and evening rituals and during her afternoons in the Queen's chapel. Everyone apparently believed she was Lina, although Zora thought that the Shield-Bearer *might* suspect the truth. She was pretty sure that Catriona knew she had been Zora. Nobody, however, seemed unhappy with the current situation. *As the Goddess said, it doesn't matter.*

Even though the Queen would wear black and be in official mourning until the Longest Night, the court was a much happier place. Lady Esme had apparently managed to spread her anger and grief further than Zora had realized. *I thought she was only angry at me. Well, at me and Lina. I guess we only got the worst of her anger, not all of it.*

Two months after the Sacrifice, the Queen began hearing petitions again. There weren't all that many—this was time of year when people who had estates outside the city went there—so Zora and the Shield-Bearer were hearing petitions only one morning a week. They had finished with the scheduled petitions, and Zora was about to recite the formal dismissal when a man walked into the room and bent his head to say something to the clerk.

Zora didn't recognize him at first. He was slim and graceful, with long, jet-black hair, and dressed in clothing that looked expensive without being gaudy. As he turned to face the front of the room she noticed that his hair was pulled back from his face, both to hold a simple golden circlet in place and to make the blue circle on his forehead visible. She recognized him just as the clerk said loudly, "Lord Ranulf, Beloved of the Goddess!"

What happened? Zora's thoughts raced frantically as her stomach tightened with nerves. *Did Kyril not make it home? Did something happen to Lina?* She turned to the Shield-Bearer, wondering what she was supposed to do now.

The Shield-Bearer said softly, "Lord Ranulf is a surviving Year-King, which is why he is called 'Beloved of the Goddess' instead of 'Chosen of the Goddess.' He was married to your mother about ten years before you were born."

I know that *much! It's in the records—even if I hadn't grown up on his estate.* "He's Kyril's father, isn't he?" Zora said aloud, forcing the words through stiff lips. "Why do you suppose he's here?"

"I'm sure he'll tell us," the Shield-Bearer said, watching Lord Ranulf walk slowly down the room toward them. "When he gets to us, give him your hand to kiss. It's the custom—although it isn't applied very often."

Zora nodded and turned back to watch Lord Ranulf cover the last few yards to stand in front of her chair. She extended her hand and tried to smile. "Lord Ranulf, Beloved of the Goddess, be welcome in our court," she said formally.

Lord Ranulf bowed over her hand, then raised his head and looked straight into her eyes as if trying to see into her soul—or figure out which girl she was. Zora shifted her gaze infinitesimally so that she was looking at the bridge of his nose instead of into his eyes. She didn't want to get into a staring contest with him, but a Queen could not afford to back down and lower her eyes.

"What brings you here?" she asked quietly.

"I wish to speak to you in private," he replied, equally quietly. The Shield-Bearer cleared her throat, and he added, "Both of you. And if you would ask Catriona to join us, I would appreciate it."

Zora glanced at the Shield-Bearer, who nodded very slightly. "Very well," she said. She rose to her feet and announced, "This audience is ended. Go in the peace of the Goddess."

She led Lord Ranulf to the sitting room, followed by the Shield-Bearer, who had paused only long enough to send a message for Catriona to join them.

"Catriona is Lord Ranulf's niece," she explained to Zora as she handed first her and then Lord Ranulf a goblet of red wine.

Zora noticed that the Shield-Bearer didn't ask Lord Ranulf whether he preferred red or white wine. *Has he spent enough time here that she knows which he likes? And was I supposed to know that Catriona was his niece, or not?* For a moment she couldn't remember again whether she was Zora or Lina, let alone whether either of them should have known this fact.

"Daughter of my sister Sigrun," Lord Ranulf said conversationally. He set down his goblet on the small table next to him and looked from Zora to the Shield-Bearer and back. "*What happened here this summer?*"

"Kyril was chosen king—" Zora began hesitantly.

"I know *that* much," Lord Ranulf snapped. "Colin told me about the Choosing when he came home."

"And Kyril?" Zora asked anxiously.

"He came home last week."

Last week? The Sacrifice was months ago! "Is he all right?" *It's not out of character for me to be concerned. Lina would be frantic.*

"Physically he appears to be fine." Lord Ranulf scowled. "But there's something strange going on. Did he form an attachment to one of his Companions?" As Zora choked on her wine he added, "And are you missing any of them?"

"An attachment to one of his Companions?" the Shield-Bearer asked incredulously. "While married to the Queen? You, of all people, know how impossible that is!"

"Then who is the boy he brought home with him—the one he won't let out of his sight for an instant?" Lord Ranulf scowled.

"Are they sharing a bedchamber, or did you try to put the new boy in the dormitory with the other students?" Zora asked. *After this summer, I'll bet Lina would live as a frog before she'd agree to be parted from Kyril.* "You needn't look so surprised, Lord Ranulf. Kyril told me about your school. We spent a lot of time together, even before he was Chosen."

"Are you still in love with him?" Lord Ranulf asked. From the shocked look on the Shield-Bearer's face, Zora guessed *that* wasn't a question anyone ever asked the Queen, but she chose to reply anyway.

"I will always be fond of Kyril, but I regard him more as a brother than a husband," she said serenely. "I accept that he has a life to live elsewhere, and, as I'm sure you know, our marriage ended with the Sacrifice. To the best of my knowledge, we are not missing any of his Companions."

"Why would we be missing any of the king's Companions?" Catriona entered in time to overhear the last sentence. She closed the door behind her. "None of *them* fell into the water."

"Your housekeeper told me about Lady Esme," Lord Ranulf said. "Did she really try to kill the Queen?"

"It all happened so quickly," Zora said, "and she was pretty crazy by the end. It's hard to know for certain exactly *what* she intended."

"Is she dead? And are you absolutely sure about that?" Lord Ranulf asked.

"Yes to both," Catriona said. "I found her body under the waterfall, and I was part of the burial detail. She's gone, and she's not coming back."

"That leaves me with only three questions," Lord Ranulf said, ticking them off on his fingers. "What happened to my son? Who is the boy he brought home with him? And what happened to the girl he came to Diadem with last spring? She's one of my fosterlings, and her mother is making quite a fuss."

I'll just bet she is, Zora thought. *I'm so glad I'm not there to hear it.*

"Oh, dear," the Shield-Bearer said. "Was that Zora?"

"All Kyril would say was that she chose to remain here to serve the Goddess."

The Shield-Bearer sighed. "That is one way of putting it," she said. "The day Kyril was Chosen, Zora—his cousin, I gather—was chosen as one of the Four."

"The four priestesses who serve during the Queen's minority?" Ranulf asked. "Did you not already *have* four of them?"

"Yes," the Shield-Bearer said. "Zora was the fifth, which made the rest of them very nervous. But she was closer to the Queen in age than the rest of them, and she could handle—" She broke off, suddenly remembering that the Queen was sitting right next to her.

"She discovered that Lady Esme was making poisons and giving them to me," Zora said, pretending she hadn't noticed what the Shield-Bearer had been about to say. "As Kyril may have told you, Lady Esme was extremely unhappy about her father's being Year-King. Not just about his death, but about losing his affection prior to that."

"Year-King idiocy?" Lord Ranulf asked.

Zora nodded.

"Year-King idiocy?" the Shield-Bearer asked incredulously.

Lord Ranulf chuckled. "It's what my wife calls the king's state of mind during his marriage to the Queen, when she is the center of his world and all other relationships are unimportant." He sobered. "I can see why that would be upsetting to his daughter."

"I understand that her mother died when she was a small child and that she was devoted to him," Zora said. "That's why I had them buried together when Catriona found their bodies together under the waterfall."

"That was kind of you," Lord Ranulf remarked. "I notice that everyone is referring to Zora in the past tense. Just what happened to *her*?"

Catriona sighed. "I suppose I'm the person best able to answer that. The ritual of the Sacrifice was like nothing we've had before—and hopefully like nothing we'll ever have in the future. We ended up with five people in the river."

"Starting with Kyril, I presume," Lord Ranulf said. "He won't talk about it, but if he turned into a fish and swam downstream, he wouldn't have known what happened after he went in—and, of course, the drugs don't help. Lady Esme was another, I gather, but who were the other three?"

"Esme took both the Queen and Zora in with her," Catriona replied, "and then I dove in after them in the hope of saving them."

"Esme's dead," Lord Ranulf started ticking points off on his fingers again, "and a good thing, if she dragged the *Queen* into the water. Kyril is alive and home, and two of you are sitting here. So Zora would be the one who's missing. Was her body found?"

Catriona shook her head. "We think it was washed out to sea. There haven't been any reports of bodies coming ashore downriver."

"Hmm." Lord Ranulf looked thoughtful. "The Year-King and the Queen were in the usual robes, correct?" He looked at Catriona. "What were you and Zora wearing?"

Oh, no! Zora wished she could kick him to make him stop talking. Unfortunately, he was too far away.

Catriona winced at the memory. "I was in full dress uniform, complete with cape. It certainly made swimming difficult, but it came in handy when I pulled the Queen out, because it gave me something to—"

Oh, no... She can't tell us apart by touch because we look alike, but she can probably guess what happened now!

Catriona's voice failed for a moment, and she stared at Zora in horror.

"Wrap me in," Zora said quickly. "Kyril told me that my half-brother Rias was a shape-changer and my father's twin sister was one, so he thought I could learn, and he was trying to teach me. I can't do much, and I'm not certain what I did that day. As you said, Lord Ranulf, the drugs don't help—but whatever I did, my clothing didn't survive it."

"And she has to be the Queen," Catriona said obviously trying to reassure herself as well as the rest of them. "If she were Zora in the Queen's shape, I should be able to tell the difference."

"Of course you could tell the difference," Lord Ranulf agreed promptly. "You've been able to see a shape-changer's true shape for as long as I've known you."

"I *should* be able to tell Zora and the Queen apart," Catriona said softly, "but I can't, not for sure."

"What do you mean?" the Shield-Bearer asked. "Why wouldn't you be able to tell them apart?"

"Because, in their true shapes, they're identical," Catriona explained. "Isn't that true, Uncle?"

"I wouldn't worry about it," Lord Ranulf said reassuringly. Zora noticed that he hadn't answered the question. "If you didn't have the right one here, I'm fairly certain the Goddess would have made her displeasure known by now."

The Shield-Bearer shuddered. "I'm certain you're right about *that*," she said. "I remember the last time—with your wife and her brother—vividly."

"I'll deal with Zora's mother," Lord Ranulf said. "As for the strange boy, he's probably a friend that Kyril made during his journey home. It did take him longer than usual to make the journey. And I can remember how alone a Year-King feels after his bond with the Queen is severed."

Kyril must have stopped someplace where no one knew him so he could teach Lina to shift properly. If she'd arrived at Eagle's Rest looking like him, *Lord Ranulf wouldn't be* here *seeking answers. And if she'd arrived looking like herself, he'd still be there, demanding answers from her and Kyril. And the Goddess only knows what my mother—I mean Druscilla—would be saying!*

His eyes locked with Zora's again, but this time there was no question in his. *He knows.*

But all he said was, "Do you feel better about the Sacrifice, knowing that Kyril survived? Are you content to be Queen now?"

"Yes, I am," Zora said steadily, knowing what he was really asking was 'Are you content to remain in Diadem and be Queen instead of coming home?' *This is my home now. Besides, I probably couldn't cross the border if I wanted to. Which I don't.*

"I hear in the city," Lord Ranulf said lightly, "my son is considered to be especially favored of the Goddess. There are even people who claim they saw him borne downstream by a dolphin, if you can believe that." He smiled and shook his head as if in amusement at some foolish superstition. "Dolphins don't live in fresh water."

As if Kyril would need any help from a dolphin, Zora thought. *And he and the Queen were dressed alike—oh, yes, Lord Ranulf definitely knows what happened now!* "Lord Ranulf," she said, realizing this might be her only chance to ask for his help. "Kyril said that you had a theory—"

"Yes, I do," Lord Ranulf said. "And I intend to continue to test it." He smiled reassuringly at her. "Perhaps I'll come to visit again next year." He paused, then added, "Do you have any message you want me to take home with me?"

"Yes," Zora said, choosing her words carefully. "Tell Kyril that I am glad to hear he is well, and that I am well also." She couldn't resist adding, "And tell him I wish him happy in his next marriage."

"You give your consent to his marriage?" Lord Ranulf asked.

Zora nodded.

"I shall be happy to carry that message," he said. "If you ever have need of me, send Catriona. She knows the way."

"Thank you," Zora replied. *If you send me a suitable shape-changer each spring, everything should be fine—if the Goddess wills it.*

And I have faith that she will.

ABOUT THE AUTHOR

Elisabeth Waters sold her first short story in 1980 to Marion Zimmer Bradley for THE KEEPER'S PRICE, the first of the Darkover anthologies. She then went on to sell short stories to a variety of anthologies. Her first novel, a fantasy called CHANGING FATE, was awarded the 1989 Gryphon Award. Its sequel, MENDING FATE, was published in 2016. She also writes short stories and edits anthologies.

She also worked as a supernumerary with the San Francisco Opera, where she appeared in *La Gioconda*, *Manon Lescaut*, *Madama Butterfly*, *Khovanschina*, *Das Rheingold*, *Werther*, and *Idomeneo*.